Whitestone

The Whitestone Stories

To my King~
my name is graven
on Your hands.

A hundred thousand thanks to Liam,
my one love and steadfast encourager.
And fondest gratitude to Kayla,
my first reader who kept me writing.

So there I lay, belly up on the Whitestone Elementary gym floor. My first day back at school. Getting back to school, they told me, would be the start of getting back to normal. The obvious question was *why?*

School made me feel a lot of things. Normal wasn't one of them. Example: the game my brain played in class, revealing answers to me with all the dazzle of a game show hostess—until Mrs. Ingram called my name. Then whisk, answers gone into the great unknown. The contestant is sent home without a parting gift. How was that normal?

School was also the place to go to feel like a klutz. To use grandma language, I was 'in a growth spurt.' Translation: giant klutz. Grandma Judy liked to ask if I was 'putting manure in my shoes.' (To be clear, this was a reference to fertilizer, not odor.) As if I would walk in perpetual cow poo in order to be taller than every girl and most of the boys in my class.

In gym class, Coach Readdie couldn't seem to see past the tallness and accept the klutz half of the equation. She expected me to be some kind of Olympic hopeful on the basketball court. I admit, this played out fantastically in my imagination. I could run. I could dribble… I just couldn't run and dribble simultaneously. Run, dribble, and shoot a lay-up? Sure, and I'd jump up and take a bite out of the moon while I was at it.

So, normal means being a dumb giant klutz. But where does a girl go when she wants to feel like a total outcast? (If you can't guess by now you're just not paying attention.)

Have you ever had that dream when you walk into class, take off your coat—no, not *that* dream—the one where you're still in your pajamas? And they're My Pretty Pony pajamas, five sizes too big, something like that? Well, imagine that feeling, except you don't get to wake up from it. Boys can make you feel like that even when you haven't done anything embarrassing. Sometimes it's just embarrassing being you.

So imagine how amazing you'd feel if you, say, wet your pants in front of the whole class (that wasn't me), or your own dad called you a loser at school right in front of your friends (not me, either). Or you had a fall-down, drooling seizure in front of the entire school.

That one's mine. Back to the gymnasium floor.

"I think she's dead!"

It was Tiffany Klipfel's raspy voice. Why did Tiffany always have a raspy voice? More importantly, who was she talking about?

"Look—Rory's dead."

So. The dead person was me. I wondered if they were right. Until recently, I hadn't thought much about what would happen to me after I died. I never imagined Tiffany Klipfel would be involved.

"Step back. Everyone back, now." I wasn't sure about that voice, a woman's. There was a kind of hollow, rushing sound, lots of voices, feet pounding. The smell was familiar. The smell of failure… The school gym. I must've opened my eyes then; there were feet all around me. Someone had a sweet pair of high tops, the kind I can't wear (because even clowns would point and stare). Above all the feet, a cluster of faces stared at me. I was on my back on the beige, rubbery floor. Miss Diakos, the school nurse, kneeled next to me.

There could be only one explanation. I had tried to run, dribble, and shoot the lay-up. But no, I wasn't in my horrible, horrible gym clothes. I had been up in the bleachers. So, there could be only one other explanation. I had fallen down the bleachers, tripped up by my size 9-½ longfellows. Cause of death: my own feet. These things never happen in the privacy of your own home, of course; it has to be during an all-school assembly. One of those unwritten life rules.

"Can you hear me, Rory? You're going to be okay," Miss Diakos said, maybe to convince herself. My classmates stood around, some whispering or trying to hide laughter and doing a poor job of it. Then I noticed someone kneeling near my head, a kid who looked awfully familiar for someone I didn't know.

He couldn't have been more than a fourth-grader. Just some random fourth-grader in a group of seventh-graders, why not? But while they were all staring *at* me, his big, dark eyes looked right *into* me. And he did something strange. He touched my forehead with his pudgy fourth-grader fingers. Then his eyes seemed to pull back, and he saw I was looking at him, and the eyes got wide. He backed away until I couldn't see him anymore.

Soon the paramedics came, and before you knew it, I was back in the hospital—the same room even. 316. My second home lately.

Turns out Mom was right. Things were back to normal. The new normal.

The new normal turned out to be nothing like the old normal. If I'd known just how un-normal it would be, I might've closed my eyes right then and refused to open them again. Because it was the things I started seeing that changed everything.

Lying there alone, my mom outside the door talking to a nurse, a machine attached to my finger giving an occasional unconcerned beep, the smell of hospital-cleanness in my nose (so different from Grandma's-house cleanness or wash-my-bedsheets-day cleanness, but sharper and digging deeper), it came back to me. In limping bits and pieces, a few more memories returned.

That chubby fourth-grader looked familiar for a reason. My breathing quickened when that ragged scrap of memory tumbled by. I grabbed it, and it had sharp edges. My heart pounded, but the beeper kept beeping at its unconcerned pace.

I looked around this room where'd I'd recently spent a lot of time, seeing it as if for the first time. Well, I had spent most of my last visit in a coma. Almost ten days, the nurses told me—told me like I'd be shocked, like I would've thought I'd just taken a quick nap. No, what surprised me was that it had been only ten days. It felt like I'd been floating for ten years.

Sometimes in my coma I had heard voices. Usually they didn't make sense, like they spoke English but with the words all out of order. But I knew my mom's voice, and I heard my Grandma Judy's a lot. I don't remember hearing my sister, Sheelan. And I never heard my dad.

I never told anyone, but a few times I could actually see. With my eyes closed. I know they were because I could see my shut-eyed self lying in the bed, my head all bandaged up, machines blinking and humming around me. That's when I really got that floating feeling.

I felt it when I couldn't feel anything else. I read once that if you swim in the Dead Sea, you float easily because there's a lot of salt or minerals or something in the water. It kind of felt like that sounds. Not like I couldn't sink, more like I could start sinking any second, like maybe I should sink but didn't. My coma was my own private Dead Sea. I also read that nothing can live in the Dead Sea, which explains the name.

Maybe it could have been the real thing—the Dead part. The dark and quiet weren't so bad. It was the perfect place to hide. See, I knew something waited for me when I did wake up. I don't know how I knew, but I sensed this thing very close by, waiting to rip out my insides and eat me alive. I didn't know what it was at the time, but I wasn't about to go find out. The dark quiet was fine.

But other things had disturbed the quiet. Like that kid. The first time I saw him wasn't today in the school gym. I remembered now, him beside my hospital bed one of those times when I was doing my coma zero-gravity thing. But that wasn't all.

That boy had been there when IT happened.

'It' was what my family called the accident—when we talked about It at all, which was hardly ever. I had my seatbelt on, but when you're skinny you can slip right out of those things. Or, in my case, I hated the shoulder strap and stupidly wasn't wearing it right. Result: banged-up head for Rory. Doctors have much fancier words for this, which they call their diagnosis. Diagnosis is a fancy word for 'what we think is wrong with you.'

I just wanted to know what was wrong with everyone else. Didn't they think it was strange that this kid, this pudgy brown boy, was always where he wasn't supposed to be? In the gym, touching my head. In this room, when I was in a coma, touching my head. And there...in the car? Near the car? Not touching my head. Holding my hand?

I still remembered his eyes, sort of wise and sad. When I was in the coma, they had looked right into me. Not the unconscious me in the bed—the me floating overhead, looking down at myself. He had looked up, and he had seen me.

Remembering it was like dreaming a dream you've dreamed a hundred times but forget until you dream it again. I felt like I'd been there a hundred times. But it wasn't a dream, because even while the boy was looking up at me, my Mom had come in and sunk into an orange vinyl chair. She looked ten years older that day, wearing a black dress I'd never seen, kind of old-ladyish and not the type of thing she ever wore, but the details too real to be a dream, the tiny pleats of the black fabric, the flat black buttons. The mousiness of her hair under the fluorescent lights.

She didn't even notice the boy. When I looked back, he was gone.

All that was weeks ago.

Mom and Dr. Flynn came back in, and I had to come back to the present moment. Having one of those penlight things shone into your eyes will do that.

"It's logical to attribute a seizure to the head trauma, at least as a starting point," he told my mom. His breath always smelled like wintergreen, though I never saw him chewing gum or mints. Dr. Flynn was okay, pretty young for a doctor, I guess—younger than the other doctors I'd seen striding in and out of the room with their eyes on their metal clipboards. Striding, clipboarding, their brains whizzing along at top speed. Speaking 'medicalese,' as my grandma called it. Dr. Flynn didn't stride around much. He was more of an ambler, and he had ruffled sandy hair and a bit of a baby face, like he probably couldn't grow a beard if he tried.

"We'll run a few tests to see if we can't determine the cause," he said.

"More tests?" I asked. You might say I whined.

"Will she have to stay overnight?" Mom twisted the strap of her purse. She wore the gray skirt and white blouse, which meant she'd had to come straight from her office assistant job. "The insurance only covers…"

"Let's look at the preliminary results and then decide. Right, Irish?"

That was me—Irish. I hardly heard him.

The kid was back.

There in the room with us. When I stared at him, his brown eyes got really big again. Caught him. Finally, time for some answers.

"Who are you?" I demanded.

Dr. Flynn smiled, but I saw him exchange a quick look with my mom. "Well, a fellow Irish American, Miss Joyce."

"No, I mean him." I pointed at the kid, who gestured like I should keep quiet, as if somehow they wouldn't observe him, standing three feet away in a place he had no business being.

Mom's and Doc Flynn's eyes bounced around the room, at me, at each other, but never at the kid.

"Did someone peek in the room, Rory?" Mom asked.

The kid shrugged as if to say, *told you so.*

They couldn't see him.

Now, the question: How soon would they move me to the psych ward?

"Um…yeah," I said vaguely.

They let it pass. After all, I'd just had a seizure. Why not freak out about some passing kid who may or may not have peeked into the room? (The kid still stood there, still watching me.) I was tired, they were thinking. Overwhelmed.

They didn't think to ask me. I felt pretty okay—my mom looked tired and overwhelmed. But I was ready to be convinced.

"Lie back, Rory," my mom said. "Just close your eyes and rest. You've been through a lot today."

So I did, and the doc went to order the tests and Mom went to get coffee. Closing my eyes was like an eraser, a screen refresh, a restart. I was alone.

I peeked out the crack of one eyelid. No, I wasn't.

"You're still here," I said. I refused to look at him.

"I've been here a lot." His voice was soft, but not as boyish as his face.

"It's getting a little annoying."

"You don't usually see me."

Now I had to look at him. "Do you not want to be seen? 'Cause there's this thing you might try, called hiding. Or leaving." But I knew what he meant, because no one else seemed to see him. Lucky them.

"I'm not leaving." He came and sat in the orange chair. The cushion sighed.

"Who are you?"

He gave that some thought, as if there could be a hundred answers to that question and he had to pick one, and the answers were up on the ceiling. His eyes finally came back down.

"I'm Rafie." He said it more like 'toffee' than 'taffy.' Too bad, I liked taffy better than toffee.

"Rafie?"

"That's good," he said, like I'd come up with the name myself. "Call me that."

"Are you some kind of hologram or something, that only I can see?"

Give me a break—I'd recently had my brains shaken loose. I swiped my hand at him, like it might pass through his

13

holographic self. Instead his hand came up and caught mine, and even though he didn't squeeze, I had the feeling he was unusually strong. I had another feeling, too, of familiarity. He'd held my hand before, at a horrible time. An awful pain in my head and a scorched, hot metal smell and a voice moaning...the smell and sound and feel of It.

And the feel of him. I pulled my hand away. "You." My voice sounded weird and warbly in my own ears. "What are you?"

His brown eyes drifted up to the ceiling again. He was going to give that question a lot of thought, too.

"Just tell me."

"I'm a friend. A friend of a Friend."

I almost groaned. "Wait, I get it. Are you supposed to be some kind of... Like that show Grandma Judy watches, *Saved by the Angels*?"

I would've laughed in different circumstances. There he sat in his striped shirt—like he'd been to Sesame Street and raided Ernie's closet—scratching his nose with the back of his hand and shrugging at my question. Some angel.

"Something like that," he said.

Now I did laugh, and gawk. "Like *Saved by the Angels*? You're kidding."

"I don't know about a show, but that's the best word you've got."

I still gawked, but without the laughing. "An angel?"

"It's not important what we're called, but Whom we serve."

Strangely, the *whom* drove it home more than anything else. Fourth-graders don't say *whom*. Then I heard the rest of it. "Did you say 'we'?"

He nodded—not a 'yes' nod but a 'look behind you' nod. I turned to see the corner of the room that no one could have reached without walking right past us.

There was another boy there, an older boy. No, more of a young man, with black hair and eyes like blue lightning, arms crossed over his chest, his eyebrows pulled together and mouth slightly frowning.

I put my head back on the pillow and closed my eyes again. But it was too late for that. Once you see something, you can't unsee it.

2

That was how I came to be Saved by the Angels.

Have you ever noticed how much life is not like a TV show? Personally, I never had a monumental problem that could be conveniently wrapped up in the space of an hour. And in real life, there's never a commercial break when you really need one, if you know what I mean.

As for the bad guys... I'd always assumed that the worst were on TV or in the movies. The magic of special effects should pretty much guarantee it. Evil in the movies can spew buckets of slime, make your brain explode inside your skull, invade the body of your Aunt Ginny, that sort of thing.

Evil in the real world always seemed kind of dull. Greedy men in suits, stone-faced tyrants in uniforms, people taking advantage of weaker people. Liars, senseless killers. Soul-numbing, change-the-channel material, not the stuff gripping tales are made of.

But my dad did always say truth is stranger than fiction.

Who would've guessed that the boogeyman was real—only worse than anything you or Hollywood imagined? Or that it was your job to guard against him? Even fight him. Who would've guessed that it was your job to wield a sword against him? Okay, maybe not a real sword. But then again, maybe sometimes yes, a real sword. Stranger things have happened.

I ought to know.

Some of life's strangeness is just ordinary strangeness, like algebra. After I got out of the hospital—again—and got back to the supposed normalness of school—again—that's what waited for me. Algebra. By this point, I was already desperately behind in most of my classes. (Everything but gym. For the first time in my life, gym class cut me some slack.) Now I had the added torment of incomprehensible math on top of it.

For the record, I wasn't a hopeless student—until I was called on in class, then I was certifiably hopeless. But art was by far my favorite by far, the one considered 'non-academic.' I did like English, too. Not the grammar so much, but I did like writing. If you could write without grammar, that would be the subject for me. Math didn't give me shivers of joy, but I could juggle numbers without smoke pouring out of my ears.

But something changed while I was in room 316 having unexplainable visions. When I came back to math class, they were adding letters. Apparently now $A = 3$, but not all of the time; sometimes it equaled four. Unless suddenly $B = 4$, then it was anyone's guess what A equaled. Don't even talk to me about X.

The worst part is that no one else seemed bothered by this. Mrs. Ingram bubbled over at the idea of adding and subtracting letters, and she explained how to do it with lots of enthusiasm. She never really explained why.

So later when I sat in the cafeteria, torn between the homework and my equally unappetizing lunch, I had no idea where to begin. Staring furiously at page 124 of my math book did no good whatsoever. I tried staring blankly at the sheet of notebook paper in front of me; it stared blankly back. A moment of inspiration led me to write my name in the upper right hand corner of the page, then to write the numbers 1 through 10 in a tidy column on the left margin. The answers to problems 1 through 10 remained a mystery.

Scratch scratch...scratch scratch scratch. Across the table from me sat Jasmine Wee, a girl from my class. Her pencil danced over her sheet of paper, also numbered in the left hand margin. I watched in amazement for two reasons: first, she was eating the cafeteria's Special of the Day, despite the fact that it was unrecognizable as food; and second, she was solving the algebra problems, one by one.

I guess I was staring, because she finally looked up at me with her dark eyes.

"You actually get that stuff?" I asked.

She put down her pencil and lifted her fork, poking the noodly mass on her plate. "It's better than those greasy chicken thingers," she said.

I was eating the greasy chicken thingers. These were more commonly known as chicken fingers, a term that always creeped me out a little. I instantly preferred 'thingers.'

"I mean the algebra," I said. "You understand it?"

Her eyes narrowed. "You assume I'm a math prodigy because I'm Chinese?"

"Huh? Um, no. Are you?"

"What, so you assumed I'm Japanese?"

"No, not that. Are you a math prodigy? Because I could use one right about now. I just don't get this adding of letters."

"Well," she said, as if in that word was the answer to my problem. She came dangerously close to smiling but must've decided against it. "Once it clicks, it's pretty easy. Give it some time. You missed a lot of school."

Don't say it, I begged her silently. Don't tell me you're sorry about what happened. Part of me curls up and dies inside every time someone says that.

She didn't say it, just took another bite of the noodly stuff.

"Any chance you might explain it to me?" I asked.

Still suspicious. "You never talked to me before."

"Sure I have."

"I don't think 'Could you get my pencil? It rolled under your desk,' really counts."

"That's not... It's just—"

"Don't bother explaining. I know. You're no different than the rest of them."

Jasmine was saying several things here. First of all, there was the Them issue. The cafeteria was the perfect place to observe the phenomenon of Us and Them.

First there was Us, the people who sat at the row of tables closest to the kitchen, where the noise of crashing silverware and the smells of so-called food poured out every time the swinging doors flew open. Closest to the food line and the disapproving eyes of authority figures. Our tables by default. We were not a unified band, by any means. We were the odds and ends, not without friends, but without organized cliques. The leftovers, to use cafeteria terminology.

Then there was Them. Those like Madi Swanson and her staff of socially skilled ladies-in-waiting (I use the term 'ladies' loosely), wearing the same navy pleated skirt and white shirt as the rest of us, but somehow making it look good. To be a part of that quintet was the secret yearning of every junior high girl at one point or another. But membership was extended only to the chosen few, and woe to the girl who violated their secret oaths and was booted out of the sisterhood.

For Jasmine to say that I was like them was something of a slam. Clearly I wasn't rich or boyfriendly enough to be one of them—to be like them merely suggested that I shared some of their less admirable qualities. Like snobbishness.

Because Jasmine was also referring to her Defining Grade School Moment.

It happens all the time: a kid does something so historic or humiliating that it forever shapes his identity. Christie Smothers ran the mile faster than any of the girls—or the boys—in P.E. Ever. She immediately became Christie Smothers, future Olympic Track and Field Star. George Ortega tried for a heroic catch in a game of kickball and ended up snagging his slacks on a chain link fence. Henceforth he was Georgie Underpants. (In a stroke of pure luck,

Georgie's family moved away the following summer, and he had a chance to start fresh in a new town.)

Jasmine's moment came as a transfer student in Miss Moorhead's fifth grade class. An unlucky and probably totally justifiable set of circumstances led her to lose bladder control in front of her teacher and fellow students. The unfortunate fact of her last name led to some predictable and mean-spirited nicknames.

I'm not proud to admit that I used one of those names a time or two. Not to her face, but in some pitiful attempt to score points with other kids. The attempts failed; I was not ushered into any cliques. But I figured something out:

1) Calling people names makes them feel cruddy, which then makes you feel cruddy. If you have a soul.
2) There's enough crud in the world without me adding mine in.
3) Cliques aren't really my thing. Too much pressure.

So Jasmine was wrong about me, mostly. I was different from the rest of them. I never meant to shun her by not talking to her. My failure to speak stemmed from the fact that, somewhere between the ages of eleven and thirteen, my ability to hold an intelligent, or at least intelligible, conversation evaporated. I suppose my body was so busy growing six inches that my brain couldn't get a word in edgewise. But by the age of thirteen, I finally realized that the best way to keep the goofus words from coming out of my mouth was to keep the big yap shut.

But how to explain this to Jasmine? "Listen," I said. "I don't care if you wet your pants in class two years ago if you can solve algebra problems today."

She snapped her book shut, scooped up her tray, and walked away.

This is exactly what I'm talking about. Big yap SHUT, Rory.

I gathered up my things and prepared for the long walk to the tray depository. It took me past the Madi Swanson table first. Were I part of this club, I would probably be 'Rori' and have luxurious red curls instead of rusty fuzz. I couldn't help but notice how their eyes automatically followed me, assessing me, though their conversations continued without a hitch. These conversations typically revolved around boyfriends and the bizarre lengths they went to in order to obtain, maintain, and dispose of them.

The next table was a rowdy boys' table, and like Madi's it had a ringleader. Kevin Sebeck was a master at disrupting class without getting caught but getting plenty of laughs. A lone girl walking past a table full of goofball boys, I was hamburger meat before a pack of dogs. I tried to look invisible.

Naturally this failed. Kevin muttered something to his buddies, and they laughed. From the corner of my eye I saw him make strange, jerking movements, earning more laughs. Not until I put my tray on the counter did I realize he was faking a seizure.

I managed to make it through English, social studies and homeroom without crying. I even made it all the way home, though admittedly I jogged the fifteen-minute hike in about nine minutes, by some miracle not slipping on the patches of ice in the road and landing on my head. I keyed open the garage door and stumbled into the dimness, colliding with a stack of boxes that hadn't been there that morning. The top one hit the concrete floor with a smack, and a jumble of shirts spilled out.

My mom's handwriting was scribbled on the box: Salvation Army. I bent and picked up a shirt. My hands shook when I lifted it to my face and breathed in. It still smelled like my dad.

The painful knot in my throat let loose, and I sobbed right into my dad's T-shirt. When I was little, he used to let me wipe my runny nose on the edge of his shirt. It sounds gross, but it meant something. The thought of it made me want to cry harder. But it was weird. The shirt stayed dry. My body wanted to cry, but my eyes wouldn't do it. I couldn't even manage to do that right.

I heard a shuffling sound; I gulped back my raggedy breaths in case it was my sister. I hated the thought of her seeing me like that. But when I turned toward the open garage door, blinking against the brightness of winter overcast sky and snow, I saw a silhouette that was definitely not Sheelan. Short but bulky, it brandished some kind of club. No, a baseball bat. It sidled in the doorway, lifted the bat higher.

"Hi, Kings," I said.

The bat lowered. "That you, Rory?" His words made puffs in the air.

"Yep."

My neighbor Kingston stepped into the shadowy garage, and I could see that he saw I was crying, or whatever it was I was doing. He didn't mention it. "I heard some noises in here and thought it might be a 'possum. The Nelsons found one in their garage last week, you know. Thought I might get to see one."

"See it, or flatten it?"

He smiled, his fudge-colored eyes sparkling in his shining brown face. "Aw, this is just for courage." He set the bat aside. "You know I'd never hurt the thing."

I did know. I'd seen Kingston catch spiders in his hammy hands and bring them outside to set them free. He was watching me in that patient way he had; I turned away and hurried to scoop the fallen shirts back into their box.

"My mama just baked cookies. Want to come over?" he asked.

I almost laughed, except I was afraid I would sob instead. Those were probably the exact words he'd used to introduce himself five years before. I had avoided him religiously for over a week, but one thing I had come to learn about Kingston is that he's unavoidable. Still, back then I was determined to blame him for ruining my life by moving in next door.

Until he came along, life on Sweetnam Lane had been practically perfect. My best friend, Jenna, lived in the other half of our duplex, and our bedrooms shared a wall. We had just devised a language of taps to communicate after our unreasonably early bedtimes of 8:30 (mine) and 8:45 (hers). Then her mother got a promotion. Three weeks later, Jenna was gone. I'd had other friends since then, but never another best friend—the closest to it were Hannah and Kimmie, and they'd gone to the Catholic middle school last year. Just another turn in the downward spiral that had started with Jenna's exit from my life.

The salt had entered that wound when another eight-year-old moved into Jenna's room. An eight-year-old *boy*—natural enemy of all eight-year-old girls. So I chose to ignore the existence of Kingston Fisher until the day he finally cornered me—in this very garage—with his offer of a snack. I was unfairly enticed by the aroma of freshly-baked chocolate chip cookies and had little choice in the matter. Ever after, I was a regular visitor in the Fisher household. Not only did Mrs. Fisher make unbelievably good cookies, but Kings turned out to be not such a bad kid.

"Oatmeal raisin," he said.

I don't know if even the chocolate chip would have won me over on this day. I just needed to crash by myself. "No thanks, Kings. Stuff I've got to do."

"Alright. I'll try to save one for you." Kingston had the physique of one who enjoyed many a cookie and saved few, but his intentions were good. As he shuffled out, he peered back into the darkest corner of the garage for a moment as if he spied something. There was nothing there but a rickety old chair my dad had been meaning to fix for about a year. So out Kingston went in search of oatmeal cookies and opossums.

I dug in my pocket for the house key and came up empty. I'd just had it. I checked my backpack. Nothing. Without my key ring, I was locked out until Sheelan came home. I looked at my watch. 3:16. That might be in ten minutes or two hours, depending on her extracurricular agenda. I could go to the Fishers and have that cookie, but Mrs. Fisher had a way of knowing when something was bothering you and a kindly knack for drawing it out. Within ten minutes I'd be reliving my week and whining like a toddler.

"Where are you, you stinkin' keys?" I muttered, stamping my foot (like a whiny toddler).

"You dropped them over there," a voice answered.

I nearly dropped.

I spun around to the rickety chair in the corner, just where it had been, only now it was occupied. A girl sat there with a large book in her lap, engrossed in its pages. She looked to be about Sheelan's age—one of her friends? I'd never seen her before in my life. Whoever she was, she could consider a career in espionage.

"Sheelan's not home yet," I said, finally spotting the keys on the floor by the Salvation Army boxes. I grabbed them up, keeping my eyes on the girl.

She looked up when I said that, and her eyes were bright, like the eyes of someone sitting in a shadow shouldn't be. Not glowing or anything freaky like that, but like hazel-green beads of glass held up to a light. Full of light.

"So, you can see me," she said.

"Well, yeah," I said, maybe a little sarcastically. Then it hit me. I gaped at her. "You mean... You're one of them?"

"One of whom?"

"You know. Like Rafie. And the other guy."

"Micah."

"If you say so." I wanted her to say so. "Are you? An angel?"

"How will you know?" she asked.

I threw my hands up in frustration. Obviously I didn't know. I couldn't tell an angel from a sophomore. What do people picture when they hear the word 'angel'? Chubby babies with wings. Or halos, white robes, golden harps. Even if you imagine them looking like ordinary people, they don't exactly look ordinary — you picture them all windswept and interesting, breezy and slightly aglow. Airbrushed.

Try this: faded blue jeans, very worn at the knees, tank top splashed with red and peach flowers, flip-flops. Corkscrew red-brown hair poking out around her head, skin like coffee with a lot of cream. She asked a good question: how could I know she was an angel, when she looked like a neo-hippy girl?

"How will you know?" she asked again.

"Well, for one thing, you're sitting on a chair that has no seat," I said, and she glanced down like she hadn't noticed this. But my answer hadn't satisfied her. "Because you say so, I guess," I tried. "Until a few days ago, no one's ever come up to me and claimed to be an angel, so I assume no one's going to say it unless it's true."

She shook her head, her hand flipping through the pages of her big book. She didn't even look at the thing, just stopped at a page and pointed, her eyes locked on mine. "Satan himself can transform into an angel of light, Rory."

Whoa...Satan? Okay, maybe I could believe in angels—I guess if I didn't at this point, I'd just have to believe that I was crazy and having hallucinations (more on this later)—but the devil? Wasn't he just a sort of... I know I was paying attention in English class the day we learned about this... a symbol of all the evil in the world? Kind of a *personification* of evil?

It seemed rude to challenge her. "So you could be the devil, is that what you're saying?"

"How will you know, Rory?"

There was something about the way she asked the question—aside from the fact that she kept asking the question—that made me nervous. It wasn't *how can you know* or *how would you know*, but how *will* you know. Like I had to be prepared for more of this.

"I don't know," I said. I suddenly felt sick to my stomach. There was too much happening all at once. Life had become a big game of dodge ball, and I felt like the lone dodger. "I don't understand."

Then the girl smiled at me, and if I'd had any doubts about her, they were mostly whisked away at the sight. I saw a kindness in her eyes that was far older and deeper than anything a sixteen-year-old girl could express; it was like the love of a thousand grandmas rolled into a lovely little package and handed to me as a gift. "I know you don't understand. That's why I'm here." She patted the book in her lap.

"You were sent to help me?"

She gestured at me as if I'd just scored a point. "See? You're already a step closer."

"To what?"

"The truth. You know that I was sent. So what's the next logical question?"

Now I was on the spot. "Um... Sent. Sent by whom?" Okay, I said 'who,' but let's pretend I'm not grammatically challenged.

"Exactly. Sent by whom? That is how you will know, Rory." She flipped some more pages and pointed at the book again. Again her eyes never left my face, as if she could read with her fingertip. "'Beloved, do not believe every spirit, but test the spirits, whether they are of God; because many false prophets have gone out into the world.'"

"So I just have to ask if you were sent by God?" Seemed easy enough.

Her finger tapped the page. "'By this you know the Spirit of God: Every spirit that confesses that Jesus Christ has come in the flesh is of God, and every spirit that does not confess that Jesus Christ has come in the flesh is not of God.'"

Oh. Jesus. It felt a little weird talking about Jesus in the garage. I was used to hearing about him in Sunday school, but we'd stopped going a long time ago. I knew he was a great guy, God's right hand man, and all that. I guess I just didn't associate him with my regular life: school and friends and home. We used to say a little prayer-poem before dinner when I was younger, 'Come Lord Jesus,' etc. etc., but now we hardly ever ate at the same time. Mom usually had to work through dinner.

And I'd always thought of angels, when I thought about them at all, in broader terms. Not just a Christian thing, but kind of spiritually generic, belonging to everyone. But if 'Jesus Christ' was the angels' secret password, that worked for me. "So," I asked, "what's your name?"

"My name doesn't matter, but Whom I serve," she said.

"Right, right. And whom do you serve?"

"I serve the King of kings, the Most High."

Was that the right answer? I had the feeling she was testing me. "And do you confess Jesus Christ?" I'd forgotten the exact words.

"I confess that Jesus Christ has come in the flesh. I confess the Christ crucified, and Him risen."

"Okay. Great…"

"Gabby," she said. "You can call me that."

"Thanks."

"But now will you test *her*?" a deeper voice asked behind me. I spun around. A tall figure stepped from behind the stack of cardboard boxes. It was the same black-haired guy who had suddenly appeared with Rafie in room 316. He was all about the dramatic entrances.

"Micah," the girl greeted him. Only then did I notice there was no puff of cold breath when she spoke. And she was wearing a tank top and flip-flops in winter.

"Gabrielle," Micah replied, also seeming to notice the tank top and flip-flops. "Why do you come?"

"Same as you, to do the will of the Most High. And look, she sees us."

Yes, and she can hear you too, I thought.

"What is it, Micah?" Gabby asked. Then she pointed a finger at him. "It troubles you that she can see."

"It is irregular," he said.

"But not impossible." She said the word as if it tasted deeply significant and a little funny.

"She does not even wear the belt."

"Then you need not ask why I have come, brother."

Clearly in angelic circles it wasn't considered bad manners to talk about someone as if they weren't in the room. I cleared my throat. "Excuse me, but is it possible for me to know what's going on here? I do have a belt upstairs if you need one."

"Who are you talking to?"

I spun around again—another voice. My sister, Sheelan, stood in the doorway, staring at me as if I was having a conversation with myself. I turned back to Gabby and Micah, my mouth hanging open. They were gone.

Sheelan just kept staring.

My presence in English class Friday was pointless.

That might be said about lots of Fridays, not to mention some Mondays through Thursdays, but today it seemed especially true. I did like this class. A handful of seventh-graders shared it with some of the eighth-graders. This made us feel pretty important until we were actually in the class, when we felt totally intimidated. But Mr. Behrens was my favorite teacher after Mrs. Greene, the art teacher. It wasn't so much his teaching style as his perfectly bald head, hypnotically reflective of the fluorescent lighting. The best part was, his first name was Hal. On the surface, a boring name, Hal Behrens, until you realize that Hal is short for Harold and he could've easily been Harry Behrens. He was the unhairiest hairy bear ever to teach junior high English.

That Friday, though, he couldn't compete with the voices in my head. My mom and Sheelan had been talking about me the night before. Mom sometimes got home from her second job after I'd gone to bed, but Sheelan usually stayed up. I lay in bed and listened to her tell my mom about my behavior in the garage.

"She was having a conversation, Mom."

"Yeah, so?" Mom was tired and half-listening.

"No one else was there."

I could hear my mom sit down. "Oh, don't you ever talk to yourself?"

"It wasn't like that. She was talking like someone was there."

"Maybe someone was."

I'd held my breath for a second, like Mom was about to suggest it might be an angel, because normal people saw and talked to angels all the time. Ha.

"Trust me, I checked," Sheelan said.

"Well, she's been through a lot—"

"And I haven't?"

"We all have, Shee. But Rory..."

"Rory got to sleep through the worst of it. Only she woke up crazy."

"Sheelan."

"Forget it. Forget I even mentioned it. Maybe we're all going crazy in our own ways." She stomped upstairs to the bathroom. I heard her begin her lengthy un-beautification routine to reverse the beautification process she performed every morning.

I heard my mom's sigh and the crinkle of the bag of pretzels I'd left on the table—probably the only dinner she'd have. "Maybe," I heard her say.

The walls in my house were way too thin.

"What are your thoughts on that, Rory?"

I jerked up at my desk. Mr. Behrens had asked the question; the class watched expectantly for my answer. I had no idea what we were discussing. "I, uh..."

"No thoughts whatsoever?" This earned a sprinkling of laughter.

Too many thoughts, I wanted to say.

"Can someone show Rory where we are in the book? And what about the empty box in this chapter—what does it symbolize? Anyone?" Hands raised to answer the second question. No one seemed interested in steering me to the right page. I grabbed a book from my backpack and flipped through it cluelessly, hoping the words 'empty box' might pop off the page.

Something tapped my elbow. A dog-eared copy of a paperback novel hovered beside me. The hand that held it belonged to the eighth grader who sat behind me. He must have seen it in the book bag beneath my chair. I'd been flipping through my history book.

"Thanks," I whispered, daring to glance at him. Typically I kept a safe distance from the eighth graders. But he didn't seem scary at all, returning my look with a quick half-smile. I only knew his first name: Sam.

"Chapter three," he said. "Page sixteen."

I noticed him later in the cafeteria, sitting with mostly other eighth-graders at the far end of the room. It was hard to tell what sort of person he was just by the people sitting around him. There wasn't a clique thing going on that I could tell. They were talking and laughing, but not obnoxiously.

I sat down at the usual table, picking a space across from Jasmine Wee. She hadn't spoken to me since my case of bumble-tongue a few days before. "Hi," I ventured.

She gave me a cautious nod. "Hi."

"Um, sorry about what I said the other—"

"Can we just forget about it?"

"Sure."

Her arm slid across the paper in front of her. She was trying to be subtle about it, but she was covering her homework.

"Algebra?" I asked.

"Mm-hmm."

"You still get it?"

"Mm-hmm."

"I still don't."

She set her pencil down. "You may as well know, Rory, I'm not going to give you the answers, so you don't have to waste your time being nice to me."

Ouch. This day was getting better and better. For some reason, my chin wanted to quiver. When had I become such a crybaby? A dry-eyed crybaby.

"I don't want the stupid answers. I just want something to make sense for once." I stood and scooped up my tray, no longer hungry for ham and cheese. But the last thing I wanted to do was to walk past Kevin Sebeck's table—the whole gang clustered like sharks and I was blood in the water. I banged the tray back down and left it there, walking towards the other end of the cafeteria. Maybe I would walk right outside and fume (cry) in the parking lot.

But that hard bubble in my throat—the kind that makes it hurt to swallow? Well, it felt like it rolled upwards into my head and popped. Pains in my head weren't any big surprise since the accident, but this was like shards of glass in my brain. I managed to walk as far as the last table, but everything went gray when I reached for the door. Was it windy outside? A whooshing sound filled my ears.

Thus began Public Seizure Number Two.

I never felt myself hit the floor, but suddenly figures gathered above me. They were gray and smeary, scribbled pencil sketches smudged by a finger, moving around me like the drawings in a flipbook where you fan through the pages fast and it looks animated. I could just make out their faces, some of them vaguely familiar—the other kids in the cafeteria.

I stared too hard, and then I saw the other shapes. People-ish, but not human-ish. They hovered over shoulders, they skulked, they watched me there on the floor with nasty glee on their faces. I went cold all over.

Then, in all that grayness, there was a pale yellowish, even a golden, light. Someone knelt beside me, and in all that riot of gray scribbly movement, he seemed solid and still.

And dressed really strangely. First there was the helmet. Not like a bicycle helmet: a warrior's type of helmet. Like a Roman gladiator's helmet, maybe? But no, hardly like that at all, and only if it could be made of light, not metal. His hair curled out from underneath it, the same black-brown as his eyes. And he wore a breastplate—and yet not. Like the helmet, it didn't look heavy or even solid at all, if something incredibly strong can be un-solid. Underneath that was a broad belt, and it was a beautiful thing. I'd never seen anything like it. It looked like it was woven from gold and silver and...fire and air, maybe.

If this weren't odd enough, he was barefoot. He said my name and told me I would be okay. Despite everything, I believed him. He seemed very believable.

As for the rest, the usual routine: crowd gathered around, school nurse, ambulance and, you guessed it, Room 316 at the county hospital.

That bothered me more than anything, that number. Funny how a bunch of big things can be happening, but you go crazy over a little thing. Like the number 316. I don't even know why it bugged me.

I lay in bed, facing the wall. "Grandma, what time is it?" I heard her close her book and turn to look at the clock on the opposite wall. "It's a bit past three, darling. Is there something you want to watch on the television?"

"It's 3:16, isn't it?"

"Well, let's see." She must've adjusted her glasses on her nose. "It's quarter past. Well, no, you're right. Exactly 3:16 on that clock. You want me to pull the TV around?"

"No, Gran." So, I was going crazy. Sheelan was right. Sheelan—who would've guessed?

"Want another drink of water?"

"No, thanks."

"What's troubling you, Rory?"

I flopped over onto my back. "A lot of different things."

"Your mom will be here in about an hour."

"Then I can go home?"

"I'm sure you can. But that gives us an hour to talk about a lot of different things, if you want." She set her book aside.

I wasn't sure what I could talk about, though. Grandma Judy always had answers to things, and she never made me feel stupid, but what Sheelan had said really got me to thinking. I didn't want to start blabbing about what had been happening to me if people were just going to think I was crazy. More than that, *I* didn't want to start thinking I was crazy. Dad liked to say that if you thought you were crazy you probably weren't, because crazy folks were usually the last to know. But best not to risk it.

The number thing seemed safe, though. "This number keeps popping up. Three-sixteen. It's weird. Has anything like that ever happened to you?"

"Oh, sure." She tucked a wisp of hair behind her ear. She had the kind that couldn't decide if it was mostly blonde or mostly gray. "Sometimes I'll come across an unusual word in a crossword puzzle, then I'll hear it used on a news program later, or I'll read it in a book. It seems like I haven't heard that word for years, and all of a sudden, three times in one day. Maybe it's just because I'm attuned to it."

"What about a number?"

"Not that I remember. Do you want me to buy you a lottery ticket?" she joked. Grandma and Dad didn't believe in the lottery—Dad called it 'the poor man's tax.' I wasn't sure what that meant, just that it wasn't good.

But to me the lottery didn't sound like such a bad idea. "Yeah, number three-sixteen. Whatever that means."

"Well, it's the day you were born. March sixteenth."

Oh, yeah. I hadn't even thought of that.

"But I can think of an even better three-sixteen." She picked up her book again, and I saw that it was her green Bible, the one she carried in her purse. *Oh, it's just her Bible*, I thought, as if it couldn't possibly shed any light on my problem. After all, old guys wrote that stuff way back when. My problem was right now.

Then it occurred to me: considering my recent odd visitors, maybe, just maybe, there might be something to it.

"Here it is." She peered down her nose through her bifocals. "John 3:16."

"Oh, that one. That's the sign you always see hanging from the stands at football games and stuff."

"If you say so. It's also one of the best-known verses in the Bible. 'For God so loved the world that He gave His only begotten

Son, that whoever believes in Him should not perish, but have everlasting life.'"

"Yeah, that's a pretty important one, I guess."

She smiled. "I can't think of anything more important than that." She closed the fat little book and laid it on my bedside table. "You keep this. If Someone is trying to tell you something, you'll want to have it handy."

"Okay. Thanks, Gran."

"You're welcome. Now why don't you try to rest, maybe take a nap before your mom comes to get you?"

"I'll try." I rolled back over and tried to bully the pillow into some sort of comfortable configuration, but it stubbornly held its original shape. All this time in a hospital bed, and I still hadn't figured out what they made their pillows out of. A huge, stale marshmallow was my best theory so far.

It didn't really matter. My thoughts refused to let me rest. I kept thinking about those creepy gray things I saw lurking around during the seizure. But even more than that, I thought about the boy in the bizarre armor with the reassuring way about him.

If it had been another angel, it would've made more sense. Not a lot of sense, but at least some. But he wasn't an angel. I was pretty sure of it, because I knew him. I'd known him all semester.

It was Sam from my English class.

4

Life became all about tests.

I didn't know at the time that life is always about tests. A lot of them are pop quizzes you don't even know you're taking. Sounds unfair, but I couldn't exactly moan: I'd already been given the answers—the Teacher's manual, so to speak. And it wasn't cheating to read it. You're supposed to. Read it, and at least you might recognize a test when you're sitting right in the middle of one.

But I was also taking the kinds of tests you know are happening to you. A noodle scan, alternately known as an MRI. Hard not to notice when you're lying in a noisy, coffin-ish tube, not allowed to move for what seems like forever. Then an algebra exam. Would you believe I passed it? Only because I had help, but more on that later.

Back to the noodle scan. It revealed that I, despite all evidence, still had a brain. And there wasn't anything visibly wrong with it. Sounds like good news, but guess again. When they can't find anything physically wrong with a girl who's having fall-down seizures and talking to invisible people, where do you suppose they send her?

P. H. McDonald, Ph.D. (What my dad would call a head-shrinker.) I got the feeling after our first meeting that psychiatrists prefer not to be called head-shrinkers. Not even just 'shrinks.' But more on that later.

Back to the algebra test. I passed—not with a D, either—a B. I had to give the credit to Jasmine Wee, and no, I didn't copy the answers over her shoulder. She actually gave me another chance. It might've been guilt that brought about her change of heart. I might've capitalized on it, just a little.

Public Seizure Number Two (PS#2) had fallen (literally) on a Friday, so I had the weekend to recover and was back in school on Monday. The fact that this pleased me just goes to show how weird my life had become.

Jasmine watched me all Monday morning. She tried to disguise the fact, but even when I didn't catch her doing it, I could feel those dark eyes boring into the back of my frizzy head. When I did catch her, she looked away with a scrunched-up sort of face.

Lunchtime proved too much for her. I sat at the usual table, but not across from her. Not so far away that she wouldn't notice me, just far enough that she would get the point. I'm not sure what the point was. I was just trying to figure out her strange behavior.

It got stranger. She pushed her tray down the table, scooting down so she sat opposite me. She swallowed a mouthful of the Special of the Day, and it didn't go down easy (shocker). I munched a french fry. I could see her gathering her courage. It made her squirm a little in her seat.

"Are you okay?" she finally asked.

I got that question a lot. It could mean a hundred different things, depending on the person asking and the tone of voice. When Mom asked, it usually meant *Are you upset with me again?* But Sheelan's usually sounded more like *Are you nuts?* My dad's "Are you okay?" was the best. His always meant *I'm just checking in with you—do you need me?*

When most of the kids at school asked, it was sort of a *What's wrong with you?* But Jasmine's was different. Hers meant *Was it my fault?*

She thought maybe she'd caused PS#2. I could let her think so. She had been rather rude to me. Maybe she had caused it. A rudeness-induced seizure. "I guess so," I said. "The jury's still out on that. But I don't think I'm on the verge of PS#3, if that's what you mean."

She tried to decode that, then brushed it off. "If you want, we can look at the algebra."

I wish I'd said, *if anything's gonna give me a seizure, it's the algebra*, and laughed, but at the time I just wasn't seeing much humor in either the seizure situation or the math one. "Yeah, okay," I said instead.

And so began an almost daily ritual of Algebra Lunches. Sometimes X equaled the Special of the Day. On those days, Jasmine actually manipulated me into trying the non-deep-fried menu selection. This she either accomplished by guilt: "How can you eat that? Do you know how those *insert animal here* are treated?" or fear: "How can you eat that? Do you know how that *insert processed food item here* is manufactured?" I argued that a vegetarian who ate fish was a hypocrite. She argued that fish weren't meat. I argued that fish had faces. We compromised on processed, deep-fried fish fingers (a.k.a. fish thingers).

The upside of my adventures in lunchland was the B on the test. I considered going vegetarian in the hopes of an A- on the next one, but that night Sheelan brought home a sack of 99-cent double cheeseburgers. She also brought home her boyfriend, which violates about five house rules and annoys the spit out of me.

Quentin wasn't a horrible person, though I wasn't secretly in love with him and insanely jealous as Sheelan liked to believe. But in the past few weeks he'd been coming over more than he ever used to, aiding and abetting Sheelan in the breaking of house rules, and I hated the idea that they were taking advantage of the new situation, with Mom working all the time. Besides, when the two of them came waltzing in, it forced me to gather up all my homework from the kitchen table and retreat to my room or else be forced to endure Sheelan's fake high-pitched lovey girlfriend voice and listen to her laugh at his dumb jokes as they watched idiotic sitcoms and tried to hide the fact that they were kissing. Why did the kitchen have to overlook the family room?

At least tonight I could hide in my room with a double cheeseburger. But my quarter pound of cheesy bliss was not to last. The first bite caused a butterfinger chain reaction: drip of ketchup on history paper, reach for napkin, book sliding off lap, grab at book, can of soda knocked off nightstand. If not for that fizzy brown puddle on my carpet, I wouldn't have trudged downstairs to discover a seriously disgusting case of lip-lock happening on the sofa.

Sheelan saw me. "Quit spying on us, Rory," she hissed.

"Please. I'm trying not to puke."

"So get lost."

"I have a right to be here." More than he did. I grabbed a kitchen towel.

"Three's a crowd, spy."

"Hey, she should bring her little boyfriend over, and it'll be a double date," Quentin said in his dopey, cheerful voice. (Weren't those two of the seven dwarves? The two with the lowest IQs?)

"Duh, she doesn't have a boyfriend."

"I got a little brother."

"Isn't he, like, nine?"

"Eleven." They snickered and sipped their glasses of soda, ice cubes tinkling like Sheelan's chilly laughter.

"Just shut up," I said.

"Don't speak that way to us," Sheelan said, like they were authority figures. "You're the one who came snooping around."

I'm not sure why, because I'd been feeling mostly annoyed and only a little bit angry, but all of a sudden I was yelling. "It's not snooping, because this is my house! I have a right to be here, unlike him! I'll just tell Mom that you've been bringing him over here all the time, and what you've been doing instead of homework!"

"You little—" she jumped up, the soda sloshing in her glass, and pointed her finger at me. "You think you can say whatever you want now, just because you're brain damaged."

"You think you can do anything you like because Dad is dead and Mom isn't around anymore!"

She could only gape at me, and I couldn't blame her. She went pale, then very red, and with no sound at all she flung her glass at me. I was still above her, though, and the glass didn't clear the iron railing. It shattered in a shower of diet cola, ice chips, and glass.

I ran upstairs, Quentin went home, and Sheelan and I spent the evening cleaning up our respective puddles of sticky soda.

Maybe I did need therapy. I heard Dr. McDonald suggest family counseling to my mom, which backed up my own personal theory (and Sheelan's, I suppose) that we were all going nuts. But my mom kind of laughed in that way that was the opposite of amused and suggested that perhaps we would in another life when she didn't have to work two jobs to pay half our bills.

So it was just me and Dr. McD, and on top of my other issues I could now add guilt because somehow my mom would have to pay for this session. I had already decided it would be only this session. Tell them what they want to hear, get a big NOT CRAZY stamped on a paper somewhere and be on my merry, certifiably sane way.

The one thing I determined not to do under any circumstance—the thing that would botch up the whole plan— was to open my big yap about the angels. Which is naturally just what I did.

Don't blame me, blame Dr. McD. That had the potential to be my new motto. First of all, she didn't come in with a clipboard. Right away that made her less like a doctor and more like a human. She was wearing this pink sweater that looked soft as a baby blanket, and when she talked to me it was as if we were both people. Before I knew what was happening, she had me talking about It, but I wasn't crying or even trapping the crying in my head while it tried to explode out my throat. That hurts amazingly, by the way.

This hurt, too, in a different way, as if a nasty creature that I hadn't even realized was on my back relaxed its claws just a bit. Then the subject of Sheelan came up, and of course the claws dug back in, along with some teeth. Somehow, talk of Sheelan made me accuse her of accusing me of being crazy, and that made me mention why: my supposed crazy conversations with imaginary people.

Oops.

So began the era of people talking about me in other rooms. Almost never in front of me, where I might have defended myself (or maybe opened the big yap and dug myself in deeper). Dr. Flynn and Dr. McD; Dr. McD and Mom; Mom and Sheelan — that always burned me up; Mom and Grandma Judy; Grandma Judy and Mrs. Ingram when Mom had to be at work.

Grandma was the only one who actually took it to the next level and talked to me. I can't say my mom didn't try, but a sort of two-way resentment hung between us: *Why do you have to put me through this right now?* we both didn't ask. Then I had my guilt issues, and all in all I wasn't very conversational and she didn't have the energy to push and pull things out of me.

Grandma had plenty of energy, but she also had a way of getting the stuff out without the pushing and pulling. She and Dr. McD must've read some of the same books.

She came by after school on one of those February days when you wonder why you had to be born in a place where you get both the soul-numbing winters and the cranium-baking summers. "I brought some soup," she announced as she shed layers of hats, scarves, gloves, jackets.

"Clean out the fridge today?" asked Sheelan, who happened to be home this afternoon. Of course she lucked out that Quentin wasn't with her during this unexpected adult intrusion.

"You bet," Grandma said. It was well known that half of what Grandma Judy dug out of the refrigerator went into the soup pot, and that you never could tell what you were going to get in each spoonful. It was surprisingly good, if occasionally scary. And today she'd brought homemade bread with it. It felt like ages since I'd eaten anything homemade.

"Give us this day our daily bread," she said cheerfully, unwrapping the loaf and carving off a thick slice. "And might as well give it to us while it's still warm." She'd even brought the butter. There was no guarantee we'd have even the basics in our fridge lately. "How's the homework coming along?"

"Slow," I said.

"This might have something to do with it." She seized the TV remote beside my books. Brandishing it like a wizard, she attempted to silence the TV but only managed to make it louder. While she fiddled with it, the phone rang and Sheelan pounced, retreating upstairs to gossip in privacy.

"I need my glasses for this," Grandma was muttering. "Which is the 'off' button?"

"Wait," I said.

"You'll get your work done in half the time without the tube on."

"See what's on?"

She looked over her glasses, which were perched at their customary odd angle on her nose. "Yeah, what? Oh, it's *Saved by the Angels*."

"You like that show, don't you?"

"Sure, but I'm not here to watch TV." She finally found the power button and the actor-angels disappeared instantly—which is probably the only accurate thing about the show. "Besides, it's just a re-run."

"Oh," I said. I didn't mention that they were all re-runs these days. "I just remember you said you liked it."

She had turned to the sink and last night's dishes still congealing inside it. "I like it alright. It's wholesome and uplifting. That's hard to find on TV these days. I can't say I agree with all the theology, if that's what you want to call it."

Somehow, with her back to me, I felt brave enough to ask, "You mean angels don't really bop around looking like people?"

"Well, that part's got some truth to it."

"It does?" I tried to sound casual. "How do you know?"

"The Bible, of course. There are stories of angels who look like people, though much of the time I think they appear more as themselves."

"What do you mean?"

"Well, what's the first thing an angel usually says when he comes face to face with a human being?"

I shrugged, though she couldn't see it. "Lo, hark, behold—that sort of thing?"

"'Fear not,' is what I was thinking. Whatever they look like, it must be intimidating. I guess they're reflecting a bit of the glory of God around them."

"But you said they could look like people."

"I'm thinking of a certain passage, in Hebrews, I think, that says not to forget to entertain strangers because you might be entertaining angels unawares. If you can offer hospitality to an angel and be unaware of it, it must sometimes look like a regular person, don't you think?"

"Makes sense," I said, scribbling on my English assignment as if it were consuming most of my attention. But I wrote *Hebrews* in the margin. "How can you be sure it's true? Oh, wait, I know—" I answered for her, "—because it's in the Bible."

"But…" She said slowly.

"But how do you know the Bible is all true?"

Once I heard people on the history network talking about all the contradictions in the Bible—before I changed to something more interesting (cartoons). But I thought about it: *if the Bible can't even agree with itself, why would anyone base their life on it?* Then I thought about it more and realized I didn't know anyone who did base their life on it, besides the pastor. The rest of us just based our Sunday mornings on it. And that's if we were being good. I mean, I knew there was a lot of good stuff in the capital-B Book. But to treat the whole thing like it's all true? Giants, big boats full of animals? Fishes swallowing men and spitting them back out? Literally true?

Grandma Judy watched me while she dried a pan. Everyone said I had her eyes, but right now hers looked a lot greener than mine. "That's a good question, Rory. If I were an expert, I could stand here and name a hundred, a thousand, examples of its reliability, it's *historicity*." She said words meant to expand my vocabulary as if tasting them. "The answers are out there, but I don't have them all stored in my brain. And you know what? That doesn't matter. There are plenty of people who can see all the compelling proofs laid out before them and still choose not to believe, or find themselves unable to believe. Myself, I just read and trust, and it's the Holy Spirit that helps me to understand and believe. And I've seen it bless my life in too many ways to ignore. Just start reading—and try praying before you do each time. You'll see what I mean." She turned back to the dishes, though I sensed she had more to say. I was right.

"If you're interested in angels, look at the concordance in the back of the Bible. It'll get you started." This time she sounded like she was trying to sound casual.

"Yeah, maybe." I went beyond casual and aimed for polite disinterest. It didn't fool her, I'm pretty sure. But that was okay since I didn't think I needed to fool Grandma Judy. And seeing as she seemed to care the most and listen the best, it made sense to listen right back.

5

Not long after this, something strange happened. I had a good week.

So my definition of 'good week' was skewed, so what? I'd take what I could get: no tests, no seizures, no visits from people of questionable origin, and even a February thaw that hinted at the spring we wouldn't feel until April. Kimmie and Hannah had no weekend school events, and we planned to hang out together on Saturday for the first time in forever. Walking home from school on Friday afternoon, I almost splashed in the sidewalk puddles, except that it reminded me of my dad. He had always laughed when we did it as little kids, whereas you could see my mom was thinking of the extra laundry.

Thoughts of Dad threatened to knock me right off my happy legs. Most of the time I dragged around a weight of remembering. Other times the shackle sprang open and I'd actually forget and feel normal, until I remembered again. Then I'd clap on some extra leg irons for the guilt. What business did I have feeling lighthearted? All this even though I knew he would want me to be happy.

I was wavering when I walked up the driveway. Then the Fishers' door swung open, and Kingston stood there munching and smiling. He didn't even have to say anything: the aroma of baking wafted around him like he was some sort of stocky angel on a cloud of yummy smell. I climbed the steps to his door without a pause. Definitely chocolate chip. And so it was that Sad and Guilty were momentarily conquered by Happy and Chocolate. (Chocolate naturally being an emotion.)

"Hello, sweetie," called Mrs. Fisher as I followed Kingston into the kitchen. She steered her two youngest daughters, Tee-Tee and Cherry—don't look at me, I didn't name them—away from the oven so she could pull out the freshest batch of cookies. She was a tiny woman with enormous oven mitts on her slim brown arms. But her small body came with a big voice. Not obnoxious, just friendly and likely to break into song without warning. A happy person, the sort the world looks at with great suspicion.

She deposited the hot pan on a cooling rack and swept over to hug me. I still got a little embarrassed when she did it, but they were natural hugs and not the uncomfortable kind that you have to give to great-aunts you hardly know who smell like lavender and liniment. Mrs. Fisher always smelled like vanilla.

Today her hug ended with an extra little squeeze that said *I know you're hurting and I care about you.* She wouldn't say it out loud or make me lie about how fine I was doing. Within half a minute I sat at the kitchen table with a tall glass of milk and two melty cookies the size of saucers. Kingston, Tee-Tee and Cherry sat around me, and soon their middle sister, Hope, joined us. She scribbled furiously in a notebook as she walked. "Finished my math, Mama," she called, grabbing a cookie. "Can I go?" She was already pulling a coat over her leotard and sweats.

"Sure can. Call when you're finished."

"The school's just down the street, Mama."

"A mile down the street, and it will be dark when gymnastics ends. We talked about this. Call and Daddy will pick you up."

"Yes, Ma'am." She kissed her mother's cheek, which was level with hers. She had Mr. Fisher's athletic build.

"Want me to check her math, Mama?" Kingston asked around a mouthful of cookie.

"Thank you, baby boy." Kings never seemed to mind when his mother called him this. "And no more cookies."

"Yes, Ma'am." He glanced over his sister's math problems like he was reading a comic book, circling one of them with a pencil as stubby as his fingers. I peeked at the page and grimaced at its unnatural mix of numbers and letters.

"Algebra?" I asked. Hope was maybe eleven years old.

"Yep."

"*I* can barely do algebra."

"Well, she got one wrong."

"Which?" Mrs. Fisher asked.

"Number seven."

"I knew it would be that one. She was rushing."

This bizarre phenomenon was known as homeschooling. Little did I know before meeting the Fisher family that attending an actual school wasn't mandatory, like a prison sentence. (It just felt like it sometimes.) Apparently it's perfectly legal to choose house arrest instead. Only the Fisher inmates didn't moan and groan about school like we at Whitestone Elementary did. Sometimes I strongly suspected that they *liked* school—not the same way the top students at Whitestone liked school, basically motivated by bloodthirsty grade grubbing. The Fishers seemed to enjoy the learning part. But hey, going to science class in your backyard or studying literature on the sofa in your pajamas sounded pretty sweet to me.

And I'd learned early on that Friday was home-ec day, and that usually meant something good from the oven.

But there was no doubt about it: the Fishers were different. Odd, according to the rest of my family. Still, no one could say they weren't good neighbors.

As gooey chocolate warmed the corners of my mouth, I decided they were excellent neighbors. I sipped milk from a pink aluminum cup, cold against my lips. It looked like a relic from decades past and probably was. Kingston's glass had long outlived the glory days of its faded cartoon character. It wasn't only the Fisher's tableware that was mismatched — this seemed to be the theme of their entire household décor. Interesting pieces of comfort and function with little else in common. There was some mysterious unifying factor, though, that pulled it all together.

"I should've come to you for help with my algebra," I said to Kingston.

"Sure, Rory. I like math." He could often be found scribbling little equations as he constructed makeshift machines out of Tinkertoys, rubber bands, and paper clips, usually for the purpose of flinging action figures across the room. The distances they achieved were carefully documented and the necessary adjustments made. This would qualify as a physics lesson for Kingston.

"Can we go play, Mama?" Tee-Tee piped up. Unless it was Cherry. The seven-year-olds weren't identical twins, but they might as well have been. Unlike Hope, they had taken after their mother and were hardly bigger than five-year-olds. Both sported enormous brown eyes and a pair of ponytails that poofed out like Mickey Mouse ears.

"Piano first. Wash that chocolate off your hands." They sighed but obeyed, each scrambling to get to the piano first. A pointless race, it turned out, since they were practicing a duet. I listened as they plunked out melody and harmony, almost in synch, but I didn't know the tune.

"Did you know opossums are the only marsupials in North America?" Kingston asked out of nowhere.

"Nope. Did you finally hunt that 'possum down?"

"Naw, never saw it. I think the Nelsons probably had a big old rat in their garage." He laughed his rolling chuckle.

"Put on the full…armor of God, so you can stand against the Devil's schemes…"

I glanced towards the family room where the girls were plinking on the piano and now singing in their piping little voices. They made a mistake and started again.

"Put on the full — "

47

"Put on the full armor of — "

"Put on — "

"Stop it, Tee! You're going too fast."

"Girls," Mrs. Fisher said in that warning tone all mothers use. Then she turned to me. "Have you been able to catch up with your school work, Rory?"

"Just about."

"You can always come here after school if you want to do homework with Kings." Kingston didn't actually have homework — or, in a sense, it was all homework for him. Usually by the time I got home he was long finished.

"Or you can help me build a dam on the creek," Kings said.

"Buckle the belt of truth around your waist…Stand firm — "

"…around your waist…Stand firm! With the breastplate of righteousness in place — "

"Stand firm!"

"Quit it!" Cherry wailed. "Mama, she's trying to mess me up."

"You'll be there all night if you don't get through that song at least once," Mrs. Fisher called back. "Don't you play, Rory? I seem to remember you taking lessons once upon a time."

I only half-heard her question. Their song had given me a weird feeling, and it wasn't just the excruciating pitch of their voices. "What are they singing?" I wondered. I must've wondered out loud, because Mrs. Fisher answered me.

"The Armor of God. From the sixth chapter of Ephesians. You recognize it?" She was giving me more credit than I deserved and probably knew it. Bible was hardly a daily subject at my school. In fact, I think it might have been illegal at my school.

"No…" I said. "Yes and no. It reminds me of something. I must've heard something, or read something recently…" What was it? Belt, breastplate…

"The shoes of the readiness of the gospel of peace…And the helmet of salvation…The shield of faith — to quench the fiery darts of the wicked — and the sword of the Spirit, which is — "

They had almost made it through the verse.

" — the Word of God! Put on the full armor of God…"

Armor.

I had been avoiding Sam with pointless dedication. Pointless because he sat right behind me in English class, dedication because I was so embarrassed about my vision of him during my last seizure—aside from having the seizure itself—that I felt pretty sure I would swallow my tongue if I so much as made eye contact with him. Making eye contact with a boy is dicey enough, but when your brain has concocted some sort of knight in shining armor picture of him against your will, it's nothing short of mortifying.

Not that he was a knight in shining armor in my seizure-vision-thingy. More of a barefoot guy wearing oddly assorted battle gear made out of light. But I was sure that if I looked at him he would somehow see straight into my brain and know what I had imagined.

No, not imagined—I take that back. Because if I imagined it, that means *I* made the whole thing up. If it was some kind of a vision, that means the picture was sort of planted in my head by Someone Else and I wasn't responsible.

Aaargh! English class was so much simpler when Sam was just some eighth grader who sat behind me.

I concocted an elaborate plan to get safely to my seat. It involved a roundabout path, an innocently dropped pencil, a swift duck to retrieve it and thus a clever avoidance of looking at Sam. Instead, my treacherous size-10s (did I mention I grew out of my 9-½s?) snagged onto the strap of his backpack, the pencil flew out of my hand along with half of my books, and I staggered to my desk only to find it already occupied. By an eighth-grade girl, no less: Shayne Something-or-the-Other.

She was sitting backwards, talking to Sam, or she had been before I practically fell on her. Now she looked up at me with an expression I found impossible to read. But not the *oh, you big loser* face I expected and probably deserved.

"You must want your seat back," she said with no apparent sarcasm, unless she was far subtler than your average eighth-grader. She stood and turned to her own desk. "See you at lunch. Meet you under the tree."

"Uh, okay," I mumbled, then realized she was talking to Sam. I felt breathtakingly stupid. Sam just smiled, his eyes all dark and sparkly. I have no memory of the rest of the class.

The tree Shayne mentioned wasn't a real tree. It was a mural painted by Mrs. Greene, the art teacher, in the main corridor outside the cafeteria. A silver-gray tree with pinkish-white flowers exactly like the one out in the schoolyard, or at least how it looked every spring. You could tell by the way she painted it that she must love that tree.

Later I actually saw Shayne and Sam meet 'under the tree,' a favorite gathering spot. A few others joined them before they went inside. They didn't notice me, but I wasn't trying to be noticeable.

Lunch was not promising, and not just because the Special of the Day was 'Ham Surprise.' (Who ever decided that surprises in cafeteria food were a good thing?) Jasmine Wee was absent that day, and the other non-clique kids were scattered and uninviting. I faced the depressing prospect of eating alone. I refused to eat Ham Surprise alone, so I got the hot dog and fries. If Jasmine were there, she would've told me that there were more surprises, and nastier ones, in the hot dog than there were in the Special. But she wasn't there, so I intended to eat my hot dog with relish—and mustard, my dad would joke.

Before I could sit down, I noticed Shayne at the last table in a group of other kids. She waved her hand in a beckoning sort of way. It almost looked like she was waving at me. I sneaked a peek over my shoulder. No one behind me. Still, she was an eighth-grader; I moved to sit down alone.

"Rory," she called. She knew my name?

I stared. She beckoned.

I had been summoned to an eighth-grade table. This could not be good.

"So what was the purpose of the school assembly?"

Dr. McD was asking. I was barely listening. Instead I revisited that afternoon in the cafeteria in my mind—and doodled on a scrap of paper from my backpack. "What? Sorry."

"Do you like to draw?" She peeked at my doodle of a crazy-haired girl. I was disturbed to see how much the girl looked like me.

"Yeah, I guess. I'm not very good."

"I disagree," she said. Today she was wearing creamy white cashmere and her honey-colored hair was swept up into a twist. She slipped something from the bottom drawer of her desk. "Here, take this. Some people like to keep a journal, but others find drawing to be more helpful in sorting out their thoughts and feelings."

I accepted the spiral-bound sketchbook from her and flipped through its pristine pages. "Thanks."

"You're welcome. Now, we were talking about the assembly, where you had your first seizure."

"Oh, yeah. It was all about Parent Night, the activities they're planning and what the different classes have to do and stuff."

"It sounds like an important night."

"I guess so. They do it every year."

"Will your mom be attending this year?"

I shrugged. "I guess, if she doesn't have to work."

"Did she and your dad attend last year?"

"Mm-hmm." Even though I was distracted, I could see what she was getting at. Might as well give her what she wanted. "I guess I was remembering that. I must've gotten upset."

"Do you remember what you were feeling before the seizure?"

"Do you think I'm getting them when I get upset? Because I was pretty upset right before the one in the cafeteria."

She was watching me closely, though she tried to disguise it by not actually looking at me. "Do you remember what you were feeling at the assembly?"

Leave it to Dr. McD to get to the heart of the problem. I suppose I should've been glad, since I'd never wanted to see her in the first place. At least she worked fast.

I said nothing. As a matter of fact, I did remember what was going on in my head at the assembly. I'd been thinking that my dad would be coming to this Parent Night, too, if it weren't for me.

It was my fault that my dad died.

6

O n TV, when someone talks to a therapist there's all that business about confidentiality. What is said in the room stays in the room, blah blah blah—the reason people can supposedly be honest about stuff. Kids, apparently, are not people. Kids pour out their wretched hearts then go home and find their deep, dark secrets the subject of dinner conversation.

This happened a few nights later, when I was least expecting it—the dinner or the conversation. We'd kind of gotten used to scrounging up our own supper, but I got home from school to discover the car in the garage and the kitchen full of grocery bags. It was like uncovering sunken treasure. Each bag offered up untold delights: yogurt drinks, microwave pizza snacks, peanut butter, bananas, boxes of cereal. The smell of brown paper bags gave me a thrill like Christmas morning wrapping paper.

"What're you doing here?" I asked my mom. I didn't mean it to sound rude. But that had started happening lately, my tone of voice not matching my mood. When I heard parents complain about their grouchy teenagers, I wondered if they were like me, not really as grouchy as they sounded. Sometimes it was only the grouchy sound of my voice that made me feel grouchy at all.

"Well, it's nice to see you, too," Mom said, rummaging for something and finding it. She brandished a cellophaned tray of meat. "And to answer your question, I'm cooking supper."

"Did you get fired or something?"

"No, Rory, I didn't get fired or something. I got paid, and I got off early, so I thought we could have a nice supper together tonight."

"Does Sheelan know? 'Cause sometimes she gets home kind of late." At first I had a wickedly gleeful thought: what if Sheelan brought Quentin home with her? She would be so busted. Then I thought of how that would ruin supper, and it was less appealing.

"Oh, it won't be ready for a couple of hours. Now please stop eating straight out of the bags and help me put these groceries away. Then you can do your homework."

I complied, but not before smuggling a package of fig bars over to the kitchen table where my books waited. Mom puttered and sliced and diced vegetables while I sliced and diced letters and numbers for my math assignment. Cooking smells hung in the air, far more mouthwatering than the odor of algebra. This went on for some time—plenty of time for a real conversation, I might add, but Mom kept it at small talk—until Sheelan came home (without Quentin) just in time to eat. She didn't seem surprised to see Mom there.

All the surprises had been saved for me.

"How did your meeting with Dr. McDonald go?" Sheelan asked at the table as she passed a bowl of peas with pearl onions.

"I didn't see her today," I said, wondering why she even cared.

"Not you. Mom."

My head whipped around; Mom pretended to be absorbed in the task of opening the new bottle of salad dressing. "It went pretty well," she said.

"You didn't tell me you were going." But you told Sheelan?

"Settle down, Rory," Sheelan said. "And show a little appreciation—she had to take the afternoon off just to go talk about your mental problems."

"That's enough, Sheelan." Mom glanced at me. "Yes, I had an appointment with Dr. McDonald to discuss your...situation. I know what a tough time you've had—"

"Oh, just her." Sheelan shut up at Mom's look.

"—but the encouraging thing is that you seem to be doing fine physically."

"Aside from falling down, twitching, drooling occasionally," I said (grouchily, and this time I felt it).

"The seizures don't seem to be caused by your injury."

"I knew she was just faking them." Sheelan was pushing it now and she knew it, but she couldn't resist.

"Faking them? 'Gee, I haven't been experiencing nearly enough public humiliation lately. Think I'll flop around on the floor for a bit.'"

"Anything to be the center of attention."

"No, that's your sole purpose in life."

"Enough, both of you." Mom stabbed at her pork chop in a way that closed both our mouths. "I didn't say the seizures aren't real. They just don't seem to be directly caused by your head injury."

"See? Mental problems," Sheelan said under her breath.

I gave her my 'if looks could kill' expression, which proved not to be fatal, maybe because my heart wasn't in it. All this time I'd been worried that if anyone found out about my angels they'd think I was nuts—I hadn't even considered the seizures. Supposing they were related?

I didn't have time to think about it. "Maybe this isn't the best time to talk about this," Mom said, giving Sheelan a chilly look all her own. "Rory and I can discuss it privately."

"Yeah, you might've thought of that before," I said. Like earlier, when I'd spent an hour doodling in the margins of my history report and she'd peeled potatoes and talked about the tabloid headlines she'd read at the grocery checkout.

"You'll have to forgive me for not thinking of it before. I've had a lot on my mind lately," she said with a voice crisper than the salad I fiddled with on my plate. We all ate without talking or tasting. Finally she added, "Since the subject has come up, Dr. McDonald would like to meet with all of us for one session."

"Really?" Sheelan put her fork down. I could almost hear the rusty gears cranking in her brain. She would love the chance to complain about how hard it had been for her and how no one appreciated that, thanks to her crazy younger sister basking in the limelight.

"She agreed to meet on Saturday evening."

"No way," Sheelan said immediately. "Tamika and Tyler and Quentin and I are going out."

"You know I can't do it on a weekday without missing more work. On Saturday I can just go into work late. And Dr. McDonald made a special appointment for us."

"Maybe Rory doesn't have anything better to do on a Saturday night, but I already made plans. And there's nothing wrong with *my* head."

"Sheelan—"

"I do have plans," I said.

They stopped and looked at me.

"I actually do have something better to do this Saturday night."

"And what might that be?" Mom asked.

"A youth group thing."

"Where? With whom?"

"At that church on Front Street. Shayne from my English class invited me."

"Shane a girl or Shane a boy?"

Sheelan snickered and I got hot in the face. "Shayne Svoboda," I said. "A girl in eighth grade."

"Svoboda?" Sheelan chewed her lip then pointed at me. "Her older brother's a junior. Jeff—only he spells it J-e-p-h. He's such a loser!" She laughed the cold laugh of a securely popular girl, a social butterfly with venom.

Mom's face had that far-away look. "Aren't they the kids who lost their mother a year or two ago?"

That's one thing Shayne and I found we had in common right away. Well, two things. We'd both 'lost' a parent, and we both hated that expression. "It's not like my mom slipped down into the sofa cushions or something," Shayne had said that day in the cafeteria, and before I could stop it I laughed out loud. She didn't seem to mind. "Whatever! Mrs. Greene just thought I should invite you to the teen group at our church. I guess since I've 'lost' my mom and you've 'lost' your dad, she thought you and I might have stuff to talk about." She shrugged.

I played with a french fry. So Mrs. Greene had put her up to this. She was the coolest teacher I had, but I wasn't so sure this was cool.

"We were already talking about asking you to come."

"Who's 'we'?"

"Us." She gestured down the table. That last, hard-to-define table of assorted, seemingly unhostile kids. The ones I'd had the cafeteria seizure in front of (by this point, who in the school hadn't I had a seizure in front of?).

"Oh." I spotted Sam and looked away quickly. Besides Sam and Shayne, there were a couple other eighth graders but also some seventh-graders, about seven at the table altogether that day. "All of you do this teen group thing?"

"It's called 'Teen Scene.' I know, lame. We're going to think up a better name. Maybe if Mrs. Greene likes it, she'll let us change it."

"What does Mrs. Greene have to do with it?"

"She's a sponsor, chaperone, whatever you want to call it. Our fearless leader."

"I didn't know she was a churchy lady." I didn't know what else to call it.

"A Christian, you mean?"

Yeah, I guess that's what you would call it. Shayne went on, "Well, she's not allowed to say much here in the school. She got in trouble once already for it. But if you come to our group you'll get to hear her testimony. Her story. It's great."

"She's my favorite teacher."

"So come and find out why she's different from the other teachers."

"Aside from the fact that she seems to like kids?" I asked. Shayne chuckled. It was as if I'd wandered into some alternate reality, one where I had the power to make eighth-graders laugh. And not just *at* me. So naturally I agreed to try out this Teen Scene thing. I was ready for an alternate reality.

Real reality, unfortunately, wasn't about to go down without a fight. And what a fight—what my dad called a slobberknocker. My mom agreed to my Saturday night plans, but it didn't mean I got out of the family session with Dr. McD. Mom managed to reschedule for earlier in the afternoon, to accommodate Sheelan's social life, I assumed. Turns out it was for mine.

"I'm glad you're making new friends," she said as we drove to the session. Making it sound like I was just starting kindergarten or something.

"And you even have a playdate today," Sheelan cooed. She was positively giddy about the session now that it didn't conflict with her evening plans. She'd been on the phone half the day bragging to all her friends about going to a therapist. I'm not sure what pleased her more, the thought of talking about herself or hearing about me. My bet was on talking about herself.

I was half right. About ten minutes into the session and Sheelan's Life According to Herself, my eyes glazed over and I was practicing the fine art of covert napping. I think I may have actually fallen asleep when something cut through the fuzz. Talking about herself had taken an alarming turn towards talking about me.

"And that's when I came home to find her chatting with her imaginary friends in the garage," Sheelan was saying. "My theory? The seizures weren't getting a big enough reaction, so she had to try some new weirdness. But honestly, Dr. McDonald, I just feel sorry for her. I didn't tell anyone about it except my mom. And Quentin, of course. He's my boyfriend."

Dr. McD skillfully wrested control of the session away from Sheelan for a while, but we didn't accomplish much before it ended. She did seem particularly interested to hear that I'd be attending a youth function at the church, and she noticed I was carrying Gran's Bible (Shayne had suggested I bring one). I didn't mention how I really wanted to bring my dad's Bible, but that I couldn't find it anywhere. That seemed like the kind of stuff shrinks drooled over.

All of a sudden I was nervous about it. For starters, Mom and Sheelan were going to drop me off at the church. I suggested that leaving me at the corner would be plenty fine. Mom nixed the idea. Should she leave me at the front entrance or the side? I didn't know. Which doors would be open on a Saturday evening? Would I be wandering around from locked door to locked door like a stooge? Suddenly I had serious reservations. And suddenly Mom had reservations about the church, a denomination different from ours. Asking why that mattered since we hadn't even been going to our church didn't score me any points.

"You're not going to come home a Baptist, are you?" she asked, half-joking.

"Mom," I said in the two-syllable way.

"I see kids going in." She pointed.

"Yeah, there's Shayne." We stopped at the curb. This was my last chance to back out.

"Ooh, I see boys," Sheelan teased. "Which one do you have a crush on?"

"Shut up, Sheelan."

"Oh, come on. Why else would you go to church on Saturday night?"

"Have a good time, Rory," my mom interjected before a real slobberknocker broke out. I hopped out, slammed the door, pretended not to see Sheelan's smug smile as they drove away, and reached for the door.

It was locked.

7

The door that had opened for everyone else was locked for me. I'm beyond being surprised by such things.

The worst possible thing you can do in this situation is to pull on the locked door again; this makes you look like a perfect loser. I peered through the glass door, partly hoping no one had seen me, partly that someone would see and let me in. I pulled again. It stayed locked, big surprise.

That's when a hand reached from behind me and pushed the door inwards. This is the moment when you transition from *I'm afraid I'll look like an idiot* to *I am an idiot*. I turned to see who had witnessed my stupidity.

Sam from my English class. He waved his hand for me to enter first.

In all honesty, I didn't have to call him Sam From My English Class anymore. I'd peeked at his English assignment when we passed them to the front of the class. Sam Newman, it said. Not that I was trying to find out.

Now I was just trying not to shrivel up like the grape that rolled under the sofa last month. I shuffled in with a mumble that was meant as a thanks and attached myself to a moving knot of kids with a speed that suggested I knew where I was going.

"Over here, Rory," a voice called from the other direction. Shayne and a girl with the name *Mary Katherine* in fuzzy letters on her T-shirt were both flagging me down. "You're in the wrong group," Mary Katherine broadcasted.

And so I was. The crowd I'd joined was made up entirely of boys. I might have known by the smell: hair gel, old sneakers, overused cologne, T-shirts that had probably been pulled out from under the bed. I fled and joined the girls.

As it turned out, both groups were filing through different doors into the same large room—a gymnasium, actually.

"I thought this was a church," I said.

"It is," said Shayne.

I gestured to the basketball nets.

"They bring in the seats for Sunday morning and take them out when they need the gym. My brother's on the set-up crew."

"This is your church?"

"Yep."

"And it will be yours, too," Mary Katherine said with a Dracula-ish laugh, "once we brainwash you into our cult!"

"Come on, Mary K. It's that kind of talk that scares away the fresh meat."

"Call me Mary K again, and you're dead meat. Anyway, I'm a vegetarian."

"If God didn't mean for us to eat animals, why'd He make 'em so tasty?"

"You sicken me."

"Gather 'round, girls!" an adult voice cut through their snickers. Mrs. Greene beckoned and everyone gathered around her. She was wearing jeans and a cardigan sweater, her shiny dark blond hair in a ponytail, and she looked like a normal person and not a teacher. "Let's start with a word of prayer," she said smilingly. Immediately she launched into a heartfelt speech that she seemed to make up right there on the spot. It sounded like a conversation—like she knew God and talked to Him all the time. More than that: like she believed He was literally listening.

I probably should've been listening, too. But I had to look like I knew what I was doing, and that took some work. Everyone else had instantly bowed their heads when she said the word 'prayer,' and Mary Katherine's brainwashing comment skipped through my thoughts. Then they were 'amen'ing and I could breathe again.

"Why are the girls and boys separated?" I whispered to Shayne as we all settled onto the floor.

"Why do you ask?" Mary K smirked. "Someone over there you want to get up-close and personal with? Let me guess: Kyle the skater dude, with his perpetual tan and blonde tips. How he achieves it in the Midwestern tundra? No one knows."

I was saved from having to answer that by Mrs. Greene's suggestion that we go around the circle and introduce ourselves. This is what adults call 'Getting to Know You' and what we call 'Getting Scrutinized in Excruciating Discomfort by My Peers.' It soon became obvious that everyone there knew each other and this was all done for my benefit. It wasn't a simple matter of name, rank and serial number, either. We were supposed to tell why we were there.

Yeah, that would be good. There was the 'well, like Shayne, I've lost a parent, also not in the sofa cushions' approach. Or the 'I've been visited by some angels and figured I'd better do some background research' line might work nicely. Then there was the third option, just kind of go blank and stammer a little. I went for that one.

"I'm Rory. Rory Joyce. Umm... Well, I'm, uh..."

Shayne cut in just before they could start to giggle. "She's here 'cause I invited her."

"Welcome, Rory," Mrs. Greene said. "It's nice to see you outside of school, where we can be ourselves and talk about what's important. You're welcome here."

I nodded, fiddling with my shoelace. What was that supposed to mean, be ourselves? What were they being in school if not themselves?

"Did anyone else bring a friend?" Mrs. Greene was asking. No one had. "Just Shayne?" She made a little mark in her roster, and I had a big *ah-ha* moment. Shayne had brought me because she earned points for doing it. There was probably some sort of competition going on, 'win a week at Jesus Brainwashing Camp' or something.

"You picked a good week to join us, Rory—we're launching a new lesson series. We'll be combining the girls' and boys' groups early today so we can start it off together. Anybody have anything they want to discuss before we join the boys?" She turned to me. "There are some things better accomplished separately, as you can imagine. Any questions you'd like to ask?"

"No. No, thanks, Mrs. Greene."

"Oh, you can call me Kellie here. Unless it makes it too confusing at school." She saw my eyes widen and laughed. "Yes, I know, an art teacher named Kellie Greene. But I was Kellie Cooper before I got married, so my parents are blameless. Anyway, it's not nearly as good as your name." She winked and turned to the rest of the girls. "Let's go join the others."

As we shuffled across the gymnasium and I tried to figure out what Mrs. Greene meant about my name, Shayne and Mary K joked about hers. "Yeah, but you know her husband's name?" Shayne asked me. I shrugged. "Forrest!"

She and Mary K. laughed. I laughed, too, trying for something between the 'man, that is *so* funny' laugh and the 'ha ha, you're making that up but score yourself a clever point' laugh because I didn't know which one applied. It ended up just sort of lame and fake sounding, like Sheelan's when she was gossiping on the phone.

"Maybe they'll name their son Hunter," I added in a moment of inspiration. It was the kind of thing that would've cracked my dad up. Their laughter sounded like the real thing, too, and I started feeling a bit better about being there. Big mistake.

While everyone jockeyed for a position on the floor, a couple of boys were sneaking in some free throws. One ball bounced off the rim and, guided by some vengeful gods who saw their chance to put me back in my place, smacked me in the back of the head.

It didn't hurt much, unless you count the crushing blow to my dignity. They began apologizing all over themselves, maybe because an older boy walked over and scowled at them. They fell in line at his command. The fact that they made an effort to conceal their laughter made me feel all warm and fuzzy inside.

"You okay, Rory?" the older boy asked. He seemed to be some kind of youth leader, but I had no idea how he knew my name.

"I'm fine…"

"Jeph. Shayne's brother. I know your sister, Sheelan."

"Oh, yeah. Right."

"She could come, too. All teens welcome."

"Mmn. I'll be sure to tell her." And be treated to her unique brand of sixteen-year-old scorn: *As if I would be caught dead in some teeny-bop Bible class with my little sister and J-e-p-h Jeph.*

Jeph seemed like a nice enough guy. In fact, if Sheelan classified him as a loser, he was probably a great guy. But I doubt he understood what I was beginning to catch on to: just because you're welcome somewhere doesn't mean you belong there. My eyes kept connecting with the clock—high on the wall in a protective little cage. Even time was a prisoner here.

A balding man with a goatee and glasses stood to address the crowd. "Well, we've finished up our visit to the Galatians 5 marketplace, where we've carefully selected fruit of the Spirit." He rubbed his hands together, delighted with his word picture, oblivious to the groans and rolling eyes.

Or perhaps not. When he asked, "Who can name all the fruit for me?" he was already pointing at his intended victim, a boy who had foolishly both groaned and rolled his eyes. "Toby?"

Toby rattled off a list that included such things as 'peace' and 'love' and 'tangerines,' or maybe it was 'patience.' Self-control, gentleness. Something something something. I must've been shopping at the wrong market, because I didn't have much of any of that stuff. If that's what it took to be a Christian…

What was I?

In the wrong place, that's what. I looked around for Shayne, but she didn't seem to think I needed someone to hold my hand. She was sitting comfortably cross-legged next to Sam from my— Sam Newman. His curly hair looked especially out of control today. I could relate. They were exchanging occasional comments, most of them apparently humorous.

Mrs. Greene was up talking now, excited about the upcoming theme. The minutes flew past like lead balloons. Would she notice if I slipped off to the bathroom for the rest of the hour? Then I could go home and check this off my list of Things I've Tried Once and Once is Enough. I mean, who could've thought that I belonged here? I spotted the door marked 'Ladies' and stood up.

"So get ready," Mrs. Greene said, "or should I say 'gird yourselves' for a powerful Ephesians 6 experience? We're going to learn how to put on the whole armor of God."

I sat back down.

It wouldn't be my only 'whoa' moment that day. Jeph and Shayne drove me home in the largest car I've ever driven in. I don't mean SUVs and other supposed off-road monsters whose greatest threat is a careening shopping cart in the grocery store parking lot. This was an old brown Buick with a vinyl and tweed backseat that could easily seat five across. The thing felt like it floated down the road, and when it hit a pothole, we bounced in slow motion. Shayne turned to say something to me, and she had to stretch to peek over the top of the front seat, which was also about the size of a sofa.

After he pulled into my driveway and shifted the long gear stick into park, Jeph actually stepped out and opened my door for me. "The handle sticks on the inside," he explained, but it was too late because my face had already turned hot. I saw the shape of Sheelan peeking through the curtain and knew I was in for it.

"Should we pick you up next week?" Shayne asked.

I had a speedy parade of impulses. 'Yes' was the first, followed immediately by 'don't commit yet.' The next one was strong, almost like a spoken voice. *You don't belong there.*

Since I was standing there with my mouth open already, I figured I'd say something. "I'll have to check with my mom," came out, and I was relieved because it was a sensible enough thing to say. Shayne and Jeph both nodded and for a second they looked so much alike that I almost laughed.

"Just let me know during the week," Shayne said.

"Tell Sheelan I said hi," Jeph added before cranking the Buick into reverse.

When I walked in, Sheelan was on the phone (gasp), still holding back the living room curtain. "You should see what he's driving," she said with a cackle. "Like a tank! No, not a cool one. Like an old grandpa tank."

"Jeph said hi," I said flatly, not stopping on my way to the kitchen, from whence good smells were coming.

"You have got to be kidding. My little sister said that he said hi. What else did he say? Rory?" I ignored her in favor of the half-eaten pizza in the cardboard box on the kitchen table. Unfortunately I could still hear her. "Can you believe that? Like I should even know who he is! Unbelievable."

I grabbed a stack of pizza slices and went upstairs to escape the sound of Sheelan's voice. I heard the shower running—I had a little while before Mom would be out wanting the details of my evening. Even with my door closed I could still hear the constant bibbidy-blah of Sheelan, so I resorted to the radio to drown her out. I bopped my way to the bed to the rhythm of a mindless pop tune. Before I could sit, the station faded to static. Dumb radio— the antenna always fell over. I turned back to fix it.

Some guy stood there pressing the buttons.

The pizza slid off my plate and my rear hit the floor. I let out a yell that was more of a gulp.

I didn't think about it until later, but in that first split second I thought I saw different things. For a heart-gripping second it was my dad. Then I thought Quentin was in my room, then for a moment it might have been Sam. Worst of all, and for the shortest flash, I thought of those shifting gray shapes I had seen in the cafeteria during my seizure. I don't know why I imagined any of it, because when I finally had a good look at him, he didn't look like any of those things.

He didn't look like anyone I knew. Older than me, blondish hair all perfectly windswept, his immaculate clothes making him look more like an impossible male model than anything else. I stared and wondered why I couldn't scream, or if I should. He tuned in a song with a driven beat and looked up with a smile.

"Good song," he said.

"I—ah—" I tried.

"Uri," he said.

I stared blankly then realized he was introducing himself.

"Ro-Rory," I said.

"Did I startle you?" He laughed. "I should've said, 'Fear not.'" He winked at me.

I grappled with it. By now I realized what I was dealing with, but he was still a stranger who had appeared out of nowhere. Okay, they all did that, but something about it happening in my room left me off-balance. (More than usual.) It's not that I thought of it as holy ground—though if it were, I guess that would be a good place for an angel to appear—but the others had shown up on more or less neutral ground. A thirteen-year-old's bedroom was a place to be left alone.

I was still just staring at him, but he acted as if he were used to it. He was what Sheelan would call drop-dead gorgeous. Yes, I had dropped, but I hadn't dropped dead, proving we had vastly different taste. Still, more than the others, he was what I would've imagined an angel looking like if the angel were looking human. Which, said a voice in my head that sounded like Dr. McD's, might suggest that I *was* imagining him.

What next? There was something… Ask for name, rank and serial number? "Um…" I started. "You're one of Them, right?"

"I'm not a virtual DJ," he said with a smile that would've made my dentist weep for joy. "I've come because you seem confused."

I raised an eyebrow. If that was what attracted them, there should've been angels bouncing around me 23 hours a day (minus the hour I spent watching mindless television).

He settled on the footboard of my bed. I picked myself up off the floor and at the same time backed away a little bit. He smiled again, and I knew he had noticed.

"I'm concerned that you might have picked up some wrongful ideas today." His smile softened into a sad sigh. "Unsound teaching."

"You mean at the youth group? Really? 'Cause I don't think I learned anything."

"You pick up a lot you don't realize. It's the company you keep."

"They seem decent."

"Sure. Shayne is a good girl. She tries to bring at least one 'friend' every week. I'm sure she'll be the one to win the bike. She deserves it."

"Bike?" Just as I had suspected. Okay, I'd suspected Jesus Brainwashing Camp, but same general idea.

"A fifteen-speed mountain bike. Nice."

Where were we going with this? "So…"

"So be alert. Be discerning. There is faulty doctrine out there, and many false teachers. It can come from sources you'd least expect."

Now I had to be suspicious of churchy folks? "Well, I do remember some stuff they were talking about. Spiritual fruit. Love, patience…"

"Love, joy, peace, patience, kindness, goodness, faithfulness, gentleness, self-control," he rattled them off like a shopping list.

"So what about that?"

"That's all true. Right there in the Book." He was watching me.

"You've got to be all that to be a Christian?"

"Intimidating?"

"No," I contradicted him automatically, as if he were Sheelan. "Well, yeah. I mean, I can be some of those things some of the time. But all of them…all of the time?"

"No one said it was easy."

"Doesn't sound like much fun, either," I said under my breath.

He fixed me with sky blue eyes. "Are you in this just for fun?"

"In what? Am I *in* anything? Most of the time I'm just confused, as you've already pointed out."

"And that's why I'm here. Don't worry, Rory. I'll be around to help you make sense of things. You could say that when things are gray, I help make them black and white."

I wanted to believe it. "You mean you'll actually have some answers for me when I need them?"

"Whenever I can."

The others hadn't offered that. Or had they? I could imagine Gabby telling me to look in the Book. Grandma Judy, too. "What about the answers that are supposed to be in there?" I pointed to the green-bound Bible Grandma had given me, where it sat on my nightstand. Under a half-empty water bottle, a lip balm and a pack of gum.

Uri blew a breath of air towards the Book and I actually saw a little puff of dust come off it.

"Oh, all of the answers are in there," he said. "If you know how to find them." He jumped to his feet. "But when you need answers fast, I'm your man."

"So what about all this Armor of God business, and the youth group? Should I go back and learn more?"

But in the time it took me to blink, I was talking to myself. Not *by* myself, though. Mom was in the doorway, towel wrapped around her hair, stress lines wrapped around her eyes and mouth. I couldn't guess how long she'd been there, but judging by her grim expression, long enough. I grabbed the fallen pizza from the carpet, but it had landed greasy side down.

Things were always landing greasy side down.

8

And so began my tour of Paranoia-land. Not half as festive as Disneyland—though I'd never been to Disneyland and unless they had Crazy Day I doubted I ever would.

But where was Paranoia-land? Simple: it was all in my head. So they tried to tell me. Paranoia: a psychosis characterized by systematized delusions of persecution or grandeur usually without hallucinations. So said the dictionary I got when by some freak twist of fate I won the sixth-grade spelling bee. (True confessions: this might have been the first time I opened it.)

But what about a paranoid who did have hallucinations? That's what they called a schizo. Not to her face, just like I didn't call Dr. McD a shrink to her face (anymore). But it was up there in one of those five-inch-thick books in her office, I guarantee. If I looked up 'paranoid schizophrenia,' I'd find a picture of me. Probably my sixth grade picture with the crooked haircut. I hated that thing.

So it's like this: when you're paranoid, you think everyone is out to get you. But the age-old question is, what if everyone actually is out to get you? Or everyone you're supposed to be able to trust, at least.

Okay, so no one but me had even so much as suggested the schizo part, and except for Sheelan I don't think I ever heard anyone say the word paranoid, but there was a lot of talking going on behind closed doors—at home, at doctors' offices, even at the school nurse's office. Was it being paranoid to assume this had something to do with me? Wasn't their behavior the kind of stuff that inspired paranoia? Could it all be a plot to make me believe I was paranoid? Could I be any more confused?

Never ask this question.

Long story short, some things were said about me, and I said some things about myself, not knowing I was incriminating myself, plus I had another seizure. This one was at home in front of Sheelan, completely freaking her out, which is one good thing I can say about the seizure. Next thing you know, they're talking about my new best friend. He came in the shape of a little white pill.

I wasn't sure I wanted to make friends. But there he was, waiting for me one Saturday morning on the kitchen table, beside a glass of orange juice. My mom was very busy in the kitchen, trying not to look like she was watching to make sure I took the pill. And I tried not to look like I noticed. Finally it was time for her to leave for work, and there was Mr. Pill still cozied up to the juice glass.

She zipped her jacket. "Don't forget," she said, pointing at it.

I shoveled cereal into my mouth and made a sound that sounded cooperative without making any actual promises.

"How about you just take it now, and we can put it out of our minds?"

"I'm already out of my mind, remember? That's why they want to drug me."

"Rory." Mom sat down at the table. She looked tired and pale under her makeup, her light brown hair almost grayish. Somehow when Dad went away, he sort of took Mom's color with him. "Everyone's doing their best to help you. These could very well stop the seizures. That's what you want, right?"

This was what Mr. Behrens called a rhetorical question, which is when someone asks you something but doesn't really want to hear your answer. Mom already knew the answer. Of course I wanted to stop the seizures.

Only I wasn't sure I wanted to stop the seizures.

So, Rory really is crazy. Or Sheelan's right, Rory's starved for attention. And she sees angels. Thinks she's pretty special. That's what all that 'delusions of grandeur' stuff means.

Wrong. I hated the seizures. It's just that something happened when I was down there on the kitchen floor doing my jittery thing. (Though later Sheelan told me that I hadn't been jittering at all — I'd been perfectly still and silent and staring with wide-open eyes. And freaking her out, did I mention that?) The thing that happened was that I saw.

Not something new, not really. The same sort of thing I saw in the cafeteria. Only this time the camera zoomed in close, with more vivid detail. The shadowy things were still shadowy, and they still moved around so it was hard to get a good steady look at them. But one thing I knew: they were bad. I only saw two of them, but it was two too many. They gave me that feeling of being in a dream when you try to scream but no sound comes out, the kind where you wake yourself up because you're trying to yell in real life, but still no sound. They had a nightmare feeling to them.

And they hovered around Sheelan. Or so I thought.

I don't remember her running away, but she did. Even in that state of mind, I admit I expected the gray creatures to follow her like they really were her shadows. But they stayed with me. They came closer, close enough that I could smell them. They were a refuse pit, a slow, agonizing death, a hatred that never ended. Despair. They had eyes, and though I didn't want to, I looked into them and felt the sensation of falling. I knew darkness would take me. Not the dark of forgetting, but the dark of no hope.

The next thing I remember, there was a light. It was totally unlike the 60-watters in the kitchen chandelier. There was a woman, small and strong, with a beautiful belt slung over her hips, and a helmet of light upon her head, shoes graceful and worn upon her feet. And a breastplate. And a shield. A hand — one

72

that usually brandished a spatula—reached across and drew a bright sword.

These looked nothing like medieval props. Somehow it all looked as natural as sunlight, as weightless as a breeze. As resolute as eternity. And she spoke words, words of power, poetic and strong.

Then I snapped out of it and there she was, bent over me and actually still brandishing something long and shining in her hand. A soup ladle this time. She set it down and put something cushiony under my head. Sheelan stood back a safe distance.

"You back with us, baby girl?" Mrs. Fisher asked with a reassuring smile.

"You've got the armor." My voice was kind of hoarse, as if I had been screaming. "All of it."

She kept smiling as if she knew what I was talking about, though she might have been humoring me. "Yes, I suppose I do."

So, the seizures. Not exactly a fun hobby. Scary. But… If I had another, would I see more? Understand a little more? Was it worth finding out?

"I'm not sure about you going anywhere, Rory." Mom came into the living room where I waited for Shayne and Jeph to pull up in the Monstermobile. "You should be taking it easy."

"I'm fine, Mom." It had been days since the seizure. I stared out the window at the half-frozen drizzle that crusted over the dirty snow along the curbs. "I just hope they can find this place. We look exactly like every other beige box on this street."

"You know, the roads could be slick. Your friend's brother can't be a very experienced driver. What if you start to—"

"Mom, really. It's fine."

I had a feeling she wasn't just worried about my delicate health or the weather. Fact was, earlier in the week I would've jumped on either of those excuses not to go. But now I had to. No way was I going to miss hearing about this God-Armor stuff straight from the mouths of true Bible-huggers. I didn't care if I was just another point towards Shayne's mountain bike.

Mom had to go get ready for her waitressing job, but Sheelan walked in sporting her best ticked-off, judgmental expression. She'd obviously been preparing her comments—there were creases in her forehead from the strain of all that thinking—but I figured it was an excuse to be in the room when J-e-p-h drove up so she could mock him and his car.

"You're being a total jerk," she announced. That was harsh, even for Sheelan. She usually worked up to her sweeping statements of condemnation.

"If you say so," I said in the bland way I knew she'd hate.

Her eyes flashed greenly at me. She was the one who got the blue-green eyes and the strawberry blonde curls. I got the murky blue-green-gray and dark tabby-cat orange. Just one more reason not to like her. She was about to give me a few more.

"You don't care about Mom at all. It's all about Rory: Rory's coma, Rory's seizures, Rory's imaginary spirits." (See? That confidentiality garbage is just...well, garbage.) "And now Rory's got to do the God thing to make herself feel even more special."

"God thing?"

"Oh, come on. Bible meetings at the Front Street Temple?"

"Youth gr—"

"Why not just shave your head and join a cult? Then Mom can worry even more."

"Worry? I'm going to a church, Sheelan, not a tattoo parlor."

"Yeah, but not our church."

"Does our church count as ours when we don't go anymore?"

She changed tacks. "Honestly, Rory, could you be any less original? As if you're going to find any answers there."

I wondered how she knew I was looking for answers—or how she could possibly know what my questions were, so that she knew where I would or wouldn't find the answers.

"You want to know why Dad died? Because a truck ran a red light. If you're looking to make sense of that, good luck. But please don't start waving this God stuff under our noses. If there even is a God, I don't want anything to do with him. What kind of God lets this sort of thing happen? Or lets kids get cancer, or thousands of people drown in tsunamis? Either he's a weak God who can't do a thing to stop it, or he just doesn't give a —" She said a word once considered forbidden in our house, one that had been slipping under the radar more and more lately. "Or, even better, maybe he likes it when we suffer. Maybe he's just evil."

My mouth must've been hanging open. First of all, I didn't know Sheelan ever had philosophical thoughts. And I wasn't sure you could say things like that about God without something bad happening. A bolt of lightning would have done the trick—not a total zap job, just enough to forever fry her curls to frizz.

There was a flash of light, but it was just the headlights of the Monstermobile turning up the driveway. Sheelan's eyes narrowed and her glossy lip curled. When I pulled open the front door, Jeph was standing there under an umbrella. What planet did this guy come from?

I called goodbye to Mom and stepped out. Jeph spotted Sheelan. *Don't do it*, my soul cried out.

His soul ignored it. "Hi, Sheelan," he said. "There's room for one more if you want to come."

I braced myself for her pul-EEZE or the witchy cascades of laughter. She just gave a disdainful little sniff and added a chilly, "No, thanks."

Jeph seemed completely unperturbed. "Maybe next week."

"Quentin and I always make plans for Saturday nights."

"Oh." Maybe he faltered a little here. "Bring him along. We can shoot some hoops."

The little sniff again. "Yeah, I'll see what he thinks about that." She stalked away, her steps as catty and light as her voice was heavy with sarcasm.

"Ready?" I asked, meaning *forget her*.

"Yeah, it's freezing. Come on." He didn't seem too crushed by Sheelan's stuck-uppishness. Not crushed at all, really. My admiration was forgotten when I saw the car. When he had said 'room for one more' he was speaking literally. The Monstermobile was almost full, front and back. I wedged in with the other girls in the backseat, most of whom I recognized from last week's meeting, all of who were laughing at the cramped arrangement.

"Accommodations fit for a sardine," said one of the boys in the front.

"Where's the seatbelt?" I asked.

More laughter. "Well, we've found five various straps but can't figure out which one goes with which," Mary K reported. "Check out the size of these buckles! Like airplane seatbelts."

"I can't find mine," I said. It didn't strike me as funny at all.

"How 'bout we just stretch this long one across all four of us," a blond girl named Allie said. I felt the car shift into reverse.

"Where's the other part of my belt?" I could hear the weirdness of my own voice, but I didn't care right then. "I need to buckle my seatbelt or I'm getting out!"

Jeph shifted back into park and everyone got quiet. I kept tugging at the various odds and ends of seatbelts until someone pressed the right one into my hands. The click seemed abnormally loud. I knew they were all thinking, *Oh, yeah, her dad just died in a car accident, and she got some crazy knocked into her head, too.* And they were right

"She's right," Jeph finally said. "Everyone try to find a belt. Let's go."

It was still quiet when we started moving, until one of the boys in the front seat clicked on the radio. A song with a good beat got everyone moving and talking again. The boy who had turned it on had dark curly hair. He looked over his shoulder: Sam.

"Good song," he said to me.

"Yeah," I said. It was a woman singing. I made out the words *Can I be made whole again?* I'd never heard it before, but it was my new favorite.

"Who can recite Ephesians six, verses ten to seventeen? Anybody? Come on, how about just the first verse? You've had a week to get ready for this, my friends."

After our separation into the boys' and girls' lines, not unlike potty break time in first grade, we had gathered together again. Turns out the man talking, the goatee guy from last week, was the junior pastor of the church, Dan d'Amico. A few of the kids referred to him as D-squared, but most of them just called him Pastor Dan. Right now he was making it feel a lot like school, kind of lame since it was a Saturday. We were even glancing around the room, the typical classroom unspoken message: I have no idea what the answer is, must avoid eye contact with the teacher at all costs.

But then, maybe because miracles are a tiny bit more likely to happen in church, someone called out, "'Finally, be strong in the Lord and in the strength of his might...'"

"Yeah! Great. Good, Caleb. Go on."

"Um..."

"Put on the..." D-squared said.

"'Put on the whole armor of God, that you may be able to stand against the wiles of the devil,'" Caleb said triumphantly.

"Yes! Keep going. 'For we...'"

"'...are not contending against flesh and blood, but against the principalities, against the powers, against the world rulers of this present darkness, against the spiritual hosts of wickedness in the heavenly places. Therefore take the whole armor of God, that you may be able to withstand in the evil day, and having done all, to stand.'"

"Amazing, Cal—" But before the pastor could finish, the entire group chimed in:

"'Stand therefore, having girded your loins with truth, and having put on the breastplate of righteousness, and having shod your feet with the equipment of the gospel of peace; besides all these, taking the shield of faith, with which you can quench all the flaming darts of the evil one. And take the helmet of salvation, and the sword of the Spirit, which is the word of God.'"

With a look that could be described as flummoxed (my dictionary was dusty, but I had opened my thesaurus a few times), Pastor turned around and discovered that Mrs. Greene had slipped a transparency onto a piece of audio-visual equipment preserved from the age of the dinosaurs, called an overhead projector. We were all reading the words projected onto the wall behind him. The group broke into laughter.

"All right, you got me. I thought it was the power of the Holy Spirit for a minute there." He grinned and ran a hand over his balding head. "Pretty powerful stuff, isn't it? Kellie and I decided to make this a combined study for the next six weeks—" there were some approving calls from both sides of the group, quickly silenced.

Then one of the guys chimed in, "Armor's for men! Let the girls learn about that Proverbs chic."

Pastor spoke over the resulting commotion. "What I was about to say, *Jake*, is that this armor is for men and women alike. Or boys and girls, as the case may be. Recognize this?" He slapped a different transparency onto the projector. It was a poster from a gladiator movie that had been popular a few years back. Things got disorderly for a minute. A few of the guys began reenacting the fight scenes while the girls took more interest in the sweaty actor in his battle-scarred gear. "Who is this guy?"

A few people called out the name of the actor; others knew the character's name from the movie.

"No, no. I should've said what is this guy? I'm going to tell you. This is what the apostle Paul was pretty much chained to when he was a prisoner in Rome."

"Lucky Paul," Mary K said under her breath.

"This or something like it. A Roman soldier, anyway. And so God provided Paul with the perfect physical representation of the elements of armor, which he used to illustrate the spiritual armor we need."

How good of God, I thought, to provide Paul with shackles and an ever-present guard. Actually, I was a bit sketchy on who Paul even was. Yeah, I knew his title was 'Apostle,' but that was just one of those church words that got tossed around a lot but no one actually stopped to explain. I suppose I could find it in my dictionary, but opening it twice in one week felt sort of dangerous.

The pastor continued. "But before we even get to the armor, let's have a closer look at verse ten. It tells us to 'be strong in the Lord and in the strength of his might.' What's that all about?"

The boy named Jake leapt to his feet and struck a pose like the gladiator on the poster. "Be strong like God," he said in an unnaturally deep voice, which would have impressed if it hadn't cracked in the middle.

"Well, yes and no. Sit down, strong man." Pastor Dan scratched at his bristly chin. "Okay, look at it this way. What do you think is the pivotal word of that phrase, 'be strong in the Lord and in the strength of his might'?"

"Lord," one of the girls called out. The rest of us nodded. It was the thousand-dollar word in the sentence, for sure. It was even capitalized, a dead giveaway.

"Strong," one of the boys countered. "Might!" another one added.

"Be," someone else suggested, probably a future philosophy professor.

Pastor Dan took a red marker and drew on the transparency. When the enormous shadow of his hand moved away from the screen, we could see that he had circled the word 'his.'

"His?" Mary K grumbled. "Only a man would think that's the most important word."

"Think about it, my friends," the pastor went on. "Before you even think of polishing up a single piece of this armor, you have to get it into your head whose battle this is. Yep, like it or not, you're in it—it's an invisible battle, it's going on all around you, and at stake is eternity itself. Your eternity. But you haven't got what it takes to win this fight."

Not much of a pep talk, I thought.

"No, not you alone. Alone, you're toast. Alone, you might not even be aware there is a war raging around you. You're all caught up in just what you can see and hear and feel, completely ignorant of the fact that every sin, every weakness, every conflict in your life, if not caused by your enemy can certainly be capitalized on by your enemy, and he will use whatever resources available to him to defeat you. Or maybe you do know there's a battle, and you think you're pretty tough, you're courageous, you're on the right side. You're ready to leap in there and show that enemy what you're made of." He brought one palm down onto the other with a loud smack, suggestive of a little person being squashed by a big something. Then, in case that didn't make the point, he made the universal lopping-off-of-the-head swipe with his hand under his chin.

"'Be strong in the Lord and in the strength of *his* might.' His might. Not your own. I know some of the garbage that's out there to ensnare kids your age. There's a lion prowling out there, looking for someone to devour—someone like you." By now he was striding back and forth. "But take heart! You don't have to muster up the guts to face it alone. The strength of His might will carry the day. And I'm going to tell you exactly what that means. Exactly what power you have at your disposal."

He stopped his pacing. Everyone was quiet. If he'd waited a few seconds longer, someone would have giggled, and it would have fallen apart. But his timing was good; he was doing his thing.

"It's the power that took a scourged, bloody, nail-punctured, sword-pierced, suffocated corpse and restored it to life—the very power that resurrected Jesus Christ. That's the power you can call upon."

9

Things started changing even more after that first Armor of God Saturday. You know, just in case I'd started getting used to the New Normal routine. Can't have any of that stability stuff in life. Got to keep shaking things up.

No, I didn't get 'saved' just because a preacher man got himself all fired up about Jesus and the devil. If anyone had asked me then if I was saved, I would've said, "From what?" I would've said it to myself, at least, in the spirit of Keeping the Big Yap Shut.

No one asked me, though. I went home that night with an on-the-verge sort of feeling. I was at a fork in the road. If I chose one way, things would just go on in their usual fashion. The other way, and I might start putting some crucial puzzle pieces together in my head that could change everything. The crazy thing was, I didn't know which way was which. Neither one looked safe.

And I say crazy for a reason. Because come on, all that talk about an invisible war going on around us? An unseen enemy? Taking up armor? It sounded so 700 years ago. But more than that, it sounded a little bit paranoid.

Aha.

That's what got to me. It sounded paranoid, and yet it fit in very nicely with all the weirdness going on in my head: the seizures, the blurry shapes, the badness I felt coming from them. The bizarrely beautiful armor on Sam Newman and Mrs. Fisher. I went that night hoping some things would become clear, and instead I got my head more twisted around. One thing was clear: if all of it were in any way true, it was huge.

As I hung up my coat (okay, threw it on a kitchen chair), my hand encountered a lump in my coat pocket. On our way out, Mrs. Greene had handed each of us a paper-wrapped parcel, which my thirteen-year-old extrasensory junk food perception had instantly identified as a candy bar. Mom was working and Sheelan was out, so it was up to me to fix myself dinner.

"Hello, dinner," I said. I slid the candy bar out of the paper sleeve. There were words printed on the inside. I flopped onto my bed, my mouth full of melting chocolate and nougat, and read:

> For though we walk in the flesh, we do not war according to the flesh. For the weapons of our warfare are not carnal but mighty in God for pulling down strongholds, casting down arguments and every high thing that exalts itself against the knowledge of God, bringing every thought into captivity to the obedience of Christ, and being ready to punish all disobedience when your obedience is fulfilled. 2 Corinthians 10:3-6

As long as it took me to devour the candy bar, which admittedly wasn't long, I kept reading it. I understood each of the words, just not all of them together. I half expected Gabby to appear with the big book in her lap, flipping pages, reading with her fingertip, maybe explaining a thing or two. I was surprised at the strength of my wanting her to be there. Was there a way to ask her to come—like praying?

I envisioned myself kneeling at the bedside, asking God to send an angel to help me understand. It didn't look as ridiculous as I expected. I started to slide down off the bed.

Just as my knees touched carpet, Uri was sitting on my dresser.

"You rang?" he said with a Hollywood-caliber smile.

"Oh! Um…I didn't even get a chance." My heart thudded in my chest. I had been ready to ask for an angel, but I wasn't quite prepared to have one materialize before my eyes. My first instinct—no, my first instinct was to yell and run—my second instinct was to make sure no one was there to see me having one of my imaginary conversations. Then I remembered, no Sheelan and no Mom. Alone in the house with Uri—it didn't exactly give me an easy feeling.

"How'd you know what I was going to pray for?" I asked. I didn't mention that it was Gabby I'd had in mind.

"We keep watch, waiting for the right time," he said, crossing his legs. He didn't look so much like the windswept catalog model this time. His clothes were simple, khaki slacks and white T-shirt and leather shoes, but they looked expensive. I supposed if you could whip up imaginary clothes out of thin air, you might as well make them nice. He smiled again, with devastating dimples. "I told you I'd be around when things got confusing."

I was still on my knees. It felt sort of awkward, looking up at him from down there on the floor, so I pulled my desk chair around and sat. "I'm not sure I'm feeling confused as much as…" I wrestled with the word, "ignorant, I guess. Most of this is new to me." I gestured to Grandma's green Bible on the desk.

"And you probably think you need to read the whole thing to really understand what this is all about," he guessed.

"Yeah, kind of. Am I wrong?"

"Nope. Reading the whole thing is recommended—only you're afraid that even if you could read the whole thing, it still might not make sense."

"I guess so…"

"Don't feel bad, Rory. Some people read that book every day, memorize passages, teach it, and they don't even understand what it really says."

That was far from heartening. "But you," I said, "you understand. I bet you can tell me exactly what all this Armor of God business is about."

"An interesting passage." He nodded intellectually. "You do realize that the armor is symbolic?"

"Yeah, I didn't think it meant I should go down to the local blacksmith for a fitting."

He laughed. I felt pretty good about myself, that I could make an angel laugh. "Good," he said. "Much in that Book is symbolic. It's not a bad rule of thumb to consider potentially everything in the Bible as a symbol—especially those things that seem impossible, or just plain unlikely, in the real world."

"The real world..." I tried to follow him. "So this idea of an invisible war..."

Uri smiled gently. "It isn't a bad way to think of it. Rather poetic. Paul was trying to describe something very abstract in concrete terms. Pastors, parents, many of the adults in your life— they are doing their best to protect you from what they consider to be bad influences. This idea of a cosmic battle is exciting to a lot of kids. Kids want to be on the winning side, of course. So you tell them that the winners are the 'righteous' ones, and then you tell them what is righteous: don't do this, don't do that. It helps to keep them on the straight and narrow. A few of them, anyway. The problem with the straight and narrow path is it's all too easy to slip off of it."

I'm not sure what I was expecting to hear, but this wasn't it. "So the armor is sort of a picture of how to live?"

"You could say that. I suppose every week they'll discuss a piece of armor and explain another way you should improve yourself. It's a popular course of study with Christians."

"Oh." The candy bar now sat like a rock in my stomach, its sweetness gone sour. Uri surely meant well, but he was making this whole putting-on-the-armor-of-God thing sound more like putting on shackles. "And what about this?" I offered him the paper that had been wrapped around the candy. He reached out and took it; his perfectly manicured fingernails put my half-broken, half-bitten ones to shame.

He glanced at it for all of two seconds before folding it in half. "Of course. This complements the armor passage perfectly."

"I thought so." I had thought so. That was about all I'd managed to think.

He ticked off a short list on his fingers, "Captivity, obedience, punishing disobedience—that's all vital content."

Sounded pretty heavy. "Do you think if I read the stuff before and after that—the whole chapter, I guess—that maybe it will make more sense to me?"

He smiled again, a face that said *I want to encourage you, but I can't lie to you.* "I would recommend reading when you're fresh, awake and alert, ready for some deep thinking. Right now you look as though you're fit for a sofa and a television set and not much else."

It sounded like just what I needed: decompression time. It was Saturday night, and my favorite show—

I stopped cold. I hadn't watched that show since the day I had grabbed at the chance to see an early movie *and* my favorite show. That was the kind of person I was, not the kind who sat in her room on a Saturday night reading her Bible. I didn't need to be reminded of how low I ranked on the Righteous Scale.

"Yeah," I mumbled. "That sounds like just what I need."

"Of course," Uri said. "If I know anything, it's people and what they need." Though I hadn't seen him folding it, he held up the sheet with the Bible verse, which was now sleekly crafted into a paper airplane. "And I do know flying," he added. A flick of his wrist sent it slicing soundlessly through the air, straight out the door and down the hall. Before it had landed on the carpet outside Sheelan's room, Uri was gone.

I went down for my date with reality TV and a bag of cheese popcorn. I should've steered clear of the reality TV.

My dreams that night were chock full of reality, and what good is that? If you can't escape to total fantasy in your dreams, then a night's sleep feels just like another day's work. I was doing algebra in my sleep, for goodness sake. (It was even more confusing, if that's possible.) I also think I might have organized my sock drawer, which is just sad.

Then reality dreaming took a detour down memory lane. There I was sitting at the kitchen table on a Saturday morning, eating my bowl of frosted something-or-others (who cares, as long as they're frosted), and across from me was my dad, sporting some major bed head and scruffy whiskers. He was hogging most of the table space with a newspaper. I didn't mind, because he was searching the movie ads. The action flick we all wanted to see was featured on the page, with a multitude of time choices listed beneath.

I watched it all from above, just like I'd watched myself in the hospital room when I was in a coma, floating and silent. I wanted so badly to reach out and shake the me of the dream, stupidly shoveling spoonfuls of sugar into her mouth, and tell her to shut up. I could hardly move; it was like I was hanging in thick goo instead of air. My mouth opened, but no sound came out to drown out the voice of the other me as it said: "No, let's go to the 4:30 show instead."

Instantly, the dream went black, and dead silent. I could move again, but my arms groped around and felt nothing. I couldn't even hear the sound of my own ragged breathing. But I knew with sickening certainty that I wasn't alone.

A tiny light sprang up, as if someone struck a match a hundred feet away. It grew bigger, seeming to take forever, but it was eternity in an instant. Suddenly the flame whizzed straight to my chest, like an arrow set on fire. The second before it struck me, its light revealed the horrible thing that had crept up beside me in the dark. I screamed.

I woke to a strangled, raspy noise. I sat straight up in bed, trying to scream. Blackness pressed against my eyeballs; the air bathed me like ice water. Immediately I plunged back under the covers, pulling them up to my nose. My eyes darted around, terrified of what they might see but too terrified not to look. I couldn't make out even the shapes of my furniture. Then a small patch of paleness separated from the dark, on my nightstand. Grandma Judy's Bible, faintly glowing, or so it seemed; the gold-edged pages reflected the red glow of my digital clock. Gritting my teeth as tears darted to my eyes, I whipped a hand out and grabbed the book, clutching it to my chest under the covers.

The air felt so cold. I tried to get a sense of Sheelan sleeping in her bedroom, of Mom further down the hall in hers, but for all I knew, I was alone in the house. Sleep was unthinkable.

Next I remember, I awoke in a colorless version of my bedroom, the shapes of objects now visible but the light still very dim. I moved, and something heavy slid off my stomach onto the mattress beside me. The Bible.

"It will only protect you if you read it," a voice said softly.

After the night I'd had, you'd think I would jump out of my skin at this, but I wasn't even startled. Gabby perched cross-legged on my desk chair, and it felt perfectly normal to see her there.

"What time is it?" I whispered.

"The sun rises."

That meant another good couple of hours of sleep, at least. I considered asking her to just stay there while I slept, but then who wants someone watching them while they sleep? Watching over, yes, but not just watching.

I slid the Bible from under the covers back to the nightstand.

"It will only protect you if you read it," said Gabby.

"Yeah, you already said that."

"I thought I should say it again. It's not a talisman, Rory. There is power in the *logos*. Read it, bind it to your head and heart, call upon it in time of need. The *logos* will become the *rhema*."

Goody, foreign words. Just what I needed, more stuff I couldn't make sense of. "I've read some of it. The part about the armor. I'm trying to understand."

"But you don't understand. Without the Word, there is no armor—no truth, no righteousness, no peace. No salvation. Until you get into the Word, you are utterly unarmed."

"Well, maybe I don't need to be armed. This supposed invisible war—what's it got to do with me?" It was hard to drive my point home with authority when I was sitting there in my flannel pajamas and couldn't talk above a whisper for fear Sheelan or Mom would hear me. "That's why there are priests and ministers and stuff. They can worry about the religious battles. It's not my problem."

She never blinked. I mean, not ever. Gabby's human disguise was very convincing, but she/it had overlooked that critical detail. Her eyes pinned me down. "Not your problem? Then what was that thing beside you last night?"

Instantly I wanted to throw up. I shook my head. "That was just a dream."

Her unflinching gaze spoke for her. Then she asked, "What about the things you see when you have your seizures? Just dreams? Did you ever think that you might be seeing these things for a reason?"

"I know the reason—because I messed up my head."

"You've received a wake-up call, Rory. A clarion call! You have an opportunity to take the offensive, but it has to start here." She stroked the book in her lap. "Can you find the Psalms?"

"Um, I..." I picked up my Bible and started flipping, giving a secret sigh of relief when the word PSALM popped off the pages in the middle. "Here."

"Turn to the 91st Psalm."

More flipping of those impossibly thin pages. "Okay."

"Read it."

"Out loud?"

"That's best."

Awkward. "Um, I might wake my sister—"

"They won't wake for an hour," she said with a certainty that made me kind of suspicious.

"Oh-kay," I said. Then I began to read: "'Those who live in the shelter of the Most High will find rest in the shadow of the Almighty. This I declare of the Lord: He alone is my refuge, my place of safety; he is my God, and I am trusting him. For he will rescue you from every trap and protect you from the fatal plague. He will shield you with his wings. He will shelter you with his feathers. His faithful promises are your armor and protection. Do not be afraid of the terrors of the night, nor fear the dangers of the day, nor dread the plague that stalks in darkness, nor the disaster that strikes at midday. Though a thousand fall at your side, though ten thousand are dying around you, these evils will not touch you. But you will see it with your eyes; you will see how the wicked are punished. If you make the Lord your refuge, if you make the Most High your shelter, no evil will conquer you; no plague will come near your dwelling. For he orders his angels to protect you wherever you go. They will hold you with their hands to keep you from striking your foot on a stone. You will trample down lions and poisonous snakes; you will crush fierce lions and serpents under your feet! The Lord says, "I will rescue those who love me. I will protect those who trust in my name. When they call on me, I will answer; I will be with them in trouble. I will rescue them and honor them. I will satisfy them with a long life and give them my salvation."'"

It was nice; I liked it. I began to nod. "So, if I learn some of this, it will sort of… protect me? Is that what you're saying?"

"That is not at all what I'm saying. It is not an incantation, reciting a magic formula. You have to understand the promises of God. You have to be able to claim those promises."

"Okay, so how do I do that?"

"They can be claimed by every child of the King."

Swords, arrows, armor…so why not a king? "So. Okay. Then I'll claim them." I waited, but Gabby said nothing. Were there papers to sign or something? But something in her eyes made me go sort of still inside. "But I can't," I guessed slowly. "Because I'm not a child of the king?" Her silence answered me. "But you mean God, don't you? Aren't we all God's children?"

Her finger glided over a page of her book. "'But to all who believed him and accepted him, he gave the right to become children of God.'"

"Believed who?"

"The Word."

I shook my head, baffled.

"Jesus, the Christ," she said. "Read the gospel written by John." For a second she had this soft sort of half-smile on her face, like she was speaking of someone she felt affectionate about.

"John," I repeated, because I felt like I should say something. "Jesus. Right." Frankly, I couldn't quite see how Jesus figured into it. With all this talk of battle and weaponry, he wasn't exactly the guy who sprang to mind. Hearing the word Jesus made me think of the gentle shepherd with the lamb in his arms, the healer, the storyteller. And yes, the broken man nailed to a cross. None of these pictures suggested warrior. I wouldn't go so far as to say weak, but definitely not warrior.

Gabby watched me closely. "Have you been talking to someone else?" she asked.

"What, about this stuff? Not really. Just you guys." I made vague gestures with my hands meant to convey the idea of angels. "And my grandma."

She stood and walked to the window, where the first pale yellow rays of the sun played on her face. My room had gone from shadow to brightness, but I had been able to see her clearly the entire time.

"You've been given a gift, Rory Erin Joyce. To see what others seldom see. But it does not compare to what can yet be given you. And it will come through this." She brandished her heavy book. "Do not forsake it." Then she was gone.

The room felt a bit chilly. I pulled my blankets back up, and the thought *what you need is some more sleep* suggested itself with all the irresistible allure of a big, lazy yawn. But the daylight on my window frame brightened, and it passed through a colorful little sun catcher I had hung on the glass a year ago and largely forgotten about. Reds and blues and golds lit my ceiling, with a stained-glass effect. I thought about other people getting up and getting ready for church, and for the first time in a long time, I felt a bit guilty about not being one of them.

I reached for my Bible and began searching for the word JOHN.

10

Lunchtime became very political. I suppose the cafeteria always stank of politics, but now it was personal.

Sure, Jasmine and I had gotten into the habit of sitting at the same table most of the time. Okay, every day, across from each other. But it wasn't like we'd signed a contract. So when the Teen Scene kids waved me over to their table—an invitation from a group, impossible for a thirteen-year-old to resist—you couldn't accuse me of actually betraying Jasmine.

Except the look she gave me as I passed her by was a little betrayed.

If I'd had time to prepare, I might've thought of a way to handle the situation more gracefully...but then grace was never my talent. Now, in my usual state of total unpreparedness, I approached the new table with my tray and a heaping helping of surefire embarrassment: spaghetti and meatballs.

And so in a way Jasmine had immediate revenge, because I had chosen the Special of the Day to make her happy. But spaghetti just wasn't the thing to eat while being ushered into a new social group, desperate to impress. I could've been daintily nibbling on french fries. Instead I would be wrangling saucy worms onto a fork and attempting to navigate them into my mouth without slurpy stragglers or splattering danglers.

Embarrassment wasn't going to waste any time this day. The moment I set my tray down, a meatball dislodged from the plate and rolled onto the table. Almost before the laughter could start, a fork plunged down and nabbed the fugitive in mid-roll.

Sam Newman brandished the meatball high while the others cheered him and I got really hot in the face. (I hated the hot face, and the more I grew to hate it, the more often I seemed to get it.) He offered it back to me without a word, and about all I could manage was to shake my head. So he popped it into his mouth.

"And the hunter savors his catch," Jake said with the voice of a nature channel narrator. Everyone laughed. I wished I'd said it.

"I doubt it's kosher, Sam," Shayne teased. She saw my confused look. "Sam's Jewish," she said, which of course confused me more.

"Messianic," Sam added, to clarify.

I had no idea what that meant. I nodded knowingly.

So this was how it was going to be, then. Not sitting for the better part of a minute and already I was out of the loop, pretending that I knew what was going on. A half step behind, story of my life. I could dribble, but I couldn't dribble and shoot the lay-up.

Directly across from me was fellow seventh-grader Jake, the wise guy from the youth group, stocky with sandy blond-brown hair in a shag cut, his gray-blue eyes always roaming in search of something to wisecrack about. His striped school tie was askew. He traded jokes with Shayne, beside me, and some of the other kids at the table. Next to him was Sam, lean and rangy-looking beside Jake, though his shirt was also open at the collar and his tie equally crooked. Sam was taller than Jake, about my height, though we both sported a mop of hair, so it was hard to say with any accuracy. He wore glasses with rectangular frames.

He looked at me through them now. "It means I'm a Jew who accepts Jesus as Messiah," he told me. Rather than allow this to sink in, I cringed inside because I must've had a completely stupid look on my face, if he thought he needed to explain. Then I noticed that his color had deepened a little, and I immediately recognized a kindred spirit. We shared the curse of the hot face.

Probably should say something… "Oh, I get it," said I. Adequate, if not profound. And not even exactly true. I gathered that he was saying he was Jewish and Christian, and I wasn't sure how that could work. But apparently it could. And because I was nervous, the big yap opened. "I didn't know you could be Jewish and Christian," the big yap said.

"Yep," he said, so much nicer than the *duh* I deserved. "If you think about it, the first Christians were Jews."

Two days ago I would've had to take his word for it, but I had just read the gospel of John—okay, some of it—so I knew what he meant. "Right," I wanted to say, but all of a sudden it dawned on me that I was having a conversation with an eighth-grade boy and that this went against natural law. Reminded of the proper order of things, my tongue froze.

I prayed he didn't notice, since plenty of other tongues wagged around us. Jake treated the table to extemporaneous song, which is a fancy way of saying he made it up as he went along. And 'treated' is a nice way of saying 'tortured.' He half-sang, half-rapped, "My name's Jake Dean, I'm a Jesus machine, I hang with my posse down at the Teen Scene—"

Groans and tossed napkin wads forced him to sit. "What?" he asked.

"Jesus machine?" Sam laughed. "What does that even mean?"

"And like you have a posse," scoffed Shayne. "But don't bother rhyming with 'Teen Scene' because we are most definitely changing that name."

"Why not the 'Jesus Machine'?" the girl Allie asked sarcastically.

"Whatever!" Shayne said. "Let's go around fast—everyone has to come up with a new name for youth group, then we'll pick the best."

Now the rest of me froze like my tongue. Trying not to look idiotic takes up a huge amount of time once you hit junior high. It was downright exhausting. Then there were the kids like Shayne who didn't seem to bother with it.

The ideas flew. *Saturday Night Life* and *Bible Babes* were instantly voted down. "Some of us aren't babes," Jake protested.

"Aw, don't worry, Jake. I think you're pretty cute," Sam reassured him.

Someone threw out *God Squad* and then came *Jesus Freaks*, and suddenly everyone was looking at me.

"Um," I murmured. "I'm not even a member..."

"Doesn't work that way," Allie said. "Come on, out with it."

I scrambled for something funny. Oh, man, how I wanted to be funny. But inside me a switch flipped; I went from being a desperate wannabe comedian to a crushingly sad, small person. I don't think it showed on the outside (strange how sometimes you can't hide your annoyance when someone takes the last cookie, but you can mask a gaping hole in your soul). I had a sense like I was a million miles away from the only thing that could give my life meaning, and I didn't have a roadmap. Or a driver's license.

"I'm a blank," I said quietly.

Three seconds of silence threatened to expand and swallow my will to live. Then Sam said, "Blank—perfect. Generic Youth Group. We can get white shirts with black letters."

"Ding ding ding, I think we have a winner," Jake announced.

"Yeah, I don't think 'Generic Youth' is going to convince anyone to change the name," Allie said.

"No, I meant mine is the winner," Jake said. "The Jesus Machine." After a few smacks he reluctantly abandoned the idea.

I forced a smile but didn't say much as they continued talking and laughing. I nudged the cold spaghetti on my plate, the farthest thing from hungry. When I looked up, Sam looked away quickly. I got the feeling that he was a watchful person. If he kept it up, I'd have a permanent case of hot face.

The next day I tore out of my last morning class, dumped my books in my locker, and made for the cafeteria like a parched traveler makes for an oasis. (Despite the smells coming from the kitchen, not because of them.) It wasn't the Special that lured me on, but the plan I had devised that morning in social studies. If I got there before the youth group gang, I could just sit down wherever and it wouldn't look like I was opting not to sit with them. Which is exactly what I was doing.

How big a fool are you, Rory? I asked myself. Decent kids decide to be nice to me, and I run the other way. But if I didn't, it was just a matter of time before they figured out that I was a big old fake. Better to drop out than get kicked out.

My plan might have worked if not for the evil genius Jasmine. My tactic of sheer speed failed to defeat her combined tactics of speed and (I had to assume) treachery. She had already cleared the lunch line and was heading for the usual table when I walked in.

Wending my way through the maze of food, grabbing whatever was quickest, I decided to follow the 'if you can't beat them, join them' philosophy. She beat me to the table, and I joined her before Shayne or Allie or Sam or Jake showed up.

She didn't look up from her tuna noodle casserole when I sat down across from her. She pulled a historical novel from her bag and made a show of being absorbed in its pages. Then I saw a couple of the youth groupies come through the double doors, and I made a show of being absorbed in conversation with Jasmine.

"So, how's it going?" I asked brightly.

She read and chewed.

"What about that paper we have to do for social studies — totally lame. I mean, seven pages? Come on. Who can write about gross national product for seven pages? Do you even know what gross national product is? 'Cause I don't."

She turned a page.

"I wonder if teachers even read these reports they assign. 'Ooh, now I can read about the chief exports of Denmark. Exciting!'" I laughed, a bit too loud, but of course I didn't know that until it came out. "Chief exports of Denmark. Heh. Really." I was definitely losing steam.

Jasmine looked up. This would've been encouraging if not for the cold, cold eyes. "Trouble with your algebra today?" she asked.

"Algebra?" To cover my confusion, I took a big bite of what was on my plate. My mouth swam with salty, fishy noodlyness. Good grief, I'd grabbed the Special in my hurry.

"Sure," Jasmine said. "That's why you sat by me at first—algebra. And after I helped you finally understand it, you started sitting with your new friends. Only now you're back, so I assume you're having trouble again."

"Wha? You think I was just using you?"

"I know you were. But not anymore, sorry."

My big yap came up totally empty, but it didn't matter so much because right then I took a private moment to have a seizure. I didn't flop face-first into my tuna and noodles—no flopping whatsoever, as a matter of fact. Just a quick fade-out.

I was paralyzed with my eyes open. Everything went sketchy again, like the smeared pencil drawings, and when I concentrated on something in front of me, it sort of rushed in close and came into focus. First Jasmine's face—nostrils flaring—then a knot of girls, Madi Swanson and her cluster at their usual table. A jumble of activity in the corner of my eye suggested boys goofing off. There was a deafening buzz of voices—not the typical cafeteria noise, just voices and nothing else, all overlapping like a hundred conversations and arguments.

Then that hint of color, the pale gold here and there, but when I tried to focus on it, it vanished as if hidden by shadows. Shadows mostly around people, even shaped like people, but not behaving in the way shadows should.

I found a brighter patch of the golden light and clung to it. Faces, faces of friends. The light didn't come from them, but it was all around them and in them somehow. Something inside me loosened around that light, a knot of fear that wanted to untie.

The next thing I saw pulled the knot tight again. Maybe the contrast just made them seem darker, but so many shadows hovered close to the light. They moved faster. There was something animal-like in their movement, clawing and clambering over each other. There were more of those things around my friends than anywhere else in the room. Almost against my will, I focused in on one of the shadows, and it turned towards me. I caught a split-second glimpse of a face from a nightmare.

My whole body jerked. Normal vision and sound slammed down around me like a cup slammed down over a bug.

Jasmine was glaring at me. "You're so mature." She swept her tray off the table and strode off.

There was laughter from the boys' table. I could tell it was directed at me. I closed my mouth, which had apparently been hanging open; then I felt a sticky noodle drop from my chin to my shirt. In my big rush through the line I hadn't grabbed any napkins. I wiped my face the best I could with my fingers and scraped the creamy tuna blob off my white shirt.

Then Kevin Sebeck was there beside me, handing me a folded napkin. "Here," he said, then rejoined his gang heading for the exit.

"Thanks," I managed. I unfolded it to reveal the black letters written inside: LOSER. The laughter behind me got louder. I pretended not to see the letters, pretended not to notice the disdainful eyes of Madi and Trina and Britnee and Alicia and Courtney, pretended not to see that I had attracted the attention of some of the youth groupies. And I used the Loser napkin because I needed it, but it left black ink smears on the greasy tuna stain on my shirt.

I could've hid out in the nurse's office for the rest of the afternoon. The seizure gave me a good enough excuse. But I figured Miss Diakos would call my mom at work, and I'd probably end up back in room 316, so I steered clear of her and just hid out in the bathroom for the rest of the lunch hour.

I refused to miss art class. It was my favorite, it was only once a week, and even though Jasmine was in it, Mrs. Greene had a peaceful gladness about her that could neutralize the darkest Jasmine aura. Just being in the room with her would help, even if I didn't mention what had happened.

I think my shirt did the talking for me. She took one look at the tuna-scented smear on my chest and gave me a smile that said *hang in there, kiddo*. When all the students were settled in with their watercolors and easels, she beckoned me over to the supply cabinet in the corner. "That fan brush is getting tatty," she said. "Come get a fresh one." When she opened the metal door of the cabinet, she held it so that it blocked our view of the class—or their view of us.

"Doing okay?" she asked quietly.

I tilted my head. "Hard week," I answered, also quietly. It all felt very secretive.

She nodded as if she wasn't surprised. "It will probably get harder before it gets easier." This was hardly encouraging, but the fact was, I'd had my fill of cookie-cutter encouragement from teachers and counselors and family friends. It was almost a relief to hear someone being real. Only I wasn't sure exactly what she was talking about.

"Did you understand the teaching Saturday night?" she asked.

"You mean the armor stuff? Yeah, sure. Well, sort of." I used the new fan brush to scratch my nose, then I sighed. "Not really."

She laughed gently. Mrs. Greene had the sort of face that could be young enough to be your sister or old enough to be your aunt, depending on whether she was laughing. The laughing made her seem older, in a good way. "What part has you stumped?"

"Well, I know the armor is just symbolic," I began, impressed at how academic I sounded.

"No, that's not true."

"Oh." I deflated. "It's not?"

"No. The armor isn't physical, in the sense that you're really strapping on pieces of metal. But it's very real. It's armor on the spiritual plane. It has to be real, because the battle is real."

I rolled the handle of the paintbrush between my finger and thumb. "I don't know. I think I like the idea of a symbolic battle better," I said.

"Who wouldn't? Then we can just read about it and go on with our normal, ordinary lives."

I didn't want to hear about normal anymore, but ordinary sounded okay right then. I had an urge to just come clean. "You know," I said, "I just don't get this whole 'spiritual war' thing. I went to church and Sunday school when I was little, and I don't remember hearing anything about it. We learned about how God is Love and Jesus is the Good Shepherd, and love your neighbor, and turn the other cheek, and all that. Now you're telling me about a war, with good guys and bad guys. And I take it that the general of the good army is Jesus—the Lamb of God? Is it just me, or doesn't it seem like…?" I didn't want to be rude, or get struck by lightning, so I stopped.

"A lamb makes a pretty weak commander?" she finished for me. "The Lamb is not the Man for the job?" She smiled again, and I knew I hadn't stepped on any toes, human or otherwise. "Ah, Rory, you have some wonderful discoveries ahead of you. There's someone you really need to get to know."

"Who?"

"Jesus. Did you know He's also called the Lion of the Tribe of Judah? And many other names. Name above all names." She had a glow like an adolescent girl in love, kind of embarrassing. "Have you read the gospels?"

"Well, I'm reading John—"

"Great! Then you know he's also called the Word."

"Uh, yeah." There was that word—that Word—again. Gabby had mentioned it, too. And I remembered reading about the Word, right at the beginning of John's gospel. But as far as confusing went, John hit the ground running.

"Did the Jesus in John's gospel seem weak to you?"

"No, I guess not. He spoke strong words, for sure." I hadn't actually read the whole thing, but I knew how it ended—on a cross.

"Read the other gospels. Or go right to Romans, if you'd rather. I have a great little reading guide that can help you get started, but I keep it in my car. Think you can come back after school, and I'll get one for you?"

"Yeah, sure, I guess—" I stopped when the expression on Mrs. Greene's face suddenly changed. She shut the cabinet door, revealing Jasmine standing behind it, empty paint tray in hand.

"What can I get you, Jasmine?" Mrs. Greene said, all chirpy.

"I'm out of black paint," Jasmine said. She was glancing from me to the teacher with narrowed eyes. I wanted to tell her to get a hobby, something besides suspicion. What was wrong with a teacher and a student talking, anyway? But even Mrs. Greene was acting a bit weird.

Then something clicked in my brain, probably a rusty gear. Shayne had said something about Mrs. Greene not being allowed to talk about her faith in school. *She got in trouble once already for it.* I felt kind of bad—and kind of good—that she was taking a chance like this for me. Maybe that's why, when art class was over and she caught my eye as I walked to the door, and she asked, "See you Saturday?" I answered, "Yeah, see you then." Even though I thought I'd made up my mind not to go.

11

Between me and Saturday lay a marathon of history tests, cafeteria dramas, annoying sisters with equally annoying boyfriends, therapy sessions and pimples. Well, just one of each, but stack them all up and you have a stress sundae with a cherry on top (that would be the pimple).

But Saturday came, and I actually looked forward to going to the Front Street Temple youth group. I rehearsed how I'd make a joke out of last week's seatbelt episode so I'd be totally casual when the Monstermobile came to get me. Mom was hurrying around getting ready for her waitressing shift when she saw me waiting by the window. She stopped in her tracks with her hands hanging in midair by her ear, her earring swinging like a tiny clock pendulum. "Going somewhere?"

"Yeah." I thought it was obvious.

"Not the church thing?"

I made the international teenage gesture for *isn't it obvious?* Some bad attitude was seeping through, I know, but it irritated me that they knew it was a youth group—probably even knew the 'Teen Scene' name—but they still insisted on calling it the Church Thing.

"I thought you weren't going," Mom said, hooking the earring in. "You told Dr. McDonald you weren't."

"Yeah, but that was ages ago." (Three days.)

Since then, I'd started sitting with the youth groupies again at lunch—not because I'd settled my soul-deep fears about truly belonging, but because it's much easier to sit with people who smile and talk to you than people who scowl at you or ignore you. It bugged me that Jasmine thought I'd only used her for her mathematical mind, but she'd believe whatever she wanted to believe. It probably hadn't helped when I told her I would just as soon go to my neighbor Kingston if I needed algebra advice.

Mom still stood there, fussing with her blouse, trying to think of something to say. It dawned on me then: she wasn't just mildly suspicious of my Saturday night activities, her Concerned Mom radar on the spin. For some reason, she actually didn't want me to go. Only she couldn't come up with a good reason to keep me home—yet.

Time to intervene, before inspiration struck and she invented a reason. I grabbed onto the last thing she'd said. "Anyway, does Dr. McDonald tell you everything I say? What's up with that?"

"I pay the bill, that's what's up with that," she snapped back. Ouch. But I'd asked for it. "And now I have to go work all night so I have the money to pay the bill, so a little courtesy from you would be appreciated." She grabbed her coat and apron while I stared out the window, except all I could see was a jerk staring back at me, my own reflection.

With the kind of horrible timing I had come to expect from life, my mom was backing the car out of the garage at the exact time the Monstermobile arrived. There was a clumsy car square dance on the driveway, and I caught a glimpse of my mom's pinched face as she sped away to a job I knew she hated.

I looked guiltily towards Sheelan as I slunk to the door, but she was on the phone and didn't even spare me an accusing glance. She and her best friend Tamika were cooking up some elaborate scheme to punish Quentin and Tyler, who by the sound of it had committed the heinous crime of making plans of their own, minus girlfriends.

Pity I had to miss the unfolding drama. I opened the door and jumped. Jeph was standing there. It wasn't raining, so it could only mean one thing: he had the guts to face Shoot-Him-Down Sheelan again.

He opened the storm door for me. "Is Sheelan home?" he asked.

Just then Sheelan walked past the kitchen entryway, cordless phone riveted to her face, decked out in her tattiest workout clothes and hair scrunchie, no make-up. She saw Jeph and gave a little shriek.

"Hey, Sheelan, any chance you'd want to come along—" Jeph tried, but she had already leaped out of sight.

"Don't even bother," I said. "It's no use. Her evil powers are far too strong."

He laughed. "But imagine if we could somehow harness them and use them for good."

Sheelan's voice came from around the corner. "Honestly, can't you see I'm getting ready for my date? It's Saturday night, and some of us have a life."

Evil, I mouthed the word and shrugged.

Jeph was still smiling when we left, which goes to prove how unbelievably nice he was and therefore how unsuitable for my sister. He was unshattered, but the whole thing bothered me. She had lied so easily. Okay, no big surprise, it was Sheelan, but the fact that she did it without a twinge was kind of disturbing. Weren't some things, like lying, simply wrong no matter what, or did everything sort of depend on the situation?

There were fewer passengers on this ride, and more seatbelts than people; I blanked on my whole humorous seatbelt skit. Things like overworked moms and casually lying sisters kind of sucked the funny right out of a person. I wondered where everyone else was; it was just Jeph, Shayne, Allie and myself. No Mary K, no Jake, no Sam. When we arrived, I scanned the faces congregating in front of the church. A car pulled up and Jake and

Sam jumped out, and my stomach got a sort of uncomfortable-in-a-good-way feeling in it.

The girls and boys separated for their initial roll call, chat and prayer time—which, I have to admit, felt a little less awkward this time—then we came together to discuss the night's topic, emblazoned in slightly crooked, out-of-focus lettering on the white brick wall: The Blet of Truth.

I snorted, a dorky sort of laugh that burst out before I could stop it. The thing about a case of the giggles is, you can never predict when it will strike. But it's a pretty safe bet that at some point it will strike in church. This was close enough.

Other people noticed the typo and laughed, but theirs was a mild case, like a sniffle, whereas I'd been instantly struck with bubonic-plague-level giggles. All I knew was, the crowd was quieting, the pastor was ready to speak, and I was shaking with the effort to stay silent. Horrified (if you can be horrified while laughing), I peeked around to see if I was making a spectacle of myself. Jake and Sam were sitting right behind me.

Jake saw me looking. He leaned over to Sam, "Hey, you've got one of those Blets of Truth, don't you?"

"Yeah. It came with the Hlemet of Salvation," Sam replied straight-faced.

The air exploded out of my mouth with a sound like a rapidly deflating balloon. Pastor Dan looked my way, and I tried to curl myself into something inconspicuous, as if. The element of fear was enough to cure my giggles for the moment.

Pastor Dan rubbed his goatee thoughtfully. "Let me start with Pontius Pilate's famous question: 'What is truth?'"

"Better question, what is Blet?" someone called out.

The pastor glanced at the projection, sighed, and scribbled BELT above the crossed-out 'Blet.' "Okay, once again: What is truth? Let's write down some thoughts. Go ahead, call them out. Truth is…"

"The opposite of a lie," Jeph's voice came from the back of the room. How appropriate, I thought. Just like he was the opposite of a Sheelan.

"Okay, good. What else?"

"The facts."

"Honesty."

"Not being a fake."

Pastor Dan nodded. "Yes, all of those. Let's ask a slightly different question. Who is truth?"

"Oh, oh!" Mary K raised her hand, though no one else was. "Jesus! He's the Way, the Truth, and the Light."

"The Life. Right, Mary Katherine. So what is Paul telling us to do, in the Ephesians 6 passage? 'Stand therefore,' he says, 'having girded your loins with truth—'" He paused while the inevitable titter at the word 'loins' passed through the group.

"I believe Paul is just referring to the middle region," he gestured over his abdomen, "and the fact that the belt held everything else in place. Remember, he was basing this on a Roman soldier's uniform. The belt wasn't a fashion statement. It was the foundation of his armor. So truth, therefore…"

"Is our foundation?"

"Yes, it's the element that all the others hinge on. Without it, the rest sort of falls apart."

I thought I could see where this was going. Step One to Being a Good Christian: Always Tell the Truth.

"So we're supposed to always tell the truth," Allie summed it up. Allie was sitting beside me, and I was glad because while she wasn't quite as tall as me, she was sort of big-boned. Sitting next to her, I wouldn't look like a complete Amazon like I would sitting beside Shayne. She did, however, have some amazing blonde hair, smooth as a tall glass of lemonade, so next to that mine certainly must have looked like a rusty Brillo pad to anyone sitting behind us. Not that I cared about anyone sitting behind us.

Pastor Dan rubbed his palms together. "Telling the truth is crucial, but it goes way beyond that. What does Paul say? *Stand* therefore. There is a sense here of standing up for the truth, and we do that by living a life of truth. But what does that mean?"

One of the boys, a high school freshman by the name of Silas, was poking at a handheld gadget. He held it up. "I searched for 'truth' in the New Testament," he said. "Here's one in John: 'Thy Word is truth.'"

"Bravo, Silas. One step ahead of me as usual. If God's Word is truth," and he held his Bible up, "then what does it mean to live a life of truth?" He waited while we all waited for someone else to call out the pretty obvious answer.

"To live according to God's Word," a voice behind me finally said. Sam's.

"And who gave us a perfect example of living by God's Word?"

"Jesus."

The pastor was still shaking that Bible. "Jesus. The Way, the Truth, and the Life. He lived as a man—fully God, yes, but fully Man—to show us how to live. And in case no one's told you, that's our ultimate goal, to become like Jesus."

This just kept getting better and better. Trying to tell the truth all the time sounded hard enough, but now I had to try to be as good as Jesus? Talk about setting the bar high.

D-squared was on a roll now, getting into his God groove. "If we are at war, my young friends, that means we have an enemy. In the spiritual realm, I think we all know this enemy's name." Regardless of the fact that we all knew it, some of the kids had to say it anyway. A hiss spread across the group as multiple mouths whispered *Satan*. It was starting to feel like a summer camp ghost story. "Now, Satan has a whole collection of names, and one of them is the Father of…"

"Lies," Shayne supplied.

"The Father of Lies," Pastor Dan affirmed. "Okay, let's take a step back. Silas, did your 'search for truth' give you another result in John—chapter eight, I think?"

"John 8:32… 'And you shall know the truth, and the truth shall make you free.'"

"Exactly so. That was Jesus talking, folks. He is the Truth, he wants you to know the truth, he wants you to be free. But Satan is all about lies. He wants you enslaved. He whispers those lies in your heart so he can lead you down a path away from salvation— or if you are saved, so he can cripple you and render you ineffective in the battle. And he's good at it. He invented it. But you have a powerful weapon at your disposal. You have the

Word, which is Truth. You have God's promises, here in black and white and red—" Bible brandished again "—but they can't do a thing for you unless you know them."

He set the Bible down. "Get to know your God and King. Learn his truth. Don't be deceived—there are absolute truths, regardless of the preferences of our culture or 'lifestyle choices.' It doesn't change from one generation to the next. You can discover it, accept it, apply it, or you can ignore it, reject it, try to cover it up. It doesn't change. That is truth.

"So truth lived out... What does that look like, exactly, in the life of a thirteen-year-old, a seventeen-year-old? This may come as a surprise to some of you, but you're in a pretty difficult stage of your life right now." He smiled at the looks of mock astonishment. "Yeah, I know, it's a regular news flash. You're bombarded by attacks on your honesty, integrity, and purity. Who's it going to hurt if you peek at the answers to next week's history test? Why not share that juicy piece of gossip about the most popular girl— she deserves to be taken down a notch, doesn't she? Why not sneak a look at that website? Why not switch to the short skirt after your parents leave? Why not try a little sip, a little puff? It's your body, right?"

There were murmurs now but no laughter.

"This is the battlefield, my young friends. A life of integrity is doing the right thing, even when no one is watching. But believe me, usually someone is watching. And what's that thing Christians are so often accused of? Hypocrisy. Not 'walking the talk.' Read the gospels, and you'll discover that Jesus reserves harsh words for the hypocrites. Those Pharisees? That's me, that's you—when we don't gird ourselves with the Belt of Truth."

He turned it over to Mrs. Greene then, and she asked for examples of what living out the truth meant in our own lives. *Here come the goody-for-me stories*, I thought. To my surprise, more of the kids had something negative to confess. Shoplifting because their other friends were, mean-spirited gossip, and several confessions of disobeying parents on some pretty major issues. They didn't seem to get it—dirty little secrets were supposed to be *secret.*

But Mrs. Greene didn't come down on them at all. In fact, she revealed some of her own dirty little secrets. "If you want an example of what can happen when you disregard the Truth," she said, "just look at my life fifteen years ago. My parents were church-going Christians, but I was running headlong in the other direction. Bad friends, bad habits…dangerous, destructive habits. I'm not proud of it, but I tell you because if it could happen to me, it could happen to anyone. I managed to fool a lot of people for a long time, but I got to the point where I had lost, sold or given away just about everything of value in my life. But someone still saw value in me."

She smiled. "And that Someone is in the restoration business. Only He could take a used-up scrap cast by the wayside, stand her up, wash her clean, put a song of praise in her heart and reserve a crown to place on her head. Those are the feet where I've chosen to cast my crown. While I'm still here on this side of heaven, I'm learning to put on His armor, starting with the belt. Let's look at the situations that you mentioned, and we'll decide how we would handle them in Truth, living according to God's Word. And what the outcome might've been if we had."

They did discuss it. Most the time, the God Way could've just been called the Hard Way, and the results weren't always appealing. Not such a great commercial for the God Way.

Strangely, though, I felt a tug in my middle, a wanting to know more. Doing the right thing even when it was hard seemed not as stupid as I expected. It felt…noble, almost. Like telling the truth might have made Sheelan seem a little less slimy to me — even if *I'd rather be at home trimming my toenails than at some Church Thing with you* wasn't any nicer than *I have a boyfriend and a life, loser.*

I had plenty to think about when Jeph and Shayne dropped me home. I also had another candy bar, wearing another Scripture jacket. I unwrapped it.

> *Another reason for right living is that you know how late it is; time is running out. Wake up, for the coming of our salvation is nearer now than when we first*

believed. The night is almost gone; the day of salvation will soon be here. So don't live in darkness. Get rid of your evil deeds. Shed them like dirty clothes. Clothe yourselves with the armor of right living, as those who live in the light. We should be decent and true in everything we do, so that everyone can approve of our behavior. Don't participate in wild parties and getting drunk, or in adultery and immoral living, or in fighting and jealousy. But let the Lord Jesus Christ take control of you, and don't think of ways to indulge your evil desires. Romans 13: 11-14

Something bizarre happened as I read it. My heart started beating hard, my breathing got faster, and I felt like I was filling up, up to my eyeballs, and my eyes even got watery like it was going to spill out of me. Filling up with what, I couldn't say, but I felt the urgency of the words as if they were the truest words I'd ever read. It's like I was filling up with truth.

I wanted to tell somebody, or have somebody tell me what was happening to me. The words pressed on me: *you know how late it is…the day of salvation will soon be here…let the Lord Jesus Christ take control of you…*

Should I call someone? Shayne, Allie, Mrs. Greene…Sam? What would I even say? *I was just reading some verses, and all of a sudden they really seemed TRUE.* Well, duh, Rory. Didn't they already feel that way? Still, my hand was reaching for my phone.

From the corner of my eye I saw a movement; I half-expected to see Uri there, reclining on my desk. He'd shown up after the other Scene meetings. And it might have been him; I had an impression of his blue eyes boring into me, but he never materialized. Behind me came a sound in my doorway.

Sheelan, Tamika beside her. Both sported intricately made-up faces and floofy hairdos, but their clothes suggested hibernation, not recreation.

I had discovered something even worse than the gathering of Sheelan, Quentin, Tamika and Tyler before their customary

Saturday night out: Sheelan and Tamika staying home, bored, resentful and restless.

"We've been waiting for you," Sheelan said ominously.

"Girl, you've got to do something with this room," Tamika said. Tamika talked like a black girl but looked more like an Asian girl, with black-girl hair. She confused me. "White walls? White curtains? We ought to give your room the makeover."

The what?

"Come to Sheelan's room," Tamika said, as if she had authority over me. For someone easily four inches shorter than me, she did have a certain air of authority—a way of wagging her head and finger that was both mesmerizing and intimidating. She walked away with the confidence that I would obey. "And bring the chocolate."

The worst had come to pass. Sheelan and Tamika were drowning their sorrows in cosmetics, and they needed a fresh guinea pig. I was about to become the victim of makeover blackmail.

This was no cozy slumber-party scenario where big sis graciously invites little sis to join the fun, braiding ribbons into her hair or painting her fingernails. I was a mere pawn, dragged into an ongoing duel between the Whitestone High student council girls ('us,' ha) and their rivals, the cheerleaders (them). Photos of made-over faces were flying over cell phones, and the texting had gotten malicious.

"I'm not doing this," I said, drawing back from Sheelan's doorway, which I was well-trained not to cross over. Unlike my generic white room, hers was a periwinkle and plum fantasy, colors I always associated with unwelcome.

"Yes, you are," Sheelan said. "Come on, Rory, don't you want to look pretty for your boyfriend? What's his name? Oh, yeah: J-e-p-h Jeph." They both laughed.

"He's just my friend's brother."

"Really? Then why does he always come to the door to meet you for your Saturday Night Church Date?"

"Shut up, Sheelan." I retreated into the bathroom, but now they had me cornered. "You know he only comes to the door so he can see you."

Tamika screeched and pushed Sheelan. "Told you so! He is *so* into you."

"Oh, please. As if!" Sheelan wasn't denying his interest in her, just the possibility that she would ever be seen with him in this lifetime. "He looks like his mama dresses him, and he's probably going to grow up to be a priest."

"Just leave me alone," I said.

Sheelan's eyes got slitty, always a bad sign. "You do this for me, or I'll tell Mom about this." And she pulled open a drawer under the sink and pulled out a plastic baggie with a cluster of tiny white pills in it.

Tamika gaped. "She does drugs?"

"Nope. This is the medicine she's supposed to be taking, only she hasn't been." I was speechless, and Sheelan smirked. "I found them in the wastebasket. I should probably tell Mom no matter what, huh?"

She had me. Sheelan wasn't the only one in the family not exactly living out the truth.

12

"Okay..." Tamika dabbed goo on my lips. The scent of strawberry wafted up my nostrils. "Perfect."

"I wouldn't go that far," Sheelan said.

"She's like a whole new girl. Ready for your unveiling, Rory?" Tamika pulled me towards the bathroom mirror.

I was most certainly not ready for my unveiling. After the poking, pulling, scrubbing, rubbing, powdering, painting, teasing and—shudder—tweezing I had just endured, I could only imagine that I must look like some kind of crazed clown marionette, with Sheelan and Tamika pulling the strings.

The face in the mirror looked familiar. A little bit like my mom, with a shade of Sheelan. And somewhere, barely visible beneath a gruesome layer of foundation, was me. They had gone for the "smoky" look with the eyeshadow and tried to sculpt me some cheekbones with shades of blusher. I had flatly refused the false eyelashes, so Tamika had settled for an extra layer of mascara and an instrument of torture I hadn't even known existed, an eyelash curler. My lips glared glossily in the unforgiving bathroom lighting. I looked like...like a crazed clown marionette, actually.

"So what do you think?" Tamika put her hand on her hip.

I stared slack-jawed at myself. Slack-jaw didn't make the look any more attractive, but I don't think it could've made it worse. "How do you wash this stuff off?" I asked.

Sheelan huffed. "Nice thanks we get."

"Not until I get my picture." Tamika was already snapping her phone in my face. (Pity there was no flash and no merciful temporary blindness.) They shut themselves off in Sheelan's room, resuming their digital duel with the other makeover maniacs of Whitestone High.

After I'd rubbed most of the paint off my face with a washcloth, I began to see something different (myself). Soon came the suggestion of how I might look with just a little bit of makeup. It wasn't so bad. And then I finally noticed my hair.

Sheelan had messed with it while Tamika assaulted my face, misting, glopping, scrunching and floofing. Now I had curls. Not the sassy, strawberry blond curls of Sheelan, but also not the ginger frizz I had come to expect and grown to despise. Sheelan had worked some kind of hair sorcery and given me auburn waves that sort of turned curlish around my face. And it wasn't even crispy. Shiny, but soft.

"Her evil powers *can* be used for good," I murmured in amazement.

"Don't even think about using any of my product," Sheelan's voice snapped in my ear, making me jump. She didn't notice — too busy scooping up bottles and tubes. "This stuff alone costs me twelve bucks a bottle." She brandished it at me then snatched it back as if I might grab it and run, fugitive for the sake of curling crème.

"But how'll she maintain her glam new look?" Tamika asked.

"With her own money. Oh yeah, she doesn't have any money." Sheelan wouldn't either, if not for Quentin's job at the pretzel place in the mall and her ability to manipulate cash out of him.

They went downstairs, but Sheelan said loud enough for me to hear, "Maybe she can pray for some cash." Tamika cackled. They'd obviously also been talking about me and my Church Thing. I considered violating the inner sanctum of Sheelan's room, taking her precious hair product and dumping it down the toilet. Like I should've done with those little white pills.

Before I could consider that crime any further, the phone rang. Of course Sheelan pounced on it.

"Hello? Oh… Yeah, sure, just a minute," I heard her say. "Rory! It's for you."

I bounced down the stairs with my bouncy hair.

"Must be your boyfriend," she whispered.

I froze. Was she teasing me about Jeph again? But he wouldn't be calling for me. My heart hammered as I raised the phone to my ear. "Uh, hello?"

"Hi, Rory. How're you doing tonight, honey?" It was a woman's voice, and if I weren't expecting something totally different, I would've known Mrs. Fisher instantly. This time it took me a few seconds, while Sheelan and Tamika snickered and poured diet colas.

"Oh, um, I'm fine I guess."

"Good. I know this is last-minute, but Zee and I have to take Hope and Kings to their chess club dinner, and Auntie Camille was supposed to sit for Charity and Trinity, but she's laid up with the flu. Can you stay with them for a couple of hours?"

I was knocking the names *Charity* and *Trinity* around in my skull and coming up blank. "Stay with…?"

"They'll be going to bed soon, so bring a book or something. There's leftover chicken, still warm. But we'll pay you in cash, not chicken." She laughed.

I seized on the word *cash*. I was happy to help the Fishers out, money or no money—even chicken or no chicken—but this certainly was convenient.

"I'll be right over. Bye." I hung up and pulled on my coat and shoes while Sheelan watched suspiciously.

"Where are you going?"

"To get some cash," I said with the sort of cheerfulness that screamed *nah*-nah-nah-*nah*-nah. A most satisfying exit.

Charity and Trinity, as it turns out, were Cherry and Tee-Tee. Mr. Fisher (I still didn't know what Zee stood for) let me in. He was broad and tall with an oh-so-shiny brown bald head, and tonight he wore a salmon-colored shirt with an oh-so-shiny tie of the same color. He smiled and said in his deep voice, "Be good for Rory, baby girls. In bed by 8:45. We'll be home in a couple of hours."

"Yes, Daddy." They obediently kissed him and he left through the garage. When he was gone, they turned back to me in their My Pretty Pony pajamas, synchronized and scheming. I was in for it. But it was only a half an hour until bedtime. How hard could that be?

An hour and a half later, I had been charaded, Old Maided, balleted, piano recitaled, and ring-around-the-rosied to the brink of exhaustion. Then came bedtime, a.k.a. the Descent into Madness: toothpaste disasters, potty breaks, multiple drink requests, two stories—actually the same one twice—and an elaborate ritual of turning off some lights but leaving others on, with closet and bedroom doors left open a little but not too much. Then came the second potty break and the process practically started all over again.

When I finally collapsed on the sofa, I nearly yelled. Tucked amongst the calico cushions I discovered a calico cat. Punkin had nothing more to say at being sat on than a squeak and a lazy stretch, sinking her claws into the upholstery. The Fishers' house was never what you'd call tidy. Very actively used, maybe: tables strewn with papers and books, corners of the floor taken over by half-finished puzzles or bizarre tools and toys I assumed had some higher purpose. The place always smelled good, though.

I moved to the other end of the sofa, finding the photocopied "Armor of God" song the girls had performed for me, rather pleased that the lyrics by now were getting to be familiar. We were going to learn about the breastplate next Saturday. Then maybe the hlemet of salvation. I giggled to myself. It was probably my imagination, but it almost seemed like Sam had been trying to make me laugh with that joke, not just Jake.

I was sitting there smiling with chicken in one hand and the sheet of music in the other when the Fishers walked in, Kingston wearing his own shirt and shiny tie—the teal version of his dad's salmon one. "Did you win some kind of award or something?" I asked him.

"Me? Naw. I like chess, but I'm not that good at it."

Hope took the steps two and a time up to the kitchen. "He's just a big softie. He gives people a chance to beat him. But I got this," and she twirled a frilly red award like a gymnastics ribbon. "Hey, I like your hair."

I shrugged and smiled, tucking a curl behind my ear. "Thanks."

She saw me put the sheet of music down on the table. "Oh, no. Did the twins make you listen to that all night?"

"They played it a couple of times."

Mrs. Fisher said, "Maybe it's time we started learning a new song."

"It's okay. Actually, we're learning about the Armor of God in youth group." Part of me wanted to shout, *And you've got it all, Mrs. Fisher! I've seen it.* But of course I didn't want some of my favorite people thinking I'd lost my marbles.

"That's at the Front Street church, right? How do you like it?"

"It's pretty good." I grabbed my coat, and she opened the front door to 'walk me home'—watch me go down their steps and up ours, that is. Then I had one of those moments when your heart speaks out of your mouth without checking with your brain first. "I like it, but sometimes I feel like... I don't know. Like I'm not exactly good enough."

"Good enough?" Usually when adults repeat your last words, it's because they aren't really listening but want you to think they are. Mrs. Fisher was really listening.

"Yeah. For the whole Christian thing. You know?" How would she know? She was a Christian, so obviously she was good enough.

Then she laughed that laugh of hers, just happy, not making fun. "Well, Rory, maybe you haven't heard, but what they say is true: First He catches the fish, *then* He cleans them."

I was still thinking about that when I tossed my coat on the kitchen chair, walked past my sister and her cosmetic-crazed best friend as they devoured a half-gallon of Fudge Sludge ice cream and watched me. I gave my fifteen dollars a jaunty little flick in the air before shoving it into my pocket. *I prayed for cash...now do you want me to pray that you'll find better boyfriends?* I would've asked if I'd had the guts.

The twins had sapped my strength, so I just got ready for bed. Grandma Judy's Bible waited there on the nightstand; I crawled under the covers and cracked it open. (After making sure my door was closed tight. I just wasn't in the mood for any more teasing.) It opened to the Book of Matthew in the New Testament. My tired eyes skimmed over the page and got caught on some of the red words: *Follow Me, and I will make you fishers of men.*

I wasn't sure what it meant, but it gave me that little tug in my stomach again, just a gentle one this time. I dreamt of water and fishes.

The next week of school was just something to get through so I could go to the Scene. I was as surprised by this as anyone.

Some high points popped up along the way, stepping stones of okayness across the river of blah. Like lunchtimes with Shayne and Allie and Jake and Sam and the others who sometimes joined them. I still felt like one of 'the others.' Not because of anything they did—I just knew I was on borrowed time. But borrowed or not, lunchtime had become the best time of the day.

English had been good, too. I spent Monday and Tuesday working up the courage to say 'hi' to Sam before class started on Wednesday. I also started paying more attention to the homework and reading so I might actually have something intelligent to say during class. Funny how things become more interesting the more you learn about them.

Art class should have been a high point, but Mrs. Greene wasn't there and the assistant principal was substituting for her. Awkward, since we were working in paints and she wore a navy business suit. She basically took cover behind a desk I'd hardly even noticed before—a big ugly thing Mrs. Greene only used for piles of stuff—and told us to continue our projects as we'd been instructed. There was something weird about the whole situation, and the fact that Jasmine kept looking at me and looking away so I wouldn't notice sapped any remaining fun right out of that class. Nobody seemed to know the whereabouts of Mrs. Greene.

Thursday eventually crawled around, that day when you start to see the light at the end of the school tunnel. A cloud hung over the day for me, though, dreary as the real ones that hung in the sky like steel scrubbing pads. I had a session with Dr. McD after school (a McSession, as my dad would've called them). Mom arranged for Sheelan—who against all logic and after failing the exam twice had actually been granted a driver's license—to transport me there. I hesitate to use the term *driving*. She was supposed to be there promptly at 3:00, but of course she was late. Probably forgot how to put the car in reverse.

A river of kids poured out of the six safety-glass doors like a bursting dam, finding parents or grandparents or babysitters waiting to rescue them in dry cars; it carried me outside. Others dashed the short distance home or, resigned to sogginess, trudged the longer distance home with or without umbrellas. Buses carted away the rest, and I was left behind in a cloud of diesel stink. I imagined myself the poster child for the Forgotten Kid. The last thing I expected was to see someone else flattened against the bricks on the other side of the doors. There was a flash of lightning.

Sam saw me at the same time. He gave me a pocket wave, the kind when your hand stays in the pocket of your coat because it's cold outside. But it was a floppy coat so it was still a pretty big wave. I gave him an arms-full-of-books wave. My mouth opened to say 'hi' when a crash of thunder seemed to split the sky. The sound that came out of me was less like 'hi' and more like "Aaiii!"

Then the rain poured down in buckets, buckets with rocks in them by the feel of it. The school doors were locked behind us, so there was nothing for us to do but dash for the only decent shelter, a tucked-in corner where the roof overhung the pavement a bit more. Some bushes blocked the view of the driveway, so Sheelan might not even see me, but I had to chance it. It might've all been God's doing, anyway.

After the nervous laughter, I tried to think of something to say. Sam beat me to it. "Who are you waiting for?"

"My sister." I made a face. "How 'bout you?"

"My grandpa." He watched the pick-up lane through rain-spattered glasses. "He drives slow."

"My sister just drives bad."

"At least she takes you places."

"Yeah, like the doctor. Yippee."

Now it seemed like he was trying to find the right thing to say. He took off the silver rectangular glasses to rub off the raindrops, and I saw him for the first time without them. It made me a little embarrassed for some reason. He had long, dark lashes.

"I suppose you're sick of doctors," he said.

"Oh, yeah. Especially head doctors." If it were possible to properly kick one's self, I would've right then. Just what I wanted him thinking, that I had to go to a shrink. But he must've thought I just meant a regular sort of head doctor.

"Because of the seizure-things?" he asked.

Maybe it was wishful thinking, but I sensed he wasn't asking just out of a fourteen-year-old boy's natural curiosity for all things freakish. He actually sounded concerned. So I answered as honestly as I could.

"Yeah."

"You had one at lunch today, didn't you?"

I blinked. He was right. But it had been a short one, a very still one. I didn't think anyone had noticed.

"Sorry, I'll mind my own business," he said.

"No, it's… How'd you know?"

"My Aunt Bekah used to have seizures sometimes. She would just sort of tune out and tune back in again. She wouldn't even know it. It's kind of what you looked like."

I'd probably looked like a drooling idiot.

"Except she always looked like she couldn't see anything. You seemed more like you were looking at something."

He was right again. I'd been looking at his breastplate of righteousness. He wasn't the only one at the table who had it, but I'd seen his the most clearly, maybe because he was sitting right across from me. I nodded but didn't say anything.

Finally I asked quietly, "Did everybody see?"

"No." He shook his head. "Just me, I think. Is that why you have to go to the doctor today?"

"No, this is just a regular appointment." An appointment at which I had no intention of mentioning the lunchtime seizure. I guarded them secretively. Time to change the subject. "What about you? Where do you have to go?"

He smiled and looked at the puddle his shoes were in. "Hebrew lessons."

"Really? You mean, the language?" Oh, crud, that was stupid.

"Yeah, sort of. Reading the Tanakh. You know, the Old Testament."

"Oh. Right." I was confused again. Maybe being a Jewish Christian was just a confusing thing, I didn't know.

"My grandpa takes me. My mom and dad think it's good, too," he added. I thought it was an odd thing to say, but later I would understand what he meant.

A car honked, so close that I flinched like it was about to run us down. It was a white sedan, sparkling in the rain. It looked like an old-people car. I peeked out, and there pulling up behind it was our dark blue hatchback, the car that hadn't been totaled in the accident.

"Looks like we're both saved," I said. Interesting choice of words. I meant *rescued*, simple as that. But I knew enough to realize that *saved* meant much more to the Scene gang. The word hung out there between us. If I'd had the hot face before, it was frosty compared to what I felt now.

Sam slung his backpack onto his shoulder. I stood there trying to decide which was worse, him saying something about it or leaving without saying anything about it. For a second it looked like he was going to leave without saying anything, period—not even goodbye. That would be the absolute worst.

He hesitated and scrubbed a hand through his mop of dark curls. "It's okay if you're not saved, Rory—I mean, not *okay* okay, but... You don't have to feel like you don't belong or anything like that. The Scene isn't a club. It's just a place for people who want the truth."

Wow. "Um... Okay. Yeah. Thanks," I stammered.

"I won't be at school tomorrow, but see you Saturday night?"

"Saturday—definitely."

Only as we jogged out to the waiting cars did it occur to me how it might look, us coming out from behind the bushes together. Sam's grandfather leaned over and opened the door for him, noticing me at the same time. "Does the young lady need a ride somewhere as well, Samuel Solomon?" He had a wrinkly but kind looking face, and a heavy accent.

"I think her sister's here."

"Yes, that's her," I said. "Thanks anyway."

"Certainly, miss. And *shalom*."

Sam had a bit of the hot face as he drove away.

Sheelan had a knowing face when I got in the car. Knowing just didn't look right on that face.

"Shut up," I said before she could say a word. *Shut up* was going to be a hard habit to break, but I decided to give it a try. Starting from that point on.

13

As it turned out, Sam wasn't the only one to miss school on Friday, though his was for happy reasons. (Absent by reason of Jewishness, he told us later.) Me, I stayed home because I was a mess.

Don't blame me—blame Dr. McD. Honestly, I was beginning to see how these head shrinkers worked: to make people feel better, first make them feel ever so much worse. Then when things begin to improve a little, it looks like a big breakthrough. Well, right now I was in the ever-so-much-worse stage of the program.

I told Grandma Judy my theory on shrinks. Oh, yes, Gran Judy was home with me. Ever since I was maybe eleven, if I had to stay home sick from school, Mom would usually still go in to work. Then it was nothing but DVDs and popsicles all day while I built a nest of used tissues around myself on the sofa. But now that I was crazy, I needed a babysitter.

Having Gran there wasn't so bad, though, because she made really good lunches. And cookies.

"Come on down," she said. "I'll show you how to turn a stick of butter, two eggs, and a cake mix into any kind of cookies you want."

I kept my face in my pillow. "Hmmf," I said.

"Come on. You can tell me about all the awful things the doctor did to you."

I sulkily rolled out of bed, already defeated and once again unfairly enticed by baked goodies. Now is when I'd have to admit that Dr. McD hadn't actually mentally abused me or anything. "She just has a way of making me feel crummy," I grumbled.

"You know, sometimes God works that way, too."

Yikes. Some heavenly Father. God really needed a new public relations guy. "So He purposely grinds us down?"

"Usually He doesn't have to. We do a good job of it ourselves. But He may let us, because as they say, when we hit rock bottom, that's when we start looking *up*. Bring your Bible, I'll show you something."

"It's your Bible, Gran." I grabbed it and thumped down the stairs.

She already had the big mixing bowl out and was dumping the cake mix into some melted butter. She cracked an egg, showing me how to do it in one swift, single-handed motion. I tried to copy her and got egg-slimed. "Now look up Second Corinthians while I stir," she said.

"Here it is." I impressed myself with my speed.

"No, you're in the Old Testament. That's probably Second Chronicles."

"Oh, yeah."

"Go to the New Testament, after Acts, Romans, First Corinthians…"

"Umm…Okay. Got it."

"Twelfth chapter. I think it's verse eight or nine. 'And he said unto me…'"

I read, "And He said to me, 'My grace is sufficient for you, for My strength is made perfect in weakness.'"

"That's the one. Broken pots, Rory. God uses broken pots. When we get out of the way, that's when we make room for Him to step in."

Is that what happened when I was in a coma? Because I'd certainly gotten out of the way then—and who should step in but an odd assortment of so-called angels? But the only thing they'd accomplished was to make me question my own sanity... Or did Dr. McD get the credit for that?

"Broken pots, huh?" I muttered, wiping a bit of egg goo from the Bible page. "What about crackpots?"

"Oh, you're no crackpot, Rory Joyce."

"What about my hallucinations?"

"Do you think they're hallucinations?"

Here we hit the core of the problem. Without actually asking me to, Dr. McD had gotten me to admit that

1) I wasn't just talking to 'imaginary people,' but
2) I was seeing other strange things when I had my seizures, and (here's the clincher)
3) it was my fault that my dad had died in the crash.

So that's why I came out of the session with my brain in a twist and my stomach in knots. I hadn't cried or anything. In fact, I held it all together pretty nicely until nighttime when I suddenly felt the need to throw up.

Just like she had a way of getting information without asking for it, Dr. McD had a way of communicating things without actually saying them. She never came right out and told me that my seizures were just some weird outlet for the guilt I was feeling about my dad. And she didn't exactly say that my 'special visitors' were sort of like another kind of seizure—ones I didn't even know I was having. But I lay awake half the night with those ideas in my head, almost like I'd come up with them myself. The fact that the seizures had become so quiet and still, not the fall down and twitch kind, made the whole hallucination thing seem possible. Was I just a girl who had an occasional quiet freak-out and imagined stuff—stuff that would make me feel better or worse or important or unimportant—whatever suited me at the time?

Gran Judy's question still hung out there. *Do* you *think they're hallucinations?* I hesitated. I'd gotten so twisted around with the mind games, I wondered if Gran was asking me questions they had told her to ask. Yes, I actually suspected my own grandma might be in cahoots with the shrinks. I was paranoid, just like they'd suggested. They were making it true.

I didn't have an answer. I didn't know what to think anymore. But, as strangely comforting as it would be to just chalk all of it up to a mental breakdown—something that could be fixed—I discovered that I didn't want that to be the truth. I wanted the Truth to be the truth. So even though I didn't know the answer to her question, I picked the one I wanted.

"No, Grandma. I don't think they're hallucinations."

She stirred for a few seconds. No men in white coats jumped out of the closet to take me away. "Neither do I, then. You've always had sense—you use the brains the good Lord gave you. If you're seeing people that others can't and you're sure they're real, I'll take your word for it."

"Thanks." I hoped she wasn't just making nice grandma talk, because I really needed an ally right then.

She added, "I just want to be sure they won't cause you any harm."

My hand stopped on its way to steal a glob of cookie dough.

"What do you mean?"

She tilted her glasses forward at a funny angle, so she could see over her bifocals. "Well, folks who can't be seen by everyone are obviously something special. Good special or bad special, that's what I'm concerned about."

My heart did some clumsy, happy acrobatics. Did someone actually get it? "You don't have to worry about that."

"Are you sure, now? I won't have any demons tormenting my granddaughter." She winked at me, but the light in her eye was less like a twinkle and more like a laser.

"No. They're not demons." I took a deep breath. "They're angels, Grandma." There, total confession.

The dramatic response never came. She never even missed a beat. "Are you sure, though? You know a devil's just a fallen angel and can look as pretty as it pleases. 'Satan himself transforms himself into an angel of light.' Even quotes Scripture."

"That's what they said. But they taught me to test them. To ask whom they serve."

"Do they proclaim the lordship of the risen Christ?"

"Yep. But I'll double-check next time if it makes you feel better." If there even was a next time. It seemed like ages since Gabby had popped in to point at the Book, or Rafie had come to lay a hand on me. Or Micah, to... Well, I wasn't sure what Micah was all about. Uri was the last one I'd seen, and he had his way of boiling things down, putting them in plain language. Not that he made things easier. Just the opposite, really.

Grandma said, "What would really make me feel better would be to talk about this with my pastor. I can keep your name out of it, if you prefer, but I know he could shed some insight on the situation." Gran went to a different church than the one we used to attend. My dad had picked ours, but when he'd had to start taking work on Sundays, the rest of us kind of dropped the ball.

Then she asked, "Have you thought about discussing all of this with your pastor?"

That would be embarrassing, considering we hadn't actually been going to church. I could barely remember our pastor's name. Then I had one of those *ding!* moments. What about Pastor Dan? He'd pretty much have to take me seriously, or else admit that everything he'd been teaching was a fairy tale.

"Maybe I will," I said slowly, but I'd already made up my mind to do it on Saturday. It was shaping up to be a big day.

I couldn't have been more right.

There are different kinds of Big Day, though. There's the special-life-changing-things-a-happening sort, and then there's the let's-put-our-hopes-on-the-curb-and-crush-'em big day. You might even get a combo. No combo on my day—it was all #2.

Things started well enough. Amazed at my own recklessness, I asked to tag along with Sheelan to what we used to call the Super Everything Store, back when we used to amuse each other. There I spent my babysitting money on some makeup and a bottle of hairstyling cream virtually identical to her worth-its-weight-in-gold *crème*, but less than half the cost. (Sheelan was a sucker.) This money would've normally gone towards junk food or what Mr. Behrens called fluffy fiction, so it was a pretty big step for me.

Okay, I did get a bag of cheese doodles.

Sheelan pried right into my bag before I could hide it, eyeing my choices with a sniff that wasn't quite disapproval. "Okay for a beginner, I guess," she said. "Don't ask me for help using it, though." As if I'd planned to.

She pounced on me when I emerged from the shower later that afternoon. "Makeup, hair product, a shower?" she accused. "Who are we trying to impress? That boy you were in the bushes with? Or are we just getting pretty for Jesus?"

I wanted to smack her, but I shouldered past her and locked my bedroom door behind me. That's when it occurred to me: ordinarily, she'd be getting ready to impress, performing her hours-long Saturday night glamification. I wracked my brain for any recent memory of her usual giggly phone chats with Quentin. He certainly hadn't been over lately, thank God for small favors.

I should've kept my mouth shut, but I think I've established that I often fail to do this at critical moments.

I stuck my head back out the door and called, "Should I call Jeph and tell him you don't have a date tonight? Maybe he'll ask you to come—if he's still interested." Then I closed it quick, in case she flung anything at me. She didn't. This should have been my first warning. Sheelan's sass was always safer than Sheelan's silence.

The makeup and hair thing was harder than I expected. While I could never go so far as to admire what Tamika and Sheelan had committed upon my person, I had to admit that the process required a certain skill. With uncommon good judgment, I decided to follow the 'less is more' philosophy of cosmetics. As for the hair, well, I didn't achieve Sheelan's magic, but it was definitely an improvement.

The clothes issue was tricky. Most of the time my friends saw me in the sad, sad school threads, but this was my opportunity to look…less sad. I was examining the back view of a certain pair of jeans when my mom knocked. "Can I come in?"

"Yeah, okay."

She wasn't wearing her waitressing uniform.

"Aren't you going to be late?" I asked.

"I'm not going in tonight."

"Oh." That was odd. Saturdays were big tip nights.

"Why don't we order Chinese and rent a movie? Something funny." She had a folded piece of paper in her hand, and she folded it again like she wanted it to disappear. "We can get the egg rolls and the crab rangoon."

She never let us get both. "Uh, yeah, that'd be alright. When I get home from the Scene—the Church Thing?"

"Oh, you can miss one night of that, can't you? Family time's important." She didn't say *more* important, but only because she stopped herself. She was picking her way through the words like a minefield. "We haven't had much chance to just be together since...everything happened." (Everything was another word for It.)

Okay, how not to sound like a jerk here? "Sounds great, Mom. But I'll only be gone for maybe two hours. I kind of have to finish getting ready..." I hinted. She didn't bite. "Shayne'll be here in ten minutes."

She sat on my bed. "No. I called Mr. Svoboda."

I froze. "What?"

"I called and told them not to pick you up."

"Why?"

"Because you're not going tonight."

I stared. "Because you want to eat crab rangoon and watch a movie?" There's a lot of ways I could've said that; I'm not proud to say I chose the nasty way, like she'd offered to let me scrub the toilets—which, a little later, I felt was exactly what I deserved. But not now. Now I was steamed.

"No, Rory, not because of crab rangoon. Because of this." She whipped open the piece of paper she still held. There was familiar printing on it, but my eyes followed the small thing that fell to the floor. A little plastic baggie with the pills I hadn't taken.

Sheelan.

14

Needless to say, there was no rangoon that night. Plenty of crab, though.

Sheelan. I clenched my fists and pounded on my pillow. An unsatisfying substitute for her face. Sheelan, who constantly teased me and put me down—I give one little jab back, and she retaliates with the whole arsenal, goes for total betrayal.

I locked them both out of my room, but not before the three-way shouting match ended in a draw. Well, it hadn't actually ended. We were all still yelling when I slammed the door, but there were definitely no winners. Now I could hear them talking about me downstairs, but not in the kitchen so I couldn't make out the words. The desire to go down and defend my case was just barely outweighed by the fact that I never wanted to see their faces again.

All I could do was watch the clock silently count down the minutes, knowing when the other kids gathered in their lines, then their groups, when they probably gathered on the gym/church floor, listening and laughing. Finally I watched the hour change again, and I knew it was over, and I'd missed it.

It's hard staying angry for that many minutes. It kind of crept away, replaced by this expanding bubble of sadness. I liked the angry better—it was easier—but when I tried to push the sad away to get the angry back, I just popped the bubble and it all came pouring out. Which means I blubbered into my pillow. (The makeup stains never came out of that pillowcase.)

A classic case of overreacting—unless you consider that I hadn't cried in all the time since I woke from the coma. Not one real tear. So I guess I had a lot stored up. Funny how something small can set off the whole chain reaction. I mean, there were plenty of big things to cry about: the secret of the pills discovered, Sheelan's dirty treachery, my semi-crazy state of mind, the stretched, ancient look on my mom's face. My dad. But it was a little thing that made the wave break. I just kept remembering Sam standing in the rain, saying, "See you Saturday night?"

Bleary-eyed, I reached for what I thought was a tissue. It was the folded paper my mom had been holding. I spread it open and read the 2nd Corinthians verse again. This time I read it with my mom's eyes. The words that jumped out: *war, flesh, carnal, captivity, obedience, punish, disobedience*. No wonder she'd freaked out. But how was it that I understood it better than her? I knew Gran Judy would understand. I hadn't joined a cult, but that's just about what Mom accused me of.

She was trying to protect me, I knew that. I finally understood what Mr. Behrens meant when he tried to describe 'irony' in English class. Mom was protecting me from the one thing that was helping me.

I looked closer at the paper and saw an odd pattern of geometrical creases. Then came the memory of Uri folding it into a sleek paper airplane, sending it gliding down the hallway. Sheelan had found it there.

I grabbed Gran's Bible and flipped the pages, relieved to find the other paper still tucked there in the book of John. Good thing Mom hadn't found that one, the Romans 13 passage. She would've just seen *time is running out...Get rid of your evil deeds.*

Shed them like dirty clothes... let the Lord Jesus Christ take control of you...

I buried it back in the pages before someone could make an airplane out of that one. To this day, I don't know if it was thinking about him that made him come, but when I turned around Uri was there leaning against the wall.

My first reaction was *why him,* why not Rafie with his soothing sort of way, or Gabby with her good advice—even Micah and his sternness would've been more of a comfort. Then I felt guilty. If God was sending an angel, even letting me see it, should I really be grousing about His choice? If He sent the one who left me feeling off-center and just as baffled as always, there must be a reason.

He must've seen it in my face. "You don't look happy to see me," he said, putting on a show of hurt feelings. He was devastatingly handsome in his hurt.

Now my third reaction. "Sorry, but your timing couldn't be much worse," I whispered. "If I get caught talking to you now, they'll send me to the room with the cushy wallpaper."

Uri picked a piece of lint off his crisp pinstriped shirt. "Would you like me to just put them to sleep for a while?" He snapped his fingers, suggesting how easy it would be.

I wasn't exactly comforted. Was he allowed to do that? What else could he do to them?

"You wish to know what else I could do to them?"

I shook my head. Why were his eyes so blue? They were unnatural. I sensed he was testing me. Testing...what did that remind me of? Couldn't remember.

So I whispered, "I know you're not a genie sent to do my bidding."

"True. I'm sent to do another's bidding, aren't I? And that can mean putting aside any obstacles."

That last word hit me. Referring to my mom and sister as obstacles reminded me—or maybe drove it home for the first time—that I wasn't really dealing with people here. They only looked like people for convenience. I was dealing with spirits, ones who had powers unknown at their disposal.

Was that how God worked? 'Putting aside obstacles' — like some kind of big Mob Boss in the sky? It didn't sound right. Uri had to mean something less sinister. "If you mean God sent you to get my mom to let me go to the youth group, it's too late for that."

He laughed. Unlike me, he was making no effort to be quiet, which I guess was fine since only I was crazy enough to hear him. "No, that is most assuredly not what I mean."

"Doesn't anyone want me to go? I figured at least it was what God wanted. Tonight was about the breastplate of righteousness, and I don't even know what that means, but I guess I'm not going to any time soon."

He was watching me. I didn't realize it until then, but usually he was sort of distracted, smoothing his clothes, cleaning his immaculate fingernails, folding paper airplanes. This stillness and staring made me feel frozen in the headlights — future road kill.

"Righteousness?" he asked finally. "That's easy. Doing right, living right. Following the rules."

That again. "Which rules? You mean like the Ten Commandments?" How bad could that be? There were only ten.

"Certainly those as a start. Then there's Leviticus and Deuteronomy."

"You mean there's whole books of rules?"

He had a look of mild surprise. "Surely you've been informed that the whole Bible is a guidebook to right living?"

"Yeah…" I suppose, but I hadn't thought of it as a rulebook. There were a lot of pages in the Bible. I really needed this to be simpler than it sounded. "So, wearing the breastplate of righteousness is the same as doing what's right, like the Ten Commandments and stuff?"

"That is part of it. First you have to deal with all that unpleasant business of sin."

"What do you mean, deal with it?"

"You must be convicted of your sin, Rory." His voice went all ominous.

Convicted. Ouch. "What's that like?" I asked quietly.

His eyebrows rose at me. "Do you expect me to know? God's angels are sinless."

"Oh, right." Then I thought about it. "Really?"

"There is no sin in heaven, Rory. You cannot enter with a single sin on your soul."

If I made a list of all the sins I'd committed just that evening, I'd be busy for the rest of the night. Instead, my thoughts turned to my dad. Just one sin could keep you out of heaven? I loved my dad, but I knew he wasn't perfect. Would God really let, say, one swear word decide where you spent eternity?

Heaven must be a pretty empty place. Jesus, some angels, maybe a Mother Teresa here and a Moses there. "It's not possible. No one could be good enough."

"Yet God has given you a whole book about how to do it. He must disagree."

Great, now I was disagreeing with God. I had gone from wanting very badly to understand all of this to being afraid to understand. I wasn't sure I wanted to hear any more. But then I had an image of Gabby explaining things, giving me the truth but hope along with it. Suddenly I asked, "Do you know where Gabby is? I haven't seen her for a while." Thinking of Gabby suddenly reminded me of what I'd promised Gran Judy. Test the spirits.

I sat there trying to figure out how to 'test' Uri again (surely I'd done it the first time he appeared, though I couldn't remember exactly what I'd said) without insulting him or looking like a moron, so I didn't notice when he didn't answer my question about Gabby. Once again he just watched me, sort of the way you watch the exotic but slightly creepy ape at the zoo.

"Um, I know this will sound sort of dumb…" I began.

"Oh, I can't imagine that." His tone had no hint of sarcasm. I think.

"Well, my grandma sort of knows that I've been talking to you guys." I made a gesture meant to signify that 'you guys' meant angels. "And she's worried about me. She believes me—she just wants me to make sure that I'm dealing with the good guys, you know." Here came the hot face.

"She wants you to test the spirits," he said, all unconcerned.

Even hotter face. "Yeah."

"So? Go ahead." He crossed his arms. "Ask me anything about the Bible, about heaven, about God."

"Um…" I was trying to remember how it went. "What about Jesus?"

"Oh, yes. Especially about him. The Holy One sent from God."

That sounded promising. Was that it, then, or was there more? It wouldn't matter, because right then the doorknob rattled and the door swung inwards. Just like that, Uri was gone.

"What? What's wrong?" Mom gasped. She had obviously flown up the stairs, and Sheelan was right behind her.

I gulped. "What do you mean?"

"You were just yelling for us."

"No, I wasn't."

"We both heard you, Rory. You sounded scared." Mom sounded scared.

"You were having a seizure, weren't you?" Sheelan accused.

I shook my head.

"She's lying, Mom."

"Am not! It's the truth! I wasn't yelling and I wasn't—"

"Rory." Something in my mom's voice shut me up instantly. "It's time to take your pill."

This time she watched me swallow it. Then she actually checked under my tongue. I just knew that idea had come from Sheelan.

And that was the end of my seizures and my angels.

Yes, both at the same time. Of course, Dr. McD and my mom congratulated themselves on getting to the bottom of the problem. Poor mixed-up-in-the-head Rory, blamed herself for choosing the matinee and getting her father killed in a car accident, couldn't deal with it alone and so created fictional people to talk to and seizures to let all the badness out.

That's how I imagined them talking about me. Funny thing was, I didn't really care what they were saying. I felt like I'd lost something—like a long-awaited letter, still unread, that the wind blew from my hand, and each time I chased it down, another gust blew it farther until finally it was gone.

After that, I sort of plodded through life. Something had changed. It wasn't like I hadn't gone for days at a time without a seizure or a visit before, but I could tell this was different. The world had gone colorless, a faded photograph. I didn't think about it much. I sat at the odds-and-ends table in the cafeteria, oblivious to whether Jasmine cared or not. The youth groupies didn't seem to know what to make of me. They probably thought I was blowing them off.

I walked into the girls' bathroom on Wednesday and caught a fragment of conversation between Shayne and Allie.

"What's up with that?" Allie was asking.

"I don't know. That's all my dad told me."

"Who first invited her to come?"

"Well, I did. But it wasn't my idea, it was—" then Shayne emerged from the stall and stopped short. I closed and locked my door quickly, but she had seen me. And the split second we made eye contact confirmed that they were talking about me. I only cared a little.

Mrs. Greene was absent again that week, but this time there was a real art teacher substituting. Not interested in anyone's leftovers, she had us put our unfinished paintings aside to begin a new project in decoupage. It was obvious she loved the word decoupage, because she managed to fit it into her instructions at least fifty times, always with an obnoxious French accent.

By now a rumor was circulating about Mrs. Greene's disappearance: she had been suspended for violating the rules of her probation. I'd had no idea she was on probation, or that teachers were even put on probation, but Tiffany Klipfel's dad was on the school board, and she reported that Mrs. Greene had been caught giving religious tracts to students, which was apparently against the law or at least against school policy. That was the cause for her probation, but she was suspended supposedly because she was talking Jesus talk right there in the classroom, and one of the students had reported her.

The whole time Tiffany whispered this across the art tables, Jasmine's eyes were glued to the decoupage. Her effort not to have me look at her was so intense I had to look. I put a few things together.

I had a chance to confirm my suspicions that Thursday. I decided to exit through the gym after school, avoiding the front door. Running into Sam, waiting for his grandpa and his Thursday Hebrew lesson, could conceivably crush what little spark was left in me. My path took me past the art room, and there was Mrs. Greene at her desk. My heart gave a leap until I saw she was putting things into a cardboard box. The leap became a swan dive.

I went in and let my big yap do the talking. "You got in trouble because you were talking to me about Teen Scene and Jesus and stuff in class that day, didn't you?"

"Hi, Rory. I'm glad to see you."

"It was Jasmine Wee, wasn't it? She ratted you out."

She looked at the small, framed picture of a smiling man in her hands and smiled back at it before putting it in the box. Then she sighed. "It's a lot more complicated than that, Rory. This has been an ongoing problem, and I've been praying about it. This might just be God's answer to my prayers."

Oh, goody for God, another strike against Him.

"Did they really suspend you for the rest of the school year?"

"They did. But I want to hear about you. We missed you on Saturday. Shayne said you cancelled at the last minute. Is everything alright?"

So I told her how alright everything wasn't at home. As I relived last Saturday's event, my bruised sense of justice flared up again. I was eager to find an ally in Mrs. Greene. "My mom's so wrong, and she can't see it. She won't listen to me." Then I heard a *ding*! "Hey, do you think you could call her, Mrs. Greene? Maybe you could talk her into letting me go this Saturday."

"Do you really think a phone call from the teacher accused of proselytizing would change her mind?" she asked gently.

Prossela-what? "Well, then, I'll sneak out after she leaves for work."

"But that's the same as lying. Remember the Belt of Truth."

I felt like the Belt of Truth was cinched around my neck. "Then I'll just have to tell her I'm going no matter what she says. It's the right thing to do."

"Do you think so?" She lifted a small book from her purse. "Have you read the entire sixth chapter of Ephesians, or just the Armor part? Here, look it up. The first verse."

I took the tiny New Testament and fumbled around until I found it. "'Children, obey your parents in the Lord, for this is right,'" I read with a dull voice. "You mean obey everything?"

"Well, God doesn't necessarily intend for us to obey things that violate His commands—that's the 'in the Lord' part—but I don't think your situation applies."

"So you think I should just sit at home and miss Pastor Dan's teaching?"

"If your mother forbids you to go, that would be the right thing to do."

She was taking my mom's side? This was not the alliance I'd hoped for. "But I've already missed the breastplate of righteousness. And what about this Saturday? What will I miss?"

"The shoes of the gospel of peace."

I was reminded of my first vision of Sam in armor, and his bare feet. I might finally understand what that meant, but no. Mom would rather I sat stupidly at home watching stupid TV shows than going to learn about the Bible. It was so... stupid.

Mrs. Greene put a hand on my shoulder. "Rory, if you obey your mother, I trust that God will honor your right choice. He wants you to be in the Word, growing in understanding. He will use this difficult situation for good, I'm sure of it."

It must be nice to be sure of things. I watched her put a few more knick-knacks in the box. We were quiet for a bit. "Are we going to see you around here anymore this year?" I asked.

"No, but you'll be seeing me, don't worry."

"Next September?" I asked. She didn't answer immediately. "You're coming back next school year, right?"

She drew in a deep breath. "I wasn't going to say anything yet..."

"You're quitting? You can't quit! That's just what they want. You can't let them win."

"It's not about winning and losing."

"Is it about giving up?" I was mad at the school, not her. She understood.

"Well, it looks like you're going to drag it out of me. The truth is, my husband and I are expecting a baby this fall." Her smile had some twinkle in it.

I gaped. "Really? Wow. That's great." I paused. "Then you'll be coming back?"

"I want to stay home with the baby."

"Sure, right." I didn't know many people who did that anymore. I gave her a smile, too. Mine was weak from lack of use. "That's your husband?" I asked, pointing to the cheerful photograph.

"Yes, that's Ericson."

"Ericson?" Ericson Greene. No Hunter, no Forrest. But there was always the baby to name.

As I prepared to leave, she winked at me. "His middle name is Leif."

15

Mrs. Greene couldn't have been more wrong.

Oh, I gave it a chance. I waited to see just how God was going to take all this trouble and make it good. And a few little seedlings of hope sprouted. Then came the fertilizer, if you know what I mean.

There was a chance things might be different this Saturday. I'd been taking my pills obediently all week—okay, I wasn't given much choice, but I didn't complain about it—and I'd even tried praying about it. The prayer went something like this:

God, if You're even up there watching, You've got to see that things are pretty rotten down here. I want to go to this Scene thing, and I thought you wanted me to go, too, but now my mom's not letting me. To be honest I don't know what You're up to. I don't really do well with subtle messages, so if You want me to learn about this Armor stuff, can you do a little zap thing on Mom and change her mind? Thanks. I'll be waiting to see what happens. Um, amen.

So maybe the prayer wouldn't accomplish much, but I had another reason to believe my mom might give in. I watched and waited on Saturday, not sure if she'd even go to work that night. I didn't know what to hope for. Then I saw her ironing her work blouse.

Sheelan packed an overnight bag, planning to stay at Tamika's. (This confirmed my suspicion that she and Quentin were no longer an item, and it wasn't looking rosy for Tamika and Tyler, either.) Ordinarily, Sheelan's absence would be most welcome. Tonight it meant something else. I watched her and my mom both getting ready for very different evenings, like any other Saturday. Well, if that's the way it was going to be, I might as well ask.

I stood outside my mom's bathroom while she pinned up her hair. "Mom…" I began.

She cut to the chase—also known as my quivering, dissected heart. "Don't ask, Rory. You're not going tonight, and Sheelan's sticking around long enough to make sure you don't try to sneak out."

I stood there speechless, then wandered back to my room. I sat and barely heard when my mom left, barely cared when later a car honked outside and Sheelan announced she was leaving. I almost didn't notice the smug satisfaction in her voice (almost). It wasn't until the phone rang—I don't know how much later—that I snapped out of it and trudged down the stairs. The answering machine picked up before I could.

"Hi, Rory!" Grandma Judy's voice on the machine was bright and chirpy, as alien in my dull world as an intergalactic visitor. "I've been wanting to call all day, but I was at the women's retreat and couldn't get a signal on my phone. I just got home, and I didn't want you to think I forgot about you. You must be out having fun. Well, I hope you kept tomorrow open, because I've got something for you. How about I come around noon, and we can all go out for brunch?" She paused to let that sink in, or just in case someone might pick up. "Okay, I'll call tomorrow morning— not *too* early. Love you, Rorykins. Happy birthday, sweetheart."

Click.

Sunday brunch wasn't what you would call a festive affair. Oh, the atmosphere in the restaurant was festive enough. It was one of those pseudo-Irish places, and this being Pseudo-Irish Day, there were plenty of green foil shamrocks plastered on the walls and big green hats on the servers. Add to this the miserable squeal of pseudo-Irish music, and you have the backdrop of my birthday brunch.

I had left the message on the machine, the little red light blinking, so my mom would see it when she got home. I actually heard her listen to it, then, a minute or two later, heard her feet trudge up the stairs. I lay in bed listening in the dark. At the first step, a surge of victory swept over me. *Ha, now you have to come crawling for an apology.* I'd won that whole evening's battle.

But with the next slow step, I heard weariness. Then anger—at herself. Regret. Grief. By the time she reached the top, she wasn't my mean mom who locked me up like a prisoner and forgot my birthday. She was a woman whose husband had died who was working herself to the point of exhaustion to support her family, a woman with a crazy daughter who was suddenly hanging around with Jesus freaks. A daughter whose birthday had gotten buried in the messy, depressing pile of fertilizer that was life.

My door opened a few inches.

"Rory?" she whispered.

My original plan was to say nothing, to pretend I was asleep and she was too late to squeeze in a lame 'Happy Birthday' before midnight. Now I said nothing because I couldn't talk around the rock in my throat.

"Are you sleeping?"

Still nothing came out. What could I say, anyway?

I heard her sigh, sounding the retreat, and her defeat.

Now we sat at a restaurant table—thankfully without Sheelan, who was still with Tamika—doing a crummy job of pretending that nothing was wrong. It was stupid, because I wasn't mad at my mom, or if I was, I was just as mad at myself. But I couldn't even begin to find the words to express this, so my silence just poisoned the air and made her believe I was furious. It would probably take a miracle to fix this mess.

Grandma Judy dragged her purse onto the table and started rummaging through it. Maybe she had a miracle in there. She had everything else.

"Ah, here it is." We'd been sharing some saucy buffalo wings, and now she pulled out a plastic baggie with a washcloth in it. "Those little wet napkins they give you just don't get your fingers clean. Rory, could you run to the restroom and dampen this for me with some warm water?"

"Sure, Gran." Any excuse to leave the table. I took my time doing it, too.

When I returned, a chocolate cake was sitting where my plate had been—not the restaurant's mini version of a chocolate cake, but Gran Judy's larger-than-life double-layer fudge cake with homemade chocolate cream cheese frosting. I would've been excruciatingly embarrassed if it weren't for the fact that it was practically worth dying for, let alone suffering a little embarrassment.

Then the servers all came over clapping and singing 'Happy Birthday,' and I was excruciatingly embarrassed.

As I plunged into my monster slab of cake, I could tell more than just some Grandma cake sneaking had happened while I was gone. I wasn't sure what, though. Mom's face looked less like granite and more like…well, face. And a fudge-scented breeze had blown a few of our dark clouds away.

Grandma pulled out a big gift bag full of clothes for me. Clothes from grandmas can be a hit-or-miss proposition as far as size and style go, but Gran Judy had stuck with good old jeans and T-shirts, so I didn't even have to put on the fake smile. There was also a little beaded bag and, sure enough, some secret Grandma cash tucked inside.

Then Mom started rooting around in her purse. I had a moment of dread. Was she going to present me with a tube of lipstick and try to pass it off as a gift? My expectations were as deflated as last week's balloon by this point, but no gift is better than a scrounged-up gift.

She pulled out a small green box and set it in front of me. "I meant to wrap it," she began. "I know you think I forgot—I did forget, but not entirely. I just forgot on the day." She sighed, then she shrugged a shrug that said *I'm sorry* better than the words themselves.

The box was velvet and hinged and fit in the palm of my hand, the kind nice jewelry might come in. It creaked when I opened it. The restaurant lights sparkled on a silver claddagh ring, two hands cupping a crowned heart.

I stared at it for a long time, not trusting myself to look anywhere else. "This was Dad's," I finally said.

"It will fit you now."

I slipped it on my left ring finger, and it did. She'd had it resized for me.

"Thanks, Mom," I said. I knew if I just hugged her, an open sore would start to heal over. I wished I could. The best I could manage was a band-aid, a smile. She squeezed my hand.

That in itself was like a miracle, but it was just the start. Things were better between us right off the bat. She would still give me my pill in the morning, but she didn't stand around to make sure I took it. And I did take it.

One night she surprised me by coming into my room while I was reading. "Homework?" she asked.

"Um… I finished it." The truth was, I had been poking around in Gran's Bible. I searched in the back, and you could look up a word and it would give you all the verses where it was used in the whole Bible. I was looking at 'righteousness'—and it's in there a lot—to see if I could somehow piece together some of what they might have talked about at the Scene two Saturdays ago. I wasn't sure how Mom would feel about it.

"Is that Grandma's Bible?"

"Yeah."

"It's okay, Rory. I think it's good that you're reading it, I really do. Your dad would've liked that."

"Yeah?"

"M-hmm."

"I've been looking for his Bible, but I can't find it. Do you know…?"

She shook her head and hesitated a second. "I know Dad felt bad when he had to start taking those Sunday jobs. He had to take any work he could get. I should've kept us all going to church. He felt like it was his responsibility and he always blamed himself. But it was my fault."

It was weird when parents actually admitted they were wrong. It never felt as good as you'd expect. "Well, Sheelan and I weren't exactly waking you up early and begging to go."

"No, you weren't. Dad used to crack the whip behind us, didn't he?" She gave a light snorty laugh. "He was a good man, Rory. I know he's with God now. I hope that helps you a little, too."

I nodded, but all I could hear was Uri saying, *you cannot enter with a single sin on your soul*. My dad was a good man, but good wasn't good enough for heaven.

And this business of righteousness. Most of the verses I looked up were about God, not people. How could an ordinary person put on the breastplate of righteousness when it only came in one size: XXLGOD?

I lay awake thinking about it at night, wishing I could sleep instead. Finally I threw some thoughts towards the ceiling, hoping they would break through and become a prayer.

God, I'm trying to understand. So many things that I do are sins, and I never even realized it. Well, I suppose deep down I knew, but I never thought it mattered much. How can I keep track of everything and get it all right, all of the time? You know I can't, I know I can't. So how does this work?

Oh, and God, these pills seem to have extinguished my angels. What's with that? Am I just nuts?

I have yet another algebra quiz tomorrow, God. Any chance I could sleep a bit?

So that's amen, I guess.

Grandma Judy liked to say that God always answers prayer. If that was true, I asked her, then what about the Flutterby Pink

GlitterCycle I'd prayed for every day the month before my seventh birthday? He hadn't answered that one.

Yes He had, she told me. The answer was no.

So to put it algebraically, if answering prayer was X and granting wishes was Y, then for God, X ≠ Y. Sometimes this left a girl wondering, Y not? Sometimes she started wondering during an algebra quiz, which might've been a good time for prayer but not so good for wandering thoughts.

Sometimes the answer was yes. I didn't know it then, but it was a pretty safe bet that if I was asking to understand God's Word better, He would always answer yes. He could've zapped that understanding right into my brain while I was reading (no zap), or He could use someone else to help me along. (Gabby was long gone. I sort of felt abandoned. If she was just a hallucination, I was pretty pitiful.) But God could use anybody.

Even those who thought 'God Squad' and 'The Jesus Machine' were good names for a youth group.

I was engrossed—emphasis on the gross—in choosing between the Special of the Day and the Greasy Chicken Thingers when Shayne and Allie ambushed me that Monday.

"Hey, Rory," Shayne said. She grabbed the chicken without hesitation. "Got a minute?"

Well, it wasn't like I could get my cafeteria slop to go. "What's up?" I asked.

"We wanted to say sorry."

Ah, this was about what I'd overheard in the bathroom. "Forget about it."

"No, really. Mrs. Greene told us what's been going on, why you weren't at the Scene."

"She told you?"

"She just told us that you wanted to go, but you couldn't."

"Yeah?"

Allie chimed in. "We thought you just weren't interested and you were blowing us off. We should've asked you about it."

I grabbed a water bottle. "Look, you don't owe me anything. It's not like it was your idea to invite me in the first place. I know Mrs. Greene put you up to it."

"Um… Actually, it wasn't her idea. She just thought I should be the one to ask you." Now I was interested, but she seemed to want to change the subject. "That's beside the point. We're bummed that you haven't been coming. Any chance that'll change?"

"I don't know," I had to admit. They had me hemmed in, so I went to their table by default. "I've already missed two weeks."

Just then Jake Dean sat across from me. "Well, looky. The prodigal daughter returns."

"Jake!" Allie shushed him.

"I knew she'd be back. Once you're sucked into the Jesus Machine, there's no escape."

I surveyed my lunch choices. In my distraction, I'd ended up with a bowl of limp green beans, a cup of jello, a bottle of water, and an energy bar. I reached for the bar, but Allie caught my hand.

"Ooh, nice ring. Is it new?"

"Yeah. Well, no. It was my dad's."

"Really?" She gave my fingers a quick squeeze and let go. "It's one of those claddagh rings, right?"

Sam joined us then. "What's that?"

"Rory's new ring. It was her dad's. It's a claddagh. The hands stand for friendship, and the crown is loyalty, and the heart is love. Right, Rory?" Allie asked.

"That sounds right."

"My great-grandma came over from Ireland. That's how I know. I don't look nearly as Irish as you do, though."

"Not all Irish people have crazy hair and freckles."

"And feisty tempers," Shayne said with a laugh.

"But sometimes the stereotypes are true," Sam put in. "Like my nose." He made a gesture as if it were huge.

It looked like a fine nose to me. High in the bridge, like my dad's had been (he'd always insisted it was a sign of nobility). But Jake made a show of falling over every time Sam turned his head. "Hey, watch where you're swinging that thing."

"Did you get the ring for St. Patrick's Day?" Shayne asked me.

"I got it on St. Patrick's Day, but it was really my birthday present. My birthday's the day before."

That was a mistake. Jake immediately stood up and began an operatic rendition of the Happy Birthday song. I attempted to hide behind my green beans until one of the cafeteria goons came over and requested that he stop.

"So you're thirteen now?" Allie asked.

A natural assumption. Most seventh graders turned thirteen sometime during the school year. "Fourteen," I said, not having much choice.

"Shouldn't you be in eighth grade?" Jake demanded. He was in seventh and clearly couldn't understand why anyone would choose not to be in eighth.

"Shouldn't you mind your own business?" Allie asked him.

"It's no big deal," I said, so that it wouldn't seem like a big deal. My humiliation radar warned that this topic had serious hot face potential, but Jake's singing had already sent me into the red zone so what difference did it make? "We moved when I was in first grade, plus I got sick and missed a lot of school, so I ended up doing the first grade over."

That diffused the bomb pretty decisively. Jake looked disappointed, like he'd been hoping for a story with a little more meat. He grabbed a different bone. "So why did you miss the last two Scenes?"

"That's easy," I shot back. I have no idea where it came from; words poured out of my mouth like a jammed slushy dispenser. And my voice was just as sweet. "I missed 'em because my mom and my shrink think I'm a crackpot. Why, you ask? Well, there's the seizures that *aren't* caused by any injury, and the supposed hallucinations, and now I go to the church where they talk about invisible warfare and making your brain captive to Christ. They think I'm about to join a Jesus freakin' cult, what do you think?"

Everyone just sat there looking at me. Then Jake shrugged and said, "So you're just barely crazy enough to fit in. Tell me something I don't know."

Allie giggled, and Shayne looked more interested in drowning her chicken thinger in ketchup. Then her head popped up. "No—

maybe *we* should tell Rory something she doesn't know." Sam nodded like he already knew where she was going with this. "We've got our notes from the past two Saturdays," she said. "Let's go to my house after school tomorrow and fill Rory in on what she's missed." She looked at me. "Your mom wouldn't have a problem with that, would she?"

16

M rs. Greene couldn't have been more right.

I didn't know it at the time, but when she talked about God making something good out of my bad, she meant a Romans 8:28 moment. *And we know that all things work together for good to those who love God, to those who are the called according to His purpose.*

I didn't know about being called to anything, but I did know that I went from sobbing, slobbering captivity in my own bedroom, banned from the Scene, to being an invited guest and — if I could use the word and not jinx it—friend at the house of Shayne Svoboda, eighth grader.

After school Allie and I waited for her by her locker. Allie's was just a few lockers down; I had seen the photos and magnets arranged on the inside of the door, and her neat stack of books, most of which ended up in her book bag. Shayne's locker, on the other hand, spewed out a pile of papers and spiral notebooks, and she rifled through them in search of her needed textbooks. There were magazine clippings taped to the inside of the door, curled up and unreadable.

While she was sorting through it all, Madi Swanson opened her locker on the opposite wall, the seventh-grade side. An empty juice bottle fell out of Shayne's locker and bounced over to land at Madi's feet. She picked it up and handed it back to Shayne. They laughed about it, like it happened all the time.

I watched it all, mystified. Shayne could talk to anybody. Inner sanctum girls like Madi, geeks and oddballs (like me?). There was something about her as rare in a fourteen-year-old as a perfect complexion. Oh, and she had that, too—and warm, shiny brown hair without a hint of split ends, all wrapped up in a petite package. She drew people to her like bees to a can of soda. I was drawn, too, and intimidated. Yet there I was walking home with her after school, with my mom's approval.

Because yes, I had asked for permission. It would've been convenient to leave out the fact that we were meeting to talk about the Church Thing, but I told her that, too—hoping for a notch in my belt of Truth, I admit—and she didn't seem to mind. I think to her, the idea of me having new friends edged out her dwindling fear of me joining a cult.

That, or she was just distracted by a different detail—I told her there would be boys present. Thankfully Sheelan wasn't around to hear that. I assured Mom that Shayne's father would be there, too.

He worked out of a home office, really just a corner of the basement. We ended up crashing in the opposite corner, where an old sofa and some beanbag chairs were scattered around a shaggy brown rug. Otherwise the floor was bare concrete, and the low ceiling had large ceiling tiles and light, but some of them were missing, possibly because the place looked like it was used more like a gym than an office.

"Hello, everyone," Mr. Svoboda called, spinning his chair around to face us. He was short with close-clipped graying hair but dark eyebrows, and comfortable clothes. Two computers hummed at his L-shaped desk. "Sam, Jake—good to see you guys.

When you're done there, come on over and I'll show you the new game I've got. It's beast."

"Dad," Shayne said in protest, maybe at the 'beast' or just the whole gaming thing.

He went on, unfazed. "Hey, Allie." The way he said it made it obvious she was a frequent visitor. Then he smiled at me. "And my peerless powers of deduction tell me you're Rory Joyce."

"Hi," I said.

"Good to meet you. Sorry I can't be more social, but the Holy Gestapo is breathing down my neck. Don't let me keep you from your homework."

Shayne saw my curiosity. "He designs websites for churches," she said. "And leaflets and bulletins and stuff."

Out of the blue I felt a sharp stab of envy, right in my gut. She had a dad, and a dad who worked at home. The more my dad had worked, the less he was home, and the less happy he seemed. It was dumb to be envious, I guess, since she didn't have a mom and I did. But I wasn't missing my mom.

Next came the crucial element of any boy-girl gathering: seating arrangements. A sofa and two beanbags would reveal the pecking order of our pack. The alpha dogs would surely claim the sofa, leaving the hangers-on to the beanbags, or even the lowly floor position. Shayne and Sam seemed to move for the sofa. Opposite ends, or beside one another?

Why did I care?

A fuzzy flying orange beanbag settled the issue. Jake launched it at Sam, knocking him neatly onto the blue vinyl bag. Jake proceeded to land on top of the orange bag, creating a Sam and Bean sandwich with a topping of Jake.

"Mercy!" Sam gasped.

"You look like a hot dog on a hamburger bun," Allie said, claiming a spot on the sofa. Shayne sat beside her, and I took the other end. The boys took the beans.

"Why do you get the furry one and I get the cold vinyl one?" Sam asked.

"Not vinyl—*pleather*. Revel in the luxury."

"Can we get on with it?" Shayne laughed. "Rory's waited long enough."

Allie jumped in. "Let's start with the breastplate of righteousness, from two Saturdays ago. Does everyone have the Ephesians six outline? How about notes?" Only she and Shayne did. "Oh, that's typical."

"I keep it all up here." Sam pointed to his head.

"Yeah, I keep it all up here, too." Jake pointed to Sam's head.

"Well, first we talked about the breastplate as a piece of armor," Allie said, tucking her smooth blond hair behind her ears. Allie's cornflower blue eyes and symmetrical oval face reminded me of my favorite doll when I was little—not fake-pretty, not plain. Just pleasant. "What its function is."

"Well, obviously," Jake said, "a breastplate is there to protect the—"

"Vital organs," Sam cut in, punching Jake in the arm. "When you think of a warrior getting mortally wounded, don't you picture it in the heart or in the guts, mostly?"

"Nice," I said.

"The breastplate of righteousness protects you from a deadly blow," Allie said, circling words in her notebook. "It really protects your *heart*."

"And when the Bible talks about your heart, it usually isn't referring to the organ," Mr. Svoboda said from the other side of the room. "It's talking about the core of your being, the place where you connect with God."

"Dad, quit eavesdropping."

"You're talking loud, I can't help it."

Sam said, "Pastor said something like that, too—that when we say no to sin, or unrighteousness, we say yes to God. But when we don't, we leave ourselves open to the Enemy's attacks. In other words, to temptations." An ongoing leg-wrestling battle with Jake somewhat diminished the wisdom of his words.

"Does that make sense so far?" Shayne asked.

"I guess so," I said.

"I suspect Rory is having trouble with the whole issue of righteousness," Shayne's dad said.

"Dad…"

"Um, he's right, actually."

"I'm almost always right," he said cheerfully.

I continued. "I don't really get this righteousness thing. I mean, I guess it means living right. Right? I looked it up in the Bible, and I could see that God is righteous, but I'm not so sure about us. One part even talked about our righteousness like a dirty dishrag…"

"Isaiah," Mr. Svoboda said, tapping away at his keyboard. He pointed at his screen. "'But we are all as an unclean thing, and all our righteousnesses are as filthy rags; and we all do fade as a leaf; and our iniquities, like the wind, have taken us away.'"

I spread my hands. "See? How is *that* supposed to protect us like a piece of armor? Filthy rags, leaves blowing in the wind?"

Shayne and Allie both bent over their notes—Shayne realizing she'd grabbed her math notebook by mistake. Jake scratched his shaggy carpet of hair, while Sam plucked at the shag carpet with a faraway look. This was it, then. This was my sticking point, this whole righteousness thing. Maybe I was the only one honest enough to admit it—I wasn't good enough to be in the Lord's army. No righteousness, no breastplate.

Mr. Svoboda was still watching with an unworried expression. "Does anyone see what Rory's talking about? Do you see the distinction?"

"I know I wrote down something about it…" Allie began.

Sam said calmly, "I know." For a second or two he looked at me, or maybe through me, and there was a light in his eyes that reminded me of when I saw him in armor. "She's talking about our own righteousness. Self-righteousness. That's the filthy rags. But that's not the kind that protects us."

"That's it, Sam." Shayne pointed to a scribble in the margin of Allie's notebook. "Here, 2 Corinthians 5:21." She flipped madly through her Bible. "It says, 'For he hath made him to be sin for us, who knew no sin; that we might be made the righteousness of God in him.'"

"Meaning…" I prompted.

"Meaning that we get our righteousness from Jesus. We put on His righteousness as our breastplate."

I tried to wrap my brain around that one. "How do we do that?"

"We don't. I mean, He did it," Allie said. "That's what that verse means. Jesus became our sin. He gets rid of it, and in its place we can take His righteousness."

"Because if you're going to take someone else's righteousness," Jake said with his commercial man voice, "you might as well take the very best."

"Oh," I said. It sounded simple enough. It sounded too simple, really. "But how do you do it? How do you take it and sort of…put it on? Like armor?" I felt a sudden queasiness. To them, important as it was, it was still pretty much academic. It was a study, and they believed it and wanted to understand and apply it to their lives, but it was mostly an idea. Me, I had this memory of grayish, moving, prowling, leaping shapes, not animal but not human—and of fear and despair. A fiery arrow plunging toward my chest. I didn't know what, if any of it, was real, but I wanted badly to feel protected.

"How?" Allie smiled. "That's easy. You did it the moment you asked Jesus to be your Savior. As long as you believe it and remember what it means, His righteousness will protect your heart."

The moment you asked Jesus to be your Savior… I didn't hear much after that. I hardly had the courage to meet anyone's eyes, I was so sure they would see the truth. I especially couldn't look at Sam, who knew the truth. But a few times I could feel him look at me.

When it was time to leave, Allie proposed that we all walk together and drop each person home as we went. At first I loved the idea, seeing where everyone lived, spending that extra bit of time together.

Then I hated the idea. What if Sam or Allie or Jake came from the west end of the subdivision, where the expensive houses were? What if I was the only one who lived in a duplex? What if

Sheelan came to the door? (Boys always detected the pretty yet seemed unable to detect the evil.)

Then Mr. Svoboda said, "It's raining. Better let Jeph drive you home."

So it was the Monstermobile again, only this time I was in the back with Sam and Jake. Jake took the middle. Allie lived the closest, only about ten houses away. Jeph could've turned towards Sweetnam Lane next, but he went left and wound around to Windham Lane, where the big brick monstrosities with professional landscaping stood. When we pulled up to a house with white columns on either side of the front door, I waited to see who would jump out. Sam. I silently thanked Jeph for not dropping me off next.

But Jake bounded out of the car behind Sam, and Sam climbed back in again, scattering droplets of rain on me. Jake squealed like a girl and dashed for his front door, clowning it up all the way. Shayne laughed so hard she snorted.

Sam's house, as it turned out, was across the highway from our subdivision. It was a quiet country road that led south to the limestone quarry (disappointingly, how the town of Whitestone got its name). That side of the highway was still mostly farmland, now being built up with new homes. Jeph drove beyond this bleak construction landscape and pulled up to a house set apart from the development. By now it was dark, but the porch lights were on, and as the big Buick crunched up the gravel driveway I could see it was a farmhouse closely surrounded by old trees. A yellow dog stood up on the front porch and gave one bark.

The rain became a drizzle. Sam climbed out, then stuck his head back in. "Thanks, Jeph. Bye, guys."

In a moment of inspiration or sheer stupidity, I heard myself cheerfully say, "Shalom."

The car door had already swung shut, and I saw him hesitate for just a second. Then he grinned and said, "Shalom." The dog barked his own shalom, and Sam jogged up the porch steps, dog leaping at his heels, as the rain came down again.

I don't really remember the drive to my house, just the fact that when we pulled into the driveway, Jeph shifted into park.

The car settled back like a hippo sitting on its haunches. He turned to look back at me, and instantly I knew what he was going to say, and why he'd saved me for last.

"Is Sheelan home?"

I groaned. "I don't know. Probably."

"Wait here a minute," he told Shayne as he hopped out of the car. She just looked at me and shrugged, rolling her eyes. Then she dug around in a glove compartment the size of a wheelbarrow and emerged with a pen and a scrap of paper. "What's your email?"

I told her, wishing it were something clever, not just my name and the numbers of my birthday like half the world uses for their email. Shayne scribbled it down and said, "We can email you some Scene stuff, too. Ooh, know what? Kellie lets us email her whenever we have questions and stuff. Do you think that would be okay with your mom?"

"Yeah, I think so. That'd be great." I was excited. Having Mrs. Greene by email was almost as good as having her in class. In some ways, even better.

"I'll send you her address."

"Thanks." I stepped from the car right into an ankle-deep puddle and pretended I hadn't. I squelched up the steps while Jeph came down. I saw a toss of Sheelan's hair as she turned in the doorway and closed it behind her, leaving me to dig around for my keys to open it again. But Jeph had a smile on his face.

"Bye," he said.

I could only shake my head. It was tragic, really. If Jeph were the hero in this tale, then Sheelan would be his fatal flaw.

After a fly-by homework session, I disregarded my mom's dinner instructions, which required both the microwave and the toaster oven, and opted for the simplicity of frosted wheat squares in the biggest bowl I could find. Then I settled down in front of the computer to open my email account. Not that I expected to have anything new, but there was nothing decent on TV.

Sheelan flounced down the stairs, phone attached to her face. "It's so unfair," she whined. "You can all text, and I'm stuck using this stupid antique. I have to talk my mom into getting me another phone. She acts like it's my fault that my last one's lost… Yeah, well, I can't exactly buy it, she won't even let me get a job yet. 'Your job is to be a student,'" she mimicked.

Poor Sheelan, I thought. She'd dumped Quentin and his job.

"Forget Jeph," she was saying. "He says he works for his dad. Probably gets allowance for taking out the trash and mowing the lawn. Can you believe he just showed up like that?" And on she went about Jeph, all uppity and self-righteous (now I knew what that meant), but her cheeks glowed with the pleasure of despising him.

I typed in my password, the last word in the history of human language that she'd expect me to choose. *S-h-e-e-l-a-n.* The little wheel spun, then the chime announced some new email. The usual advertisement for hair replacements, and something from shaboda@chapelweb.net, which I clicked on.

Rory, here's Kellie's email. Everyone else, here's Rory's. Meet again Thursday? -Shayne

I was the only "To" person listed, but in the "Cc" line were four other addresses, not one of them the boring old name-and-birthday variety. AlliG8r was surely Allie, and EZBNGreene was obvious. That left PBnJake and samIam. Now they all had my email address. This set the stage for major thrills or severe dejection, because I could conceivably get email from any one of them. Or I could get nothing, only it wouldn't be the same as getting nothing before.

Twenty minutes later I sat reading in the recliner when the computer chimed again. I leaped up like I'd been wearing an electrified dog collar.

It was from PBnJake.

Got instant messaging? Here's a download if you need it. It's not texting, but IMing's at least better than email. The Jesus Machine is high performance.

I clicked on the little icon attached to his mail, but my attempts to install it were wretchedly unsuccessful. I finally smacked the keyboard, certain there was IMing going on and I was missing it. *Dad can figure it out*, my brain offered. My heart reminded my brain about the facts.

I went to bed but couldn't sleep. My dad's absence hit me, hard and unexpectedly. It's what dad called a sucker punch. That was the way it happened sometimes. The reality of it—that he wasn't just working late, or out of town, or even on the other side of the planet—would suddenly squeeze inside my chest. He was farther away than I could even understand, not coming back, and I wouldn't see him again for the rest of my life. Every single day of who knew how many years, he would be gone. And after that? Who knew?

"You know, don't You?" I whispered up at the ceiling. "You know where he is now, and You know where I'll end up, I suppose." But no, how could that be? If God really knew everything, He already knew where I'd spend eternity. How was that different from Him choosing it all in advance? And if He was the one choosing, what difference did it make what I believed?

"God, I'm having a hard time understanding You. Is it possible, or shouldn't I even bother trying?" Maybe He was just too big.

But when I fell asleep, I dreamed of a carpenter who hung out with fishermen.

17

Hey, kiddo. Glad to know you're out there. If you ever want to "chat" about anything, I'm here. Miss seeing you and your wonderful artwork in class! ~Kellie ("Mrs.") Greene

P.S. I love your email address. Told you your name was special.

And I still didn't get it. I smiled anyway because I could almost hear her smiling voice when I read her words. I clicked on the next email, sent by Shayne an hour ago.

Guys, can't meet at my house after school tomorrow to talk about the SHOES. My dad's meeting with a client and won't be home yet. How about your house, Allie? —SS

Allie's reply popped up just as I finished reading Shayne's.

Fine by me. My grandma's always home. That okay with the rest of you?

I was about to reply when I heard a little *bloop*, and a new window popped up on the screen, asking if I'd allow an instant message from PBnJake. I fumbled around then clicked Okay.

PBnJake: *Yo. You out there?*

I typed, hunt-and-peck style: *Yep. My neighbor helped me set it up.* That had been Kingston, who knew even more about computers than my dad.

PBnJake: *Groovy. I'll tell the others.*

A minute or two later, I was accepting a message from AlliG8r.

AlliG8r: *Welcome to online insanity!*

Thanks, I tapped out.

AlliG8r: *Can you meet at my house tomorrow instead of Shayne's?*

I kept it simple. It still took as long as it had taken her to write her whole sentence. *Sure.*

Another request for clearance popped up. This time it was samIam. I knocked the mouse off the desk and had to reel it back in before I could click Okay.

samIam: *cool user name.*

That again? I looked at my user name, which had been popping up whenever I sent off a message. What was the big…? I laughed, because I finally saw it, staring me in the face. Duh and double-duh. I kept laughing, by now more of a nervous hyperventilation as I set my fingers to the keyboard.

REJoyce316: *thanks. just my name and birthday.*

samIam: *that's why it's cool*

Now I was in danger of actual hyperventilation. Naturally Sheelan chose this moment to enter the family room and start reading over my shoulder.

"Do you mind?" I hissed.

"Hey, I'm supposed to be babysitting you, so it's my job to see what you're up to."

"You have got to be kidding." I never thought it would come to this, but I think I liked it better when Quentin was around. At least Sheelan stayed away from me.

"Chatting with boys? Don't try to deny it—you're all red in the face. You do realize that they're probably forty-year-old men pretending to be thirteen, don't you?"

"Would you please get lost?"

"I think you've been on long enough. It's my turn."

"Since when do you ever want a turn?"

"I have to check my email."

I wanted to strangle her so bad my fingers itched. "You're just being a jerk, trying to boss me around." Another *bloop* sounded, and she smacked my hand away before I could cover the screen.

"Ooh, it's from Sam Lam."

"It's Sam I am, genius."

"Aw, too bad, it looks like he's turning you down."

samIam: *can't come tomorrow. Thursday, Hebrew lesson.*

I should've just ignored Sheelan and answered, but just the feel of her hovering behind me, spiteful and obnoxious in the most calculating way, made me understand those expressions about skin crawling and blood boiling. My voice actually quivered when I spoke. "Will you give me five minutes?"

Bloop. Bloop.

"Five minutes?" She looked at her watch and made a show of thinking about it. "Is that enough time to spend with your instant messagefriend? One who speaks Hebrew? Will I tell Mom you have a Jewish boyfriend?" She laughed, and I do believe right then it surpassed the dentist's drill and became my least favorite sound in the world. "Oh, I guess I could give you five minutes. Starting now." And she took a seat in the recliner, still way too close for my taste but at least not breathing down my neck.

Bloop. There were several new messages:

AlliG8r: *Sorry you can't come, Sam. Grammy will really miss you.*
PBnJake: *Great, now she'll be pinching MY cheek the whole time.*
samIam: *take it like a man.*
PBnJake: *I'll take it like a Newman.*

Wait, I wanted to say. Let's meet on a different day. A day when we can all be there. My fingers twitched over the keys, but I couldn't find the right letters. *Bloop.*

samIam: *gotta take out the trash. over and out.*

I gave up, clicking fiercely until I'd exited the IM program. Stupid thing. And where had the others learned to type so fast? I tramped past Sheelan and muttered, "I'm done, your highness."

"Oh, never mind. I'm watching *The Fastest House Flip*."

It was time to scream into my pillow.

All was not lost, though. The next day something wonderful happened: Jake was home sick. (Oh, just a cold.) At lunch I offhandedly suggested that we could wait and meet when two of us wouldn't be absent.

Allie was skeptical. "We'll do fine without them, considering they don't even take notes."

"Hey, I resemble that remark," Sam said.

"Nah, let's just do it Friday instead," Shayne crunched around a carrot stick.

But it was quickly established that Allie's grandma, who was always home, wouldn't be home on Friday due to bingo. They turned to me. My mind raced, imagining the countless ways

Sheelan would devise to embarrass me if they came to my house. "My mom's working, and my sister is... Does 'evil incarnate' sound too harsh?"

"It's a bit harsh, yeah." Shayne nodded.

"Has she gone over to the dark side?" Sam asked politely.

"Gone over? She started there and never left." That wasn't really true. I could remember playing together as kids, liking the same dolls, making pillow and blanket forts, her picking me up when I'd fallen off my bike. Where had it all gone wrong? I couldn't pinpoint a single event, just a sense of Sheelan drifting from dolls to boys. That was it. Puberty.

"Speaking of going over to the dark side, we could always meet at your house, Sam."

He shook his head. "It's not so dark there anymore. They've already got streetlights up in that new subdivision." This didn't seem to please him. He shrugged. "But yeah, you can come, my mom and dad won't mind. I just wasn't sure if you were allowed to go across the highway."

"Only if we look both ways first," said Shayne.

"And hold hands," I added with a straight face. There was nothing straight about my insides. The term 'butterflies' didn't do it justice — my stomach felt like curly fries.

"Watch the third step. Kind of loose."

We all followed Sam up onto the porch of his house. I stepped completely over the loose board. Although my number one goal this night was to try to understand some more about the Armor, my secondary goal was not to say or do anything painfully embarrassing. In other words, the usual.

Then a shaggy yellow missile collided with me, and my backside introduced itself to the porch while my carefully applied cosmetics were licked off my face.

"Roddy, down," Sam called sharply. The dog backed off, pink tongue lolling cheerfully out of his mouth. "Sorry about that. Guess he likes you."

"He likes, therefore he licks," said Jake. As I scrambled to my feet, Jake took the opportunity to sneeze without covering his mouth.

"Gross!" Allie ducked behind Shayne. "You're spreading the plague."

"I beg your pardon. I prefer the term 'black death.'"

The screen door squeaked as each one of us passed through. We entered a front hall with pale gingham wallpaper, a wide wooden staircase and carved banister on the right and the door to what was probably once called a parlor on the left. Sam led us into the parlor.

What struck me before we even entered was the smell: moist, cool spring air and something else familiar that I couldn't put my finger on until I walked into the room. Books. The walls were wrapped in built-in bookshelves, and every shelf was filled. The smell was that of a library—one with all the windows open.

There was a desk at the far end of the room near a small stone fireplace. Stacks of more books balanced on the desk, and behind them stood a very short, dark-haired man.

"Hey, Pop," Sam said.

Then the head rose up, and I realized it was not a short man standing but a tall man sitting. When he did stand, he stretched to an easy six-foot-four. "Sam." He took in the rest of us. "And others. Hello."

"Remember I told you we were coming home to study after school today?"

"Right, right," he said slowly. He came out from behind the desk. "I'm Isaac Newman," he said, extending his hand. I glanced from side to side and decided he was offering it to me. I shook it. It was a large hand, not thick and meaty, just long to match the rest of him.

"This is Rory Joyce," Sam said for me.

"Pleasure to meet you."

"Nice to meet you, Mr. Newman," I finally managed.

"Dr. Newman," Jake corrected, ever so helpfully.

"I think you've met Allie Rousseau," Sam said.

"Yes, Dr. Newman, we met at the Christmas party at the Front Street Temple last year."

"Right, very good. Hello again, Alessandra. Jake, Shayne," he added. Dr. Newman seemed nice, but I suspected at least half his thoughts were still back in those books on his desk. "I apologize if it's cold in the house. Your mother has opened all the windows."

"Spring cleaning," Sam said, and they both nodded like they were sharing an old understanding. "We'll go in the den."

The air was cool in the house, but the colors were warm, all old hardwood and earth tones. The den was no different, just a bit warmer because it had only one small window. Sam closed it.

"Should we meet your mother?" Allie asked.

"When she comes in from the garden," said Sam. Something in his voice made it sound more like an if than a when.

Jake studied Allie. "Alessandra?"

"I can't believe he remembered. I wasn't sure he remembered me at all."

"Alessandra Rousseau. Sounds like a French movie star," I said.

"I always thought it was way too frou-frou."

"It's pretty. At least it's a girl's name, unlike Rory."

"Rory is a boy's name?" Jake laughed. "Couldn't the doctor tell the difference when you were born?"

I didn't have to think of a return slam. Sam took care of it. "You might know something about that, Jacob *Leslie* Dean."

Jake's sandy hair seemed to bristle. "That's not my name. I'm telling you, it's Jake Elwood Dean."

"And I'm telling you I'll believe it when I see the birth certificate."

"Okay, children," Shayne cut in, "can we begin our study of the Shoes?"

"Here," Jake said, and he kicked off his fancy-brand running shoes and began waving around a most unfancy odor.

"Holster those weapons, Stinky McReeksome," Shayne said.

"Fussy O'Funwrecker."

"All right," Allie cut in. "Who's got notes—oh, forget that. Rory, how about I give you the basic outline and we can see what these guys remember from last Saturday, if anything." We settled in various armchairs and sofas. Shayne grabbed a pillow and sprawled out on the floor.

"I remember all of it," Jake bragged. "Like the fact that a Roman soldier's sandals were actually cleats."

"So they're not for sprinting, they're for standing your ground," Shayne said.

"I guess that makes sense," I said. "There's a lot in those verses about standing. But why are they shoes of the gospel of peace? It's all about battles and weapons, then all of a sudden he's talking about peace."

Allie brandished her notebook. "Here, I've got it."

"Of course she does," Jake said under his breath.

"The gospel brings peace. Peace *with* God, because Christ fixes our relationship with God after sin broke it. And the peace *of* God, which gets us through the sad and scary stuff, because we know everything's going to be okay."

"I still don't see what that has to do with armor," I admitted.

"Well, like I just said," Allie said, maybe feeling a need to defend her notes, "peace helps us to stand firm."

Sam opened a cabinet and pulled out a bag of chips. "My secret stash," he whispered dramatically, passing it around. He munched a minute, then asked, "Don't you think it's more than that, though? It's not just about *our* peace and *us* feeling secure. I mean, we're talking about shoes here. Roman soldiers had to stand firm and all that, but they also had to march all over the place. Shoes are about going places. What I heard Pastor Dan saying was, when we're sent out with the gospel, we're fitted with these 'shoes.' So we can bring other people the good news about our peace with God."

"Sent by who?" Allie asked. "Sent where?"

"The Big G. Wherever He wants."

"The Big Shoemaker in the Sky," Jake said. "And he always knows your size."

"Do you think," asked Shayne, "He would remember to put odor eaters in Jake's?"

I can't say much more was accomplished after that, other than a potato chip war and a sudden urgent need for beverages. Shayne did give me some valuable advice, though.

"You should email Kellie. She'll explain it in a way that actually makes sense—or at least point you in the right direction so you can figure it out yourself."

Pretty soon I needed directions to the bathroom, and Sam pointed me up the stairs. It was possibly the chilliest room in the house, all white tile and an old claw foot tub that crouched like a fat tabby too lazy to follow through with its pounce. I hurried in and out but lingered in the warmer hallway. The walls were hung with several framed photographs. The closest to me was of two toddlers digging in the sand, their brown curls tossed by the wind, eyes huge and dark.

"Samuel and Benjamin," a low voice said. I turned and discovered a woman right behind me. She wasn't any taller than me, but where I had angles and awkwardness, she was curves and grace. My hair frizzed, hers flowed, black-brown with a streak of silver that framed her face. But I saw something in her eyes that reminded me of myself, something we shared.

I looked back at the photograph. "They look like twins."

She nodded. Her dark eyes said all that was needed, and I didn't want to hear the words spoken out loud. I already knew. Sam's twin brother had died.

This put a terminal leak in the floaty ring of hope I'd been pumping up in my head, the hope that if *I* were one of God's children, I would be safe. Protected from evil, shielded from sadness, blessed. But apparently God didn't play favorites; He took swipes at believers and unbelievers alike. With a friend like that, who needed enemies?

18

Sure is great to find you in my mailbox! I'm glad you're getting together with Shayne and the rest. They're a great bunch. Don't worry if you don't grasp all of this Armor stuff right off the bat. Some people want to "pray the armor on" like following a recipe, but it's a lot more than just words, isn't it? It's a whole way of living.

Sounds like you're still unclear about the whole righteousness issue. People interpret this in different ways. Yes, we do take on the righteousness of Christ, but we also endeavor to **live** a life of truth. Because you know what? If you're living with unconfessed sin, you're putting out a big neon sign that says, "Enemies, here's my weak spot. Attack here!" Right living is its own defense.

Bear in mind, though, even when you're sincerely trying to live in a God-pleasing way, the enemy will still harass you—in fact, you should expect it, because you're becoming a more effective soldier and drawing attention to yourself. Don't worry: Greater is He that is in you than he that is in the world! Just watch out for the voices of doubt that make you *feel unworthy—or make God seem impossible to please. Those come from the enemy. If you want to know the true nature of God, just look at Jesus. He came to show us the Father's heart. He's the image of the invisible God!*

Have you noticed a progression with the Armor? From the foundation (belt), to basic body protection (breastplate), and then the shoes. Sam was right on when he talked about 'stepping out' with the gospel (smart kid!). Saturday we'll talk about an essential piece if you have taken that step out: the Shield of Faith. If you can't come, I'll send you my own notes, if that's okay with your mom.

Better go before I type your ear off! Stay in touch. —KG

My ear was still firmly attached, but my breakfast cereal had achieved a state of severe soggification. I ate it anyway. I was too busy digesting Mrs. Greene's reply to my email to care. If I had the courage, I'd tell her I wasn't scared of God the big cranky Judge peering down, annoyed by my blunders. I was afraid that He didn't care at all.

Or was that just Sheelan getting into my head?

I had rolled out of bed that morning with two objectives:

1) Finish my social studies report. Okay, I also had to start it. It wasn't due until after spring break, but the last thing I wanted was Denmark hanging over my head the whole vacation. It's the band-aid philosophy—one quick rip is better than slowly prolonging the agony. And,

2) Get out of the house rather than mope around watching the clock while I missed another Scene meeting.

Denmark seriously ate into my leisure time. It wasn't until midafternoon that I put the finishing touches (punctuation) on my paper and escaped the Danes—who, I learned, had stopped all that raiding and pillaging long ago, and in fact seemed to have adopted 'Posing no threat to our neighbors for hundreds of years' as a sort of unofficial national slogan.

I grabbed my jacket with an "I'm going out!" on my way through the front door. I walked down to the convenience store at the end of Sweetnam Lane, the Speedee Saver, mostly to get out but also to buy chocolate. When I got back home, Kingston was in the Fisher's half of the front yard, arranging stones along the edge of the flowerbed.

"It's kind of like doing a puzzle," he said, his way of inviting me to help. I did, though the day was clear and cold and the river rocks felt like ice. I told him that 65% of Denmark's total area is used for agricultural purposes. He told me that Denmark grows lots of strawberries, and that Hans Christian Anderson was Danish. Then he asked me if I wanted a danish, because his Auntie Camille had brought some from the bakery that morning. I was tempted, but just then my mom pulled out of the garage on her way to work. She didn't see me in the flowerbed until she was already driving past, then she waved and made a gesture back towards the house. I waved back, not understanding.

I ended up having supper with the Fishers, because when Auntie Camille and Mrs. Fisher cooked together, you'd be an idiot to go home and eat microwaved leftovers.

Much later (after dessert, to be exact… "Apple Brown Betty in a happy white Rory," as Auntie Camille said. Auntie Camille herself looked sort of like a glossy brown apple), I wandered back home. I discovered Sheelan upstairs putting the finishing touches on hair and makeup. She and Quentin had probably patched things up. She gave me what my dad called 'the old once-over,' eyeing the dirt stains on the knees of my jeans and the gooey apple dribble on my shirt. To my amazement she said nothing.

I went down to read Mrs. Greene's email again. Maybe I would reply. I'd never had a chance to talk to the pastor about my visions, and part of me was glad I hadn't, now that they'd stopped. I wasn't ready to call them 'mental illness' and sing the praises of the little white pills, but I was in wait-and-see mode. Even so, I toyed with the idea of probing the subject with Mrs. Greene.

Sheelan observed me from up in the kitchen. "Are you planning to go like that?"

"Go where?"

"Didn't Mom tell you?" She cracked open a bottle of her designer water and took a long drink while I waited. "I'm going to bring you to your little church thing."

"What are you talking about?"

She shrugged. "She changed her mind about it, I guess. I thought you knew. Doesn't it start in, like, ten minutes?"

Five minutes, actually. I flew up the stairs, and as I passed Sheelan I saw the gleam in her eye—she'd known all along that I had no clue. I silently railed against her black, wicked heart as I scrambled for clean clothes. Then I remembered: Gran Judy's birthday gift. I pounced on the gift bag, still sitting in the corner of my room, and pulled out jeans and a T-shirt. There was no time to fully rectify my alarming hair situation; I spritzed it with some product Sheelan had forgotten to hide (served her right), ran my hands through it, and galloped down the stairs. She looked me over, sniffed, and grabbed her coat and keys.

The ride was tortuous, Sheelan coasting along at a leisurely twenty miles per hour, hitting every red light. When we pulled up to Front Street Temple, I was ready to spring from the car, but Sheelan didn't stop.

"Where do I park?" she asked.

"Just let me out here."

"Can I park there on the street? Wait, here's a space."

"Why do you have to—" I choked as a horrible thought occurred to me.

"I told you, Mom said I can bring you."

"You're staying?" I breathed.

"A little gratitude? It wasn't my idea to babysit my sister at church on a Saturday night." She finished her cockeyed parking job and hopped out of the car. For an unwilling chaperone, she wasn't exactly dragging her feet. I watched her with narrow eyes. What could I do? I led her through the front doors.

The two lines had already filed into the gym, and the girls' and boys' groups were still in separate discussions. Sheelan's eyes glittered as she surveyed the scene. Her shell pink lips curled upwards in one corner. No way was I going to bring her to my group. I contemplated deserting her.

Then Jeph spotted us, and he crossed the gym floor in a few long strides.

"Hey, Sheelan, you came."

"I had to. My mom wants me to keep an eye on Rory."

"Well, first the older kids meet over in the corner, then we all come together. You can meet some of my friends."

She glanced over at the older group, and I read the words so plainly on her face: *And why would I care about your friends?* But she said nothing, just shrugged and began walking towards them. Jeph followed, after throwing me a glance with raised eyebrows and a little grin.

Mrs. Greene looked up when I approached, and her dazzling smile made everyone else turn. "Rory," she said, "I'm so glad you could make it today."

The others made room for me and reached out to pat me on back or the arm. This so completely caught me off guard, I could only nod back at them.

"We prayed you'd be able to come back," a girl named Caroline whispered to me.

"I guess it worked," I was able to whisper back.

Mary K leaned over and said in my ear. "Someone from the other group seems happy to see you."

My eyeballs slid over to the cluster of boys on the free throw line. Jake and Sam were on the outer edge. Sam's hand was raised up, but he was looking at Pastor Dan, and when the pastor pointed at him he began talking. Jake was looking my way, and when our eyes met, he gave me a nod.

"I think he likes you," Mary K mouthed at me with sing-songy tilts of her head.

I gave her dagger eyes, but she just giggled. All the time we were praying, Mary K's words ricocheted in my head. Jake? Jake the goofball, three-inches-shorter-than-me Jake? Why Jake?

When we moved to join the boys around the overhead projector, he somehow ended up behind me again. Mary K gave me a knowing look.

"New jeans, Rory?" Jake asked. I just glared at him. "Hmm, I could tell everyone your size. What's it worth to you to keep me quiet?"

I reached around and found a paper tag still stitched to the back pocket. I ripped it off, feeling the heat rise in my face. At least

Sam wasn't with him. I was letting out a long breath of relief when I spotted Sam, sitting beside Shayne. The breath became more of a sigh.

Sheelan leaned against the wall under the little caged clock, arms crossed.

Pastor Dan stood in front of us, saying nothing. We gradually quieted, helped along by the shushers in the crowd (every crowd has some). Still he didn't speak. Kids began glancing around at each other, moving very little, and for the first time I could actually hear the ticking of the clock on the wall.

Pastor cleared his throat. "I almost didn't come today," he said. We just watched him, and he cleared his throat again. "On Monday, I started thinking about what I needed to say today, and on Tuesday, I questioned how I was going to say it. By Friday, I was just about convinced that I had absolutely no business standing up here trying to teach you this stuff. I mean, who am I? Just a sinful man who makes mistakes every day. Unworthy."

He plunged his hands in the pockets of his khaki pants, paced a few steps, then pulled them out again. "Good thing we're studying the Armor. Good thing I was preparing to talk about spiritual attacks. Otherwise I might not have recognized one when it came at me."

He scribbled a word on the overhead transparency. *Diabolos.*

"It means Accuser. We forget sometimes that one of the weapons in our enemy's arsenal—maybe *the* weapon, subtler than straight-out temptation—is accusation. He wants us to forget the joy of our salvation and abandon our reliance on the gospel of Christ. So he throws our sins back in our faces. And don't we give him a lot of ammunition?"

He scribbled furiously on the glowing face of the overhead: a stick figure with a stick sword, a helmet like a bowl, a shield that looked like a big donut. "Okay, I wasn't an art major," he confessed. "But you get the picture. We talked about this two weeks ago." He drew a big circle around the figure. "A believer has God's hedge of protection around him. But when he sins and allows the sin to fester, unrepented, active in his life..." He smeared out gaps in the circle. "...he punches holes in his hedge. It's an invitation to the enemy."

He paused to draw arrows penetrating the circle. A voice came from the other side of the gym. "What if you're not a believer?"

At first I turned to stare like everyone else, checking out this stranger who so coolly challenged our pastor. For a second it didn't compute that it was my sister. It was a wonderful second. Then it evaporated. *Sheelan.* I closed my eyes and prayed that I would evaporate.

She wasn't finished. "Does an unbeliever get attacked? Because I know a few, and they don't seem to be experiencing all of these attacks you're talking about."

Now I prayed that Sheelan would evaporate.

Pastor Dan's pacing resumed at twice the speed. "Excellent question. I'm glad you asked." Surely 'glad' was a nice way of saying 'annoyed.' But he started scribbling away on the transparency, and up popped another stick figure, this one with no circle around it. "Unbeliever. No hedge of protection, but you know what? Not a lot of arrows, either. Maybe no arrows to speak of."

"Seems preferable to me," Sheelan said with a sniff. I hardly knew this girl. Yes, Sheelan could be a pain, but it just wasn't her style to pick a fight in a crowd of strangers. She was much more the behind-your-back, treacherous type.

Pastor Dan still seemed pleased. "It seems simpler, doesn't it? That's the lure of the world. You see..." and he drew directional arrows pushing behind the stick unbeliever, "...this person is completely influenced by the world and the flesh. It's a harsh fact, folks, but we're all born headed for hell. Deservedly so. This person is already on his way. Why would the enemy mess with that? Just a little nudge now and then keeps him skipping towards destruction. No overt attacks are necessary.

"In a strange way," he sighed, rubbing a hand over his balding head, "it's a positive sign when you sustain a spiritual attack. It means you must be making progress. This is when it's vital to have the Shield of Faith. Let's talk about that. And you in the back, thanks for the input. If you want to talk more about it after we're done here, I'd be glad to do that." Sheelan gave her *right, whatever* shrug.

"Okay, who can describe a Roman shield for me?"

Several voices and pointing fingers volunteered Sam for the job, including Jake. "His dad's a professor of ancient and medieval history," he told me. "Sam knows all about this stuff."

"You told me he was a doctor," I accused.

"No, I said he's *called* Dr. Newman. Hello, that's what you call a professor."

Sam cleared his throat and said, "The shield was made with layers of wood strips and it was molded into a curved shape to deflect missiles. Then they were covered with leather. And there was a metal boss in the center that made it an offensive weapon, too."

"Right. What did the layers accomplish, do you know?"

"They could soak them in water. If the enemy fired flaming arrows, the fire would be extinguished when it penetrated."

Pastor pointed at him. "Yes. Thanks, Sam. It would do what, folks? 'Quench all the flaming darts…' Sound familiar? Sure. The Shield of Faith quenches all the flaming darts of the evil one. What might some of these fiery arrows be? Anyone, just call them out."

"Temptations?" someone called. It sounded like Jeph, from the back.

"Yes. We've talked about those. They come in all shapes and sizes—and there are countless temptations marketed just for your age group. What other arrows does the evil one fire at us?"

"Lies about ourselves."

"Hate thoughts."

Pastor nodded. "That out-of-the-blue, violent thought. The overpowering urge to act on it, or to act on any other kind of sinful thought. Or that sense of being the lowest of the low, unlovable even to God—especially to a perfect and holy God. Any others?"

Caroline poked a timid hand up and pulled it down again, like a naughty puppy on a leash. It was enough to catch Mrs. Greene's eye. "Yes, Caroline?" she asked.

"I don't know, I was thinking maybe a feeling of depression? Probably not, though."

Pastor Dan took a deep breath and let it out slow. "No? Well, that's exactly how I felt when I woke up this morning. Like an emotional millstone was tied around my neck. I had no reason to feel that way, but it was enough to make me want to cancel this." He gestured over the room. "I'd have to say definitely yes. And there's another big one. Can anyone think of it?"

Nobody came up with it, though Pastor Dan kept fishing. My heart began to pound as a word leaped behind my lips and demanded to be let out. I bit my tongue. I mean literally. I bit it, hard, and I couldn't stop the "Ow!" that followed.

"What was that?" Pastor pointed towards me. "From over here."

"Doubt?" I said lamely.

He clapped his hands together once. "Aha. Doubt. But if you're a Christian, you don't have any doubts, right?" He made a game show wrong-answer sound. "Everyone wrestles with doubt sometimes. God understands. He'll even use your doubts to draw you closer to Him, if you seek the truth with all your heart."

He slapped a new transparency on the overhead projector, but left it covered. "So, what might you say is the opposite of doubt?"

"Trust?"

"Belief?"

"Hope?"

He pondered these, tugging at his goatee. "Wow, those are all pretty profound, when you think about them. And they're all right. But the word I'm looking for is a little more obvious. Big hint: it's our topic today…"

"Faith," a chorus of voices called out.

He revealed the transparency and the bold capital letters: FAITH. "And what is faith?"

"Believing what you can't see," Silas said.

"That's true, and a lot of people have a problem with that. They liken having faith in God and His promises to believing in fairy tales. But let's see what God says about faith, shall we? How about Hebrews 11:1. Someone got it?"

Pages flipped in the mad race for Hebrews. Allie got it first. "'Now faith is the substance of things hoped for, the evidence of things not seen.'"

Pastor Dan scribbled *substance* and *evidence* on the overhead. "Faith is not a flimsy, wish-upon-a-star thing. This verse is actually a description of what faith does. Faith treats those things that we hope for as real things, and it proves that what is unseen is real. Okay, how about Romans 10:17?"

Silas had this one. "'So then faith comes by hearing, and hearing by the word of God.'"

"You've got to know it, folks. The word of God—in other words, the gospel. Unless you hear it, you can't be convicted of its truth. Unless you know it is true, you can't begin to trust in it, and you'll never have absolute confidence in God's power and His promises and His plan for your life. And this confidence, this faith in Christ's victory over sin, death and the devil—this is your Shield."

19

1 tried so hard not to yawn that my face hurt. Finally I had to lift the bulletin and yawn behind it, hoping that two thousand people around me didn't notice. Maybe they didn't, but my mom did. She raised an eyebrow at me.

I couldn't help it. She'd dragged me out of bed at eight o'clock on a Sunday morning. Now we sat listening to an energetic Reverend Someone Special explain the Seven Steps to Spiritual Success or something like that. Steps that all started with an S, blazing in full-color animated glory up on a huge screen.

My mom had brought us to church. Not our old church with its dim sanctuary and wooden pews worn smooth by many backsides, its pastor in his white robe—and not Gran Judy's church with its folding chairs and people who raised their hands while they were singing or answered 'amen' back to the minister. She'd picked the new church off the first interstate exit north of Whitestone. A shimmering spectacle of glass and steel with a sweeping amphitheater of cinema-style seats, it all centered around a semi-circular stage where young Reverend Snazzy Suit strode back and forth, preaching his heart out. When he was done, the choir behind him exploded, at least a hundred and fifty people singing their lungs out.

Me, I was just yawning my brains out. Not that the sermon wasn't engaging (peppered with jokes) or the music inspiring (loud and professional). It's just that I'd been up until way past midnight chatting online. And while the minister seemed to have everyone else riveted, I kept thinking about what we'd learned at the Scene. I put the glossy bulletin up to my face to cover another yawn and saw a little imprint on the back cover: *ChapelNet*. Wasn't that Mr. Svoboda's company? There was a little logo of a net scooping up the symbol of a fish with a cross inside it. Maybe these guys were the Holy Gestapo he'd mentioned.

"What a place," Mom said after the service while we lined up to drive out of the parking lot. There were even a couple of policemen directing traffic at the stoplight. "Now that was an experience. With all those people, I expected to feel lost in the crowd. But the minister was good—I felt like he was talking right to me, didn't you?"

"He had a nice suit," Sheelan answered. It was her trademark expression of approval.

"And his sermon was so real. Not just Sunday-morning speak. I actually feel like this could change the way I do things this week. What about you, Rory?"

I almost felt guilty for not sharing the enthusiasm. After all, she'd probably conceived the whole notion of going to church to appease me in some way. "I'm still thinking about it," I said.

"You napped through the sermon, in other words," she said, half joking. Mom could accuse me of dozing, but the charges would never stick. I bet I gave it more thought than she and Sheelan did. After their initial praises, they resumed their ordinary Sunday afternoon activities, but I kept thinking about it. It bugged me, because I couldn't put my finger on what bugged me. It was a seamless church service, uplifting and encouraging. The preacher was passionate, determined to convince us of all the

179

ways God longed to bless us, and he had plenty of Bible verses to back it up. And I believed his message. But there was a weird empty feeling in the middle of it.

I slid into the computer chair, pulled up Mrs. Greene's last email and clicked 'reply.' *Is being a Christian just believing that God and Jesus have taken care of everything, given you a free ticket to eternal life, and you just have to hop onto the boat and coast into heaven on a wave of blessings? Or is it this a battle where you have to be constantly on guard and constantly fighting and always in danger of failing?*

I clicked 'send' before I could rethink it. Only then did I notice an unread email, sent by Mrs. Greene early that morning:

Just wanted to remind you guys that we'll be gone all week visiting my mom and dad downstate. They don't have internet service but I've got my cell if you need me. Don't forget, Teen Scene is still on for Saturday. You can tell me everything you learned about the Helmet when I get home. Be good 'til I get back!! Love, KG

Serious bummer. So far the Svobodas were going on a fishing vacation for spring break, Allie was spending the week with her aunt, Sam's father had some ancient historian's conference in another country, and Sam and his mom got to go, too. (Somewhere that started with 'Bel'—Belgium? Belgrade? Belarus? Somehow I had nearly finished grade school without any significant knowledge of geography.) As far as I knew, Jake was still in town. Of course. My own spring vacation was looking more and more like a week on a deserted island.

I did have about a thousand questions to keep me company— like a swarm of flies keeps you company. Questions I'd planned to ask Pastor Dan the night before but couldn't after Sheelan's performance. I couldn't risk hanging around afterwards, and she wasn't about to wait for me. Then there were the questions I had reserved for Kellie Greene, who was on her way to the last house in the hemisphere with no internet access. There was always Gran Judy, but she'd probably want to take me to her pastor, and I was all pastored out.

So I rummaged through my Scene notes. There was a paper that had been wrapped around another candy bar. It was a short verse: *There is therefore now no condemnation to them which are in Christ Jesus.* Romans 8:1

No condemnation. It made me think of something Pastor Dan had said: 'We forget sometimes that one of the weapons in our enemy's arsenal is accusation.' I glanced at another page and saw I had written the word *accusations* and underlined it twice before adding a little question mark. I hadn't attached a word to how I'd been feeling lately, but *accused* hit pretty close to the mark. *I'm not good enough to be a Christian. I'm not Christian enough to be their friends. I'm not smart enough to understand all this. And I'm definitely not sinless enough.*

Pastor make it sound like these were some of those fiery darts shot by the enemy, but that couldn't be right. First of all, they were my own thoughts. Second, they tended to be loudest after Uri had talked to me. It didn't make sense.

I had a week to mull it over.

I was still mulling the next day, home alone, my Mom at work and Sheelan out somewhere. I was so sick of the sound of my own thoughts that I pulled out my Denmark report, actually regretting that I had finished it early. My fantasies of unlimited hours of hanging out with the Scene crew over spring break, late night chats online, and unrestricted sleeping in had crashed and burned, so the hours and days loomed large before me. I dug out a sheet of poster board, a sack of rice and a bottle of white glue and settled at the kitchen table, determined to construct an extra credit relief map of Denmark.

Who knows how long I worked on that thing, my fingers stained with green food coloring, rice sticking wherever I accidentally touched the glue. When I started, my mind was noisy with thinking. Concentration took over, and I entered the comfortable doing mode, abandoning the thinking mode.

When I did have a thought that was more than *too much glue there* or *get off me, rice* or *why did I make a relief map when the highest point in Denmark is only 173 meters above sea level?*, the thought was, "It's so quiet in here."

I said it out loud, so that it wouldn't be so quiet, but that only made the quiet after my words seem quieter. No background noise of TV, no Sheelan somewhere on the phone, no stereo or dishwasher or hairdryer. Just the faint scratchy sound of rice on poster board and my breathing. Now even that seemed loud.

If I had only turned to the left, towards the stairs down to the family room, things might have gone differently. I would've hopped down, flicked on the TV. The spell of too-quiet would've broken, and Denmark would have its Yding Skovhøj. Instead my eyes moved to the right, just enough so that the kitchen window was in the corner of my vision. Just enough that I saw a shape there, a face right behind the glass.

I jerked around. No one was there. Nothing, no shape to even suggest a face and trick the corner of my eye. Just fading sky. I took a slow breath; it shook a little. Too quiet.

Then, behind me, I felt someone standing in the kitchen doorway. *Sheelan*, I thought with relief. But when I turned, nothing. I swallowed. *Okay, Rory, you're just getting a little freaked out. Relax.* A cool sensation rushed over me, like water or a breeze or a clean smell, and suddenly, strangely, I wanted to be upstairs reading the Bible.

It will only protect you if you read it.

It was just the memory of Gabby's voice, but it was comforting anyway. As I turned, ready to go up the stairs, I heard a creak. I knew it well. The squeaky floorboard in my bedroom.

My feet grew roots. My brain whizzed through the possibilities: Sheelan (impossible), the house settling (unlikely), Uri or Gabby (irrational). My heart thumped out a simpler impulse: *run, run, run.* Run to the Fishers.

But the Fishers weren't home. When they were home, you just knew it. There was a sense of life in the place, even if you didn't hear anything specifically. It was gone now.

My bedroom floorboard creaked again, quieter this time.

I flew down the steps into the family room, slapping on every light switch along the way. I fumbled with the remote until the TV flicked on. Creeping, sinister music warned me, but the picture lit up before I could change the channel: a panicky teenage girl trying to dial a phone, a shape rising up in the doorway behind her. Screaming, a flash of metal...

I mashed the remote and the picture vanished, but the feel of it crawled all over my skin. I found a 24-hour news channel and left it there for the dry, droning voices. I'm not sure how I thought the anchorman was going to protect me from whatever was in my bedroom. It was like hiding my face and hoping I wouldn't be seen—if I couldn't hear it, maybe it wouldn't be there.

The news wasn't reassuring. Shooting, bodies in the street. Children with huge eyes and big bellies, too weak to swat the flies away. Earthquakes swallowing villages whole, crushing and suffocating. Finally I changed channels again, to a preacher confidently promising that a healed body and a healthy pocketbook were only a phone call and a thousand-dollar donation away.

I twisted away from the TV screen, turned to the computer instead. No new emails; no one online to IM with. I clicked around on the internet, but aimless surfing only led me into a virtual dumpster; some innocent-sounding sites spat up shocking pictures and ugly words. I put the computer to sleep. When had the world become such a toilet?

Why had God let it become such a toilet?

Either he's a weak God who can't do a thing to stop it...

I hated when Sheelan was in my head. Wasn't it bad enough that I had to hear the real thing all day and half the night?

Or maybe he likes it when we suffer.

Okay, that's it, I thought. No way could Sheelan be right. The only way to prove her wrong was to find something official-sounding in the Bible that contradicted her. Problem was, the Bible was still upstairs. I was 98% convinced that there wasn't really anything lurking in my bedroom, but 2% was enough to keep me downstairs. Surely there was another Bible around somewhere. If I could just find Dad's with the black leather cover. I used to see it around, but not since...

I scanned the bookshelf (when I thought of Sam's house with its walls and walls of books, our one bookshelf seemed pitiful). Nothing. I dug around in the drawers of the computer desk.

Mostly bills, by the look of it. One caught my eye: P. H. McDonald. How much money was Dr. McD charging to torment me? I lifted the envelope, but it was unopened. Underneath was a glossy pamphlet.

TEEN SCHIZOPHRENIA

"You've got to be kidding," I said to the pamphlet. There was a picture of a girl with dark, serious eyes looking right at me from the cover. She seemed to say, *You, too, huh? Bet you didn't even know it.*

Was Dr. McD trying to convince my mom that I actually was schizo? Or did my mom ask for the information? I unfolded the leaflet, and my eyes fell on a list under **Warning signs of possible onset of teenage schizophrenia:**

- **Confused or displaced thinking**
- **Difficulty telling dreams from reality**
- **Vivid, bizarre ideas**
- **Paranoia**
- **Delusions and hearing voices that are not real**
- **Severe anxiety and fearfulness**
- **Confusing television with reality**
- **Extreme moodiness**
- **Regression into childish behavior**

I read it twice, then again. I read it about ten times. Then my eyes drifted to the facing page.

> *An individual affected by schizophrenia may have an underlying genetic vulnerability. If this is triggered by an environmental stressor such as psychological trauma or head trauma, the individual will then fully express the illness. Teens who exhibit early warning signs should be evaluated so an individualized treatment plan can be developed. This may include individual therapy, family therapy, social skill training, psychiatric medication and monitoring.*

The little white pills. To 'stop the seizures,' Mom said. And they *had* stopped the seizures. That's all they were, anti-seizure medication. Right?

But they'd stopped Gabby, and Rafie, Uri and Micah, too.

Delusions and hearing voices that are not real…

I let the leaflet fall back into the drawer. The girl in the photograph watched me with regret. *Sorry,* her eyes seemed to say. *You had to find out sooner or later.*

I wrapped myself in an afghan and burrowed my face down into the sofa.

20

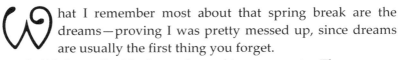hat I remember most about that spring break are the dreams—proving I was pretty messed up, since dreams are usually the first thing you forget.

I didn't totally blank on the waking moments. They were a dark, greasy smear in my memory. I don't think I ate much, and I could hardly listen to what my mom, Sheelan, and sometimes Grandma Judy said to me. The voices in my head were louder. Sometimes they spoke to me, but mostly they argued with each other about me. One said I was being prepared for hell; another said that there was no hell, there was only loss and sadness and pills and eventually nothing. They fought back and forth over it. While they did, a third voice whispered in my ear that I already was in hell.

I don't remember how I got there, but I did spend a little time in an unfamiliar room, like a hospital room, but not 316. And then I could sleep, and I dreamed the dreams that took me away from the voices. I dreamed of the Fishers standing in a circle with linked hands, their heads bowed. There was a Presence above them, and though their lips were moving, it was the Presence who spoke the words for them. Then Kingston opened his eyes and turned to look at me. He smiled and pointed at a narrow path jumbled with stones, twisting and climbing into a distance I couldn't see.

I dreamed of walking beside my dad along a narrow beach. He looked down at me and smiled. When I tried to look up and smile back, I had to squint and blink against the sunlight streaming from behind him. His face was lost in silhouette, but I reached out and took hold of his hand. I knew my dad's hand, big and thick with tough skin that was surprisingly smooth. But as my fingers slid across his palm to wrap themselves into his fingers, they passed over the rough ridges of a shocking scar.

I dreamed of Gabby and Rafie. I would see them if I glanced over my shoulder, and they seemed to be trying to talk to me. They were too distant; I couldn't hear. I had a flickering impression of Micah once. His face was grim.

Once I thought I dreamed of Pastor Dan d'Amico standing outside my hospital room, speaking quietly but intensely. Later I suspected that he had actually come but wasn't allowed in to see me. It might have made me angry, but I wasn't able to find anger in my file cabinet of emotions. I couldn't even find the file cabinet.

Soon I was home again, and Grandma Judy stayed when Mom had to work. Sheelan was spending most of her time at Tamika's house. One afternoon I sat at the kitchen table and watched Gran make me a tuna salad sandwich for lunch. She put hard-boiled egg in her tuna salad—the only way I liked it.

"What day is it?" I asked. She stopped chopping celery to look at me. I think they were the first words I'd spoken since Monday.

"Friday," she said. "A little mustard or a lot?"

"A lot."

She squirted some into the tuna mixture, stirred it and plopped a spoonful onto a toasted bagel.

"Grandma?"

"Yes?"

"We were wrong, weren't we? About the angels."

She sighed. "Rory, the Bible is never wrong, and it tells us about angels. Whatever happens, you can believe that God is taking care of you, and the angels who guard you have special access to His throne. Jesus himself said so."

"Okay. But I mean the things I was seeing…"

She put a pickle on my plate and set it in front of me. "If I did or said anything to make all of this more confusing for you, I'm very sorry. I wanted so much to encourage you. It's been so hard on you, losing your dad. I suppose I wanted that reassurance, too. Proof that you were being watched over. Scripture should be the only proof I ever need."

I didn't know it until right then, but tucked up in a corner of my heart was a lingering hope that there had been more to all of this than trauma and delusions — that I had been allowed to take a peek behind the curtain of the everyday visible and see the battleground of the invisible. But the puzzle pieces of logic and reason and modern medicine fit together too perfectly. Now Gran Judy snapped the last piece into place. I let the dream — or the delusion — die. I never could eat tuna again without reliving a shadow of that feeling.

"Do you think they'll let me go to my youth group tomorrow?" I asked.

She didn't answer immediately. "I'm not sure they'll think it's such a good idea."

"They think that's what caused my freak out?"

"No. They see it more as fuel on a fire that was already burning. Does that make any sense?"

"I know what you're saying, but they're wrong. Besides," I said, more to myself than to her, "they've already stamped out the fire."

As it turned out, Mom did let me go. Probably because she knew I was going there to say goodbye.

Sheelan drove me, but she refused to come in. When I climbed out of the car, she cranked up the radio, pulled out a magazine, and said nothing. It obviously took some effort.

The two lines were already in the gym, but the girls were being led by one of the older teens since Kellie was still out of town. I tried to slip into the back of the group. Shayne's eyes passed over me and then snapped back. Her face went blank for a second, then she whispered a quick word to the older girl and came over to me.

"Hey, I wasn't expecting to see you tonight," she said simply. The other girls greeted me, a bit weakly, I thought. They all knew something.

A hand settled on my shoulder. I turned to find Pastor Dan's intense, dark blue eyes studying me. "Rory, how are you? Do you need to talk? Kellie's not here, but we can go into the office, let these guys play some basketball for a bit."

"No, I'm okay."

"Or after group's over, if you can stay."

"I'm not sure. It's alright. I'm fine."

'Fine' is that word you use to see if a person is just looking for a quick escape route or if your answer really matters to them. I could tell Pastor wasn't satisfied with my 'fine.' "Well, I'm glad you're here."

"Just tonight, probably," I said, eyes on my shoes.

"It's good that you're here." He gave me a light pat on the back and returned to the boys' group. I didn't see Jake or Sam.

The preliminaries were over quickly. When Pastor clicked on the overhead projector light, it wasn't with his usual sense of barely-restrained energy. He moved more carefully. "There are faces missing tonight," he observed. "Some of us are traveling this spring break, I assume." He squeezed the back of his neck like there was a pain there. "I hope that's all it is.

"People tend to react strongly to this subject matter—as they should. Many don't like to admit the reality of the spiritual war. I know some folks who are gaga about angels but don't even know if they believe the devil exists. Or the ones who see a demon behind every bush. The demon who makes them swear, the one who makes them overeat. The bad hair day demon." He waited for the chuckle to pass through the group. "Seriously, though. That's why we need this." He held up his Bible.

"Faith in God isn't a buffet table, where you pick and choose which truths you like to believe. It's a complete package. And there's enough in here to teach us what we need to know about the spiritual war—both sides of it, angels and demons—but you'll notice, not *too* much about either. Maybe because as humans we're fascinated with the supernatural, to the point where we can misplace our interest and adoration. They're still created beings. Keep your focus on the Creator."

He paced, but in a wandering way. "It's all here in black, white and red. But I get more complaints and expressions of concern from parents when I teach this than over anything else. Parents want to protect their children. God, our heavenly Father, wants to protect us. One way He does this is by equipping us. Today we'll talk about the piece of equipment Paul calls the Helmet of Salvation. And by 'we'll talk' I mean 'me.'" He rubbed his hands together. "Palm Sunday tomorrow—it's Easter week, so tonight I'm all business. Allow me to hammer out the helmet, then take next Saturday off and we'll meet again the following Saturday."

He uncovered the word **SALVATION** on the overhead screen. "Okay. I think we all know what a helmet is and what it protects. But do we really know what salvation means?"

"Being saved," one of the boys said.

"Yes, that Christian buzz-word. *Saved.* But imagine you never read the Bible. Say you just step out of your space ship and someone comes up to you and asks, 'Brother, sister… Are you saved?' What would you say?"

That was easy. "Saved from what?" I asked. The words just flowed out easy as you please, without any agonizing over them first. Man, this medication took a lot of the Rory right out of me.

"Saved from what." Pastor Dan said it like a statement. "The moment you ask Jesus Christ to be your Savior, what are you saved from?" He didn't look for an answer in the crowd. He uncovered another word on the transparency.

Hell

"You're saved from the punishment you so richly deserve. Eternal damnation, which is separation from God. Why are you saved? Because God winked at your sin and brushed it under the rug? Nope. What is the wages of sin?"

"Death," several voices called.

Pastor uncovered the next word.

Death

"The wages we earned. Sin cannot be denied, young people — each comes with a price tag attached. The price must be paid. Not because God is a big bossy guy who likes handing out punishment. God is not willing that anyone should perish — the Apostle Peter even says that this is one reason why Jesus hasn't come back yet, to give more people time to repent. But repent we must. That means doing a 180, turning from our sin into His forgiveness.

"Trying to enter His presence with your sins all over you is like…jumping through a bonfire with your clothes soaked in kerosene. And dynamite in your pockets. Because He is *holy*. Sin cannot draw near such holiness — think about it. Heaven wouldn't be heaven if there were one sin there. When you are saved from Hell and Death, it is because one person, the God-Man, willingly paid your way. He took your sins upon Himself. He died in your place. So instead of hell, you are ushered into the presence of your heavenly Father, and instead of death, you will enjoy a glorified body that no hurt or decay can touch. The assurance of this can give us a hope and a joy that are as powerful in the battle as any weapon.

"But there's more. Our salvation equips us in the daily battle because we are saved from something else."

He opened his Bible. "Here's what Peter has to say about it. And if you're imagining a white-robed and bearded *Saint* Peter standing at the pearly gates, just stop. This was the fisherman who was always jumping out of boats and often opened his mouth when he should've kept it shut — the one who said, 'Go away from me, Lord, I am a sinful man,' when he realized he was in the presence of God's Son. Peter knew about sin. He writes, 'He personally carried away our sins in his own body on the cross so we can be dead to sin and live for what is right.'

He uncovered the last word.

Sin

"Dead to sin. Thanks to the victory on the cross, the *power* of sin is broken in the life of the believer. The Accuser is stripped of his greatest weapon when you live as if your sins have been nailed to that cross in the body of Jesus Christ. We still struggle with the flesh, but the true power of sin is broken when you live according to that truth. To do so is to put on the helmet of salvation, because it is a truth that renews your mind."

Renews your mind.

He went on. "In Romans Paul writes, 'And be not conformed to this world, but be transformed by the renewing of your mind...'" I stared, because his voice faded out. But his lips kept moving.

And I—sitting and listening with polite interest like someone listening to the truth, but truth that had nothing to do with me—with no warning whatsoever felt like I was being squeezed in a giant fist. The air squeaked out of my lungs, and I couldn't take a breath in to replace it. My eyes darted around, but every other part of me was paralyzed. Pastor's lips were moving, but I only heard my blood pounding in my ears. I was being crushed to death in a room full of people who didn't even know it.

Help! God, help me.

Suddenly air tore into my lungs, and I sprang up off the floor like every muscle had been tensed to the limit and released. I ran out of the gym and into the girls' bathroom.

I slowly became aware of thumping, and voices right behind me. I was sitting on the floor with my back against the door, bracing it shut with my legs against the facing wall. I wasn't crying. I wasn't anything.

"Rory, it's Shayne. Just let me in, okay?"

"Come on, Rory," other girls' voices said. "Let us in."

Let us in, Rory.

The last voice made me go stiff. It was deep and masculine and very familiar. For a split second, it was my dad's—but not quite right. Then it reminded me of Uri, only like there were three or four of him talking in perfect synchronization. The hairs stood up on my arms.

Being alone wasn't so appealing anymore. I slid over and opened the door a crack. "Just you," I said to Shayne.

She ducked inside, with Allie right behind her. "She said—" Shayne began.

"Hey, whatever's going on, we're all in this together." Allie leaned on the closed door. "So, what is going on?"

"I thought everybody knew," I said.

"We heard that you were in the hospital again. We figured you were having more problems with your head."

I almost laughed, but I'd forgotten how. She meant my head injury. I'd forgotten about that by now. "With my head. Exactly."

There was a loud knock on the bathroom door.

"We're alright. Just talking," Allie called.

The knock came again.

"We're talking. We'll be out in a minute." Another knock. She rolled her eyes, "Oh—what..." She opened the door a few inches and a face pressed into the opening.

"What's going on?" Jake Dean asked.

"You can't be poking your head into the girls' bathroom," Shayne said.

"We got here late. We missed what happened. What's wrong with Rory?"

"Can't you mind your own business?" Allie tried to push the door shut, but Jake had wedged his foot in.

"It is our business. We're the Jesus Machine." Suddenly his face pulled back from the door, followed by his foot, and the door closed on him. "Okay, take it easy," we heard him say to someone else outside.

"Is Rory okay?" a new voice asked.

"Sam? You're back," Shayne said.

"Just got back from the airport. What about Rory?"

Shayne and Allie looked at me. "I'm...here," I said.

"Anything we can do?"

They looked at me again.

"This is so..." I started, then I just sighed. "Oh, just let them in."

"But it's the girls'—" Allie stopped when Shayne gave her a look.

"Maybe we could go out?" Shayne suggested. I hunkered down on the pink tile floor in answer. For whatever reason, this place felt safe. And beyond these four people, I didn't want anyone looking at me.

Shayne shrugged, pulled the door inwards and beckoned. Jake and Sam entered warily.

"The inner sanctum," Jake whispered.

"Oh, please," Allie said. Eventually they all followed my example and settled on the floor. Sam's dark eyes had shadows beneath them, and his curly hair was askew—the look of someone who'd tried to sleep on a plane.

"So what's going on?" Jake asked.

"Do you want to tell us?" Shayne added.

I took a deep breath, testing myself. Nothing, no embarrassment, no fear. Why not tell? "Sure."

And I did tell them. Not all the details, but basically everything, starting with the accident and ending with that evening. Sometimes one of them would ask a question; sometimes they would exchange looks. Mostly they just listened.

When I finished, Jake gave a low whistle. "So the stuff she's been learning here sort of got mixed up into her seizures, and it caused weird hallucinations," he said.

"And they're sure about that?" Shayne asked. The others looked at her sharply. "Well, with everything we've been learning, you know... It could be true."

Allie jumped in. "And that's why it was so confusing. But think about it—no seizures, no demons or angels after she started the medication."

"How do you feel now?" Sam asked. He hadn't said anything up until that point.

"A little smudgy around the edges," I said. "I think it's the pills."

"Sounds like how I feel," he said. "I think it's the jet lag." He was trying for humor, and I practically smiled, but behind the joke I could see he was bothered by something.

There was a knock on the door. "Shayne?"

"Yeah, Jeph."

"Rory's sister is out here looking for her—"

"Excuse me," Sheelan's voice said, then her face appeared in the doorway. She surveyed the scene with a look of distaste. "You told me she was upset. Looks like a potty pow-wow to me."

"Potty pow-wow." Jake laughed. "Good one."

"Come on, Rory. I've waited long enough. If you're not in the car in two minutes, I mention this to Mom." She breezed out again.

"She's cute," said Jake. "How old is she?"

I ignored him and climbed to my feet, stretching out the kinks. "I'd better go. Thanks for everything."

"We didn't do anything," Shayne pointed out.

"You did. I just…I appreciate…" This was the part where I was trying to say goodbye. My exit, my backward step out of their lives where I'd barely fit in before and now was utterly out of place. Only they didn't know it was a goodbye, so it wasn't working.

"Hey, don't worry about it," Allie said. "We'll see you Monday, right? Or just call or IM if you need us."

I nodded and we filed out of the bathroom to the curious stares of all the non-potty-pow-wowers. Pastor Dan caught me before I could slip out, and by the time I convinced him that I was okay and apologized for disrupting his teaching, I knew my two minute warning from Sheelan had long expired.

She didn't seem to notice. Jeph stood at the driver's side window and she leaned with one elbow on the steering wheel, looking dangerously close to half-smiling as he talked to her. When I climbed in the car, he asked her, "Can I call you sometime?"

"I'm not home much," was her reply before she shifted into reverse and backed away. But when I glanced back as we drove off, I saw him smiling because she hadn't said no.

He was crazier than me.

21

The last Sunday in March burst forth with the glorious, springlike weather that strikes fear in Midwestern hearts — the kind of weather usually followed by a blizzard or an ice storm. This one was no exception. That night the wind howled, and Monday, the first of April, dawned like a fairyland, every bush and tree right down to the tiniest twiggy branch looking as if it had been dipped in liquid glass. Everyone enjoyed the splendor as much as they could while swinging fishtails in their cars and chiseling their mailbox doors open.

The circular driveway at school was a mess of partially-scraped cars trying to pull up without sliding into each other. Just as I was shuffling up to the front doors, a huge tank-like SUV rumbled up, and Kevin Sebeck jumped out. I prayed I wouldn't fall on my head in front of him.

Honestly, I didn't pray that he would fall on his head instead, but he did. The landing of his jump was solid, but his first step betrayed him. His feet flew up and he landed square on his back. It must've knocked the wind out of him, because he lay there for a second looking very different than the usual Kevin — that is to say, looking scared — then he sucked in a raggedy breath and picked himself up off the concrete. The driver of the big yellow tank saw the whole thing. I heard a short laugh, more like a bark, and the driver said, "Nice move, loser!" Everyone who had stopped to admire the tank heard him say it.

As he picked himself up off the ground, Kevin put on the look of death so no one dared say anything to him. I stole the briefest glance at him just in time to make accidental eye contact. I had a feeling he'd make me pay for that.

At the lockers I overheard Jasmine say to Tiffany Klipfel, "Kevin's brother must be a total jerk."

"Yeah, probably," Tiffany said. "But that wasn't his brother. That was his dad."

Ouch. I didn't want to feel sorry for Kevin. It was much more convenient to think of him as a total jerk. But I guess every jerk has a story.

Maybe Jasmine was thinking the same thing about me, because she spoke to me in the lunch line. "Are you ready for the big algebra test?" she asked while selecting lime jello with captive mandarin oranges suspended inside.

"As ready as I'm gonna be, I guess," I sighed.

"I'm going to work on the review pages right now. If you want, we can do them together."

"Oh...Thanks."

"Unless you're going to eat with your friends."

I hadn't figured this one out yet. I had planned to detach from the group. It just seemed easier. Safer. They knew too much — I'd told them because they were going to find out some of it eventually, and I wanted them to hear it from me. Now I would gracefully step away (not graceful in the literal sense, of course) and save them the awkwardness of having to endure me.

But I looked at them at the table, and my stomach gave a little squeeze. *I don' wanna leave*, it said. I looked at Jasmine, and I had a thought. I resisted it at first, because I wasn't sure about her. I still suspected she had something to do with Kellie's suspension, though common sense told me the problem hadn't started with Jasmine, even if she had helped it along. But I had a suspicion of a different sort: could living a life of truth mean forgiving and not holding a grudge?

Simple enough to test it. Forgiving Jasmine: the easy thing to do or the hard one? Hard one. Okay, that must be the right thing.

"Why don't you come eat with us?" I asked.

"No," she said immediately, shaking her head.

"Come on."

"Okay."

"Oh." That was sudden. "Good."

"You didn't expect me to say yes," she accused, pointing a celery stick at me. "You probably don't really want me to come."

I grabbed the Special and gave her a hard look. "And they say I'm paranoid," I said. "Come on. Decide for yourself whether I invited you to be friendly or for revenge."

She wasn't sure whether I was joking. Neither was I. But she followed me.

"Can you fit two more?" I asked the gang.

They shifted down and left a space at the end of each side of the table. I sat beside Sam and left Jasmine the space beside Jake. He blocked it before she could sit down.

"Not until you swear the blood oath," he said in his ominous voice.

She gave him her cold eyes. "How about I use your blood?"

Jake withdrew his hand with a soft whistle.

"I like her," said Allie. "Hi, I'm Allie."

"I know."

"Oh. Great. And…"

Jasmine didn't catch the hint, or she ignored it, so I said, "This is Jasmine—" At the last second I decided not to mention the Wee part.

"How about we call you Jazz?" Jake asked, though I doubt he was asking for permission. "I'm Jake Elwood Dean."

"Yeah, we've only been in the same class for two years, Jake."

"I know. I just like to say *Jake Elwood Dean*. 'Cause it's my name."

"And not Jacob Leslie Dean," Sam told her.

"And he's not Shemuel Shelomoh Newman," Jake shot back.

"Samuel Solomon," I corrected without thinking. A big yap/hot face moment, to be sure. "I heard your grandpa call you that," I added lamely.

Sam grinned.

"Same thing," Jake said.

"Sam, what were you about to tell us when Rory came?" Shayne asked.

His grin faded, and his eyebrows scrunched towards each other. "Oh, that. Nothing." He didn't look at Jasmine, but I knew it was something he didn't want to say in front of her.

The rest of lunch felt out of synch. The conversation didn't flow with the usual random purposelessness I had come to enjoy. It wasn't that we always had deep theological discussions, but God talk was sprinkled here and there throughout our normal conversations. No one seemed quite sure how much of that Jasmine would be comfortable with. Oh, if we were honest with ourselves, we'd admit that we didn't want to hear what sort of sharp remark she might make about our religion and all that.

Then maybe a little Jasmine rubbed off on me, because the more I thought about it, the more I wondered if they were also a bit uncomfortable around me. It occurred to me that maybe the thing Sam hadn't wanted to say in front of Jasmine was actually something he didn't want to say in front of me. Now I remembered why I was going to take that backward step out of the circle. It might hurt to pull away, but a push, even a gentle one, hurt more.

As it turns out, it was just going to be a day of uncomfortable meals. Mom didn't have to work that night, so she fixed a 'sit-down dinner,' as she called it. This was where we not only sat at a table to eat, but we actually sat there at the same time. A situation that often ended badly.

The apple-roasted chicken and mashed potatoes didn't help. They were delicious, but this was one of Dad's favorite meals, so it was sort of like eating delicious rubber and ashes. The flavor was right, but it felt wrong in our mouths. It's probably why the conversation took a bad turn.

"I found out that Ruthie at the restaurant goes to the big church," Mom said, trying for a laugh. "There are probably a hundred people there I know, only you could go to that place and never run into them, the size of it."

Sheelan nibbled the edges off a cucumber slice. "Gianna Marsala told me they have tons of programs for teens," she said, not looking at me. "I mean, where they actually get to travel places, not just sit on a gym floor or hang out in the girls' bathroom."

I rolled my eyes. Mom said, "I'm sorry we missed it yesterday. My last customers took their sweet time Saturday night. It was so late when I got home. But we'll definitely make it this Sunday for Easter."

"Why, do we earn extra brownie points for going on Easter?" Sheelan asked. "Oh, I bet Rory would know. She's getting very religious."

"What are you talking about, Shee?" Mom wiped her mouth with a paper napkin.

"Don't get me wrong. If we have to go to church, this one suits me fine. I'm just not sure I see the point."

Mom's mouth pressed into a firm line. "Your dad used to see the point," she said quietly.

"And look where it got him."

My fork hung forgotten in the air halfway to my open mouth. I stared at Sheelan. It was just like that night at the Scene, when she'd been asking all those questions. It looked like Sheelan and sounded like Sheelan, but it had to be her even-more-evil twin.

"What's that supposed to mean?" Mom did an impressive job of sounding calm.

"Dad was the only one who really thought church was important, and now he's dead. God sure has a funny way of showing His appreciation. Or was He angry because Dad started working on Sundays? Then I guess we'd better go to church, or He might come after us next."

"Sheelan!"

"Oh, wait. He's already gotten to Rory, hasn't he? Didn't kill her, just made her nuts. Now she's crazy enough to want to go every week and hear about all the demons who are out to get her—you know that's what they're teaching her at that church, don't you? Do you even care? And she doesn't just believe in them, she actually sees them. I mean, look at her. She doesn't even look like she can see us. She's probably having a mental conversation with the angels and devils right now."

Hey, it wasn't my fault if I had big, glassy eyes. That was one of the side effects of my pills. It said right there on the box: *May cause staring at obnoxious sisters with big, glassy eyes.* Right after *May cause sleeplessness, drowsiness, constipation, diarrhea, skin sensitivity and numbness.* They cover basically everything just in case. Sheelan was right, though. I wasn't good for much other than listening to them, my eyes bouncing back and forth table-tennis style.

You could see Mom was chewing herself up on the inside, but she was struggling to do a Dr. McD. "You're feeling a lot of powerful emotions, Sheelan, and that's normal. I know you're hurting. But I don't feel it's appropriate to blame God for everything bad that has happened—"

"Why not?" Something about the way Sheelan spoke left me cold. She wasn't playing the fiery drama-diva role she so enjoyed. This Sheelan was calm and positively frosty. It was the difference between a showy sword duel and a hidden drop of poison. Both could kill, but one just seemed more lethal.

She went on. "Who better to blame than the all-powerful God? Unless you're saying that God isn't all-powerful. Those seem to be the choices: either I go to church to worship an almighty God who controls everything—right down to the minute we choose to leave the house to see a movie, so we can be right on time for a sleeping truck driver to ruin our lives—because maybe going to church will keep God happy and He'll leave the rest of us alone."

"That's not what God is. God loves—"

"Or," Sheelan cut in, "we can go sing praises to a loving God who can't actually protect those He loves."

"We can't blame God for everything that happens in our day-to-day lives," Mom said. "God is there when we seek Him in our quiet moments, but He's not some puppeteer constantly pulling our strings. I've always felt that God was there for me in the big things, but the daily stuff was up to me."

"Big things? Does it get any bigger than death, Mom? Where was God when our lives were on the line? He wasn't anywhere near Dad."

"We're responsible for our own decisions, our own lives—"

"I'm responsible, you mean." For the first time, Sheelan's calmness had a quiver of emotion in it.

"Well, yes. For your choices, just like I'm res—"

"Just say it, Mom. You think it's my fault."

My ping-pong eyes bounced to Mom, but she just stared at Sheelan with her forehead all creased up, so they bounced back to Sheelan.

"You think it's my fault that we were there when that truck came through. Because I said—" Her voice cracked, but she clenched her jaw and forced it into submission. "I said I wouldn't go to the 7:00 show. I had plans. I said if he wanted me to come, it would have to be the earlier show." She stood up, and we just stared at her. "And he wanted me to come. You think it's my fault."

Mom's breath trickled out with a whispery sound. "No, Shee…"

Sheelan didn't stick around to hear more. Her hands lashed out and flipped her plate over, scattering globs of potato and splattering her glass of water over my plate and the tablecloth. She fled up the stairs, with my mom right behind. I heard a door slam, then the sounds of Mom trying to persuade Sheelan to open it.

I ate my food out of the puddle on my plate. Then I cleared the table. It was my night to do it.

Upstairs there was shouting.

I checked my email. Mrs. Greene was back—she had replied to the philosophical ramblings I'd sent just after she'd left town.

Rory, I wish I'd been home to get this when you first sent it. You ask all the right questions! Never be afraid to question and seek answers. 2 Peter 1:16, Jeremiah 29:13!!

In a sense, God's grace is a free ticket to eternal life. Free in the sense that it is a gift given to us that we could never earn, and we only have to accept it. But just because it's free doesn't mean it has no value. It was a very costly gift, indeed—it cost the life of God's own Son.

But yes, the battle rages on for a little while yet. The Enemy is going down, but not without a fight. Yes, be on your guard, ready to fight, but know that God also promises rest and peace. As far as the danger of failing goes, not to worry. It doesn't rest on your shoulders or mine. Our King has already won the war. We don't fight FOR victory—we fight FROM victory. That's what we'll celebrate this Sunday.

I hear you've had a hard week. You're not the only one of the Fearsome Fivesome who needs a little encouragement—maybe we could arrange a gathering at my house this week? Let's try to plan something, maybe dinner on Wednesday or Thursday? —KG

I typed back:

Sounds good. Thanks. —REJoyce

I just didn't know how to ask her which of Sheelan's Gods was the true God. It had to be one or the other, logically speaking. Either He was all-powerful or He wasn't. Either He could've stopped my Dad from dying and He didn't, or He wanted to but just couldn't manage it.

I heard another door slam upstairs and, very faintly, muffled sounds of crying. I went up to my room, picked up Gran's Bible, and brought it back downstairs. It took me a while to find Jeremiah. I read 29:12, 'And you will seek Me and find Me, when you search for me with all your heart.'

Ah, there was the catch. With all my heart. What did that mean? How would I know if all my heart was in it? What if I forgot a little corner of it, or if part of it had just shriveled up by now?

The crying upstairs was louder now.

I typed a group IM.

REJoyce316: *Anyone out there?*

Jake had told me there was a way I could tell who was online if I set it up that way under preferences. I had no idea what he was talking about. So I tossed the message out there with about as much hope as a marooned guy on an island when he throws out the bottle with the note.

Nothing happened. I fiddled around with the mouse, exploring the menu options, but it was mostly a mystery to me. The thought *I should get Dad to help me* actually began to cross my mind before I could stamp it out. Deep down, like the pea under the princess's mattresses, I detected a hard little lump of emotion. There was a sorrow buried there that I couldn't ignore, but it was too much for me to manage. The best I could do was to keep it down there. But the thing wouldn't stay put. It was a shard of glass in the flesh. I could work it out and bleed, or it could work its way towards my heart.

My head came down on the desk. It stayed there for a long time. If it was minutes or even hours, I can't say, but it was a small *bloop* that brought it up again, stiff and bleary-eyed.

samIam: *just me I guess*

I stared at it for a minute, and it finally sank in. A glance at the computer's clock revealed it was after midnight.

samIam: *fall asleep at the computer?*

I scrambled to find the right place for my fingers on the keyboard.

REJoyce316: *I think I did*
samIam: *it's a school night. go to bed.*
REJoyce316: *you go to bed*
samIam: *I did. With my dad's laptop. Can't sleep.*

204

I thought of a dozen things to say, from the bland and safe to the stab at humor that could fail miserably. My fingers wouldn't commit to anything, and I just sat there with my hands hovering over the keyboard.

> **samIam:** *you okay?*

This I could manage. Barely.

> **REJoyce316:** *No*
> **samIam:** *what's up?*
> **REJoyce316:** *I just don't get it*
> **samIam:** *??*
> **REJoyce316:** *I don't understand why God let this happen to my family*
> **samIam:** *oh*

Suddenly I thought of that picture hanging in the upstairs hallway at Sam's house, the two dark pairs of eyes.

> **REJoyce316:** *why does he let bad things happen?*
> **samIam:** *I wonder too sometimes*
> **REJoyce316:** *don't suppose you could explain*
> **samIam:** *can I get back to you after Bible college?*
> **REJoyce316:** *ha ha. I guess it's kind of late to be getting all deep and philosophical*

That took me a while to type. He didn't take so long.

> **samIam:** *I'm never very philosophical. But I like to listen to people who are.*
> **REJoyce316:** *So?*
> **samIam:** *So, do you believe God made the world?*
> **REJoyce316:** *Yes*
> **samIam:** *and it was perfect?*
> **REJoyce316:** *not for long. Adam and Eve ate the wrong fruit and ruined it for everyone, right? Why did God even put that tree there?*

samIam: *I guess because they had to choose to love (obey) or not to.*

REJoyce316: *???*

samIam: *He had to let A & E choose. If he just made them love him, it would be like slavery. Does that even make sense?*

REJoyce316: *You're saying love is only love if it's given freely*

samIam: *hey, you're good*

REJoyce316: *but what does that have to do with my dad?*

samIam: *just that's how death got started in the world*

REJoyce316: *So you're saying that all the cr@# we deal with now is because of one man and woman's bad choice. How is that fair?*

samIam: *I think because we all do the same thing. We don't have a tree that's off limits, but there are lots of other ways we make that bad choice every day.*

He meant sin. I could never get away from that.

REJoyce316: *Makes me wonder why God bothered to create us in the first place. if he knows everything, he must have known how it was going to end.*

samIam: *sure. ever heard Jesus called the Lamb slain from the foundation of the world?*

REJoyce316: *I think so*

samIam: *God had it worked out in advance*

REJoyce316: *??*

samIam: *He knew we'd make the wrong choice, so he had a plan B, or plan J, even before he made the world.*

REJoyce316: *but Jesus isn't in the Old Testament*

samIam: *He's all over the Old Testament. The whole Bible is about him.*

REJoyce316: *I don't get it*

samIam: *Adam and Eve show how sin began and why we need Jesus, and God gave the first promise of a savior right there*

REJoyce316: *okay*

samIam: *the Law shows us how God wants us to live holy lives*

REJoyce316: *what's that got to do with Jesus*

samIam: *Can you keep all those laws?*

REJoyce316: *Not even the few I know*

samIam: *exactly*

REJoyce316: *you lost me...*

samIam: *the Law shows how much we need a savior. We can't ever be good enough on our own. And the sacrifices*

REJoyce316: *I never understood why God wanted animals killed and all that*

samIam: *that points to Jesus, too. All the sacrifices were to make up for sins, but there could never be enough sacrifices*

REJoyce316: *So?*

samIam: *So we needed one perfect sacrifice*

I pulled my hands into my lap. That made sense.

samIam: *all the prophets in the O.T. talk about needing to fix things between us and God, and a lot of them talk about the Messiah*

REJoyce316: *how do you know all this?*

samIam: *Oh, I'm a prophet, too.*

REJoyce316: *I knew it.*

samIam: *well, not really. I'm just Messianic. they make us learn this stuff.*

REJoyce316: *so*

samIam: *so...*

REJoyce316: *So the Bible is just one long story about Jesus?*

samIam: *why we need him, how he came, and what he had to do. And then there's the part about when he comes back.*

REJoyce316: *but*

samIam: *what?*

REJoyce316: *that's not what most Jewish people believe*

There was such a long pause that I felt a twist in my stomach. I'd said something wrong. Finally there was a *bloop*.

samIam: *I have to go*

REJoyce316: *sorry if I*

samIam: *no, I just got busted by my mom*

REJoyce316: *oops*

samIam: *see you tomorrow*

REJoyce316: *okay*
samIam: *over and out*
REJoyce316: *copy that*
samIam: *roger*
REJoyce316: *surely you didn't just call me roger*

It was one of my dad's favorite dumb jokes. Sam wouldn't get it, but that was okay.

samIam: *don't call me Shirley*

Unbelievable.

samIam: *I'm on the verge of getting into deep doo doo now*
REJoyce316: *so go*
samIam: *bye*

I squeezed my fists, then stretched my fingers back to the keys.

REJoyce316: *Sam*
samIam: *yes*
REJoyce316: *thanks*
samIam: *go to bed. It's a school night.*

I almost smiled as I shut down the computer and crawled into my pajamas and bed. The rest of the house was quiet. My brain was anything but quiet, spinning with new thoughts, and in my chest I had the sensation of filling up with something that made me feel strong and trembling at the same time. The closest thing I can compare it to is how you might feel if you thought your hometown was the entire world, and then someone showed you the view of Earth from the space shuttle. Huge, scary, but awesome. And it made a lot of the little bits that didn't make sense on their own suddenly rush together with a satisfying *click*.

I dreamed that night of a mountain. From a distance I could see a figure running along a narrow path, climbing over rocky obstacles. A cloak covered most of him, but now and then a glimpse of brightness shone from underneath it, like sunlight, or the sun glinting off metal. Then I was closer, and I could see the dark hair curling out from under the helmet. On his feet, sandals, simple and strong.

22

Ericson Greene was an amazing cook. He actually made pizza from scratch, even the crust, and we got to help him roll the dough then add the toppings before he slid it into the oven. We created a monster meat pizza with double extra cheese. Kellie laughed later when we tried to bite into it and pulled foot-long strands of stretchy cheese away from our faces.

The Greenes lived in Westhaven, the town just north and east of Whitestone, a ten minute drive from my house. Jeph chauffeured us, and he picked me up last. He seemed pretty disappointed that Sheelan wasn't home. I must've seemed pretty relieved, because I was. She was a ticking time bomb, and Jeph could easily act as her remote detonator.

He dropped Shayne, Allie and me off at a small brick ranch in a neighborhood of small brick ranches similar in feel but with no two exactly alike. The trees were tall and budding, still a couple of weeks away from having leaves. That smell of thawed earth and hidden green growth was in the air; the ice had long since melted and the chill been replaced by a sense of spring frenzy. I walked eagerly into the house, and even Kellie's hug didn't make me feel very self-conscious—even though I wasn't sure why I was there. I kept thinking I had to break away from these people, but somehow it wasn't happening.

"Welcome, girls. Thanks for coming. Here, Rory, meet Ericson, my husband. Eric, this is Rory Joyce."

"Hi, Rory. Glad you could all come, ladies. Let me take those coats." He was an average-looking man, medium height, medium build, medium brown hair, gray-blue eyes, blue jeans and blue polo shirt. But there was something in his smile that wasn't medium at all. It was a little mysterious, actually.

By the time Sam and Jake showed up, we were already up to our elbows in flour, kneading and rolling dough in the kitchen. Once Jake learned it was for pizza, he tried to grab the dough to toss it in the air.

"Wash your hands at least," Allie said. Within a minute, dough was spinning in the air, and only Ericson's quick reflexes saved it from an untimely death in a sink full of soapy dishwater.

"Maybe I'll take it from here," he said. But we all helped spread the sauce and sprinkle on a blizzard of shredded cheese. Then Ericson stopped suddenly. "Oh, wait. Sam, can you eat the meat toppings with the cheese?"

I looked to Sam, curious, and happened to catch his eye. Neither of us had mentioned our IM conversation of several nights ago, but the unspokenness of it hung between us, maybe more awkward than talking about it would've been.

"It's okay," he said. "I decided not to keep kosher when I was bar mitzvahed last year."

"Really? Interesting. So you just follow your conscience when it comes to the dietary laws?"

"Yeah. I mean, my dad doesn't do kosher but my mom sort of does. She doesn't have a strictly kosher kitchen—it's more about the types of food she fixes. Since she does most of the cooking, I guess I eat semi-kosher at home. It's just her preference, not something we disagree on. My dad and I decided to go by what

Paul said, you know, whatever you eat or drink, do it for the glory of God."

Kellie said, "And Jesus said that it's not what goes into a man's mouth that makes him unclean, but what comes out of his mouth—out of his heart."

"So what you're saying is yes to extra pepperoni?" Ericson asked.

"Yes to extra everything," Sam said seriously.

"I like the way you think." Ericson sliced and diced the meat and peppers. "So you had your bar mitzvah ceremony when you turned thirteen?"

"Yeah."

"Sam's a *man* now," Jake told us like we were a kindergarten class.

Being an expert, I could see that Sam was fighting the hot face. "Mostly I did it to make my grandpa happy." He had the facial equivalent of a cloud passing over the sun, then he quickly went on. "Oh, yeah. I just remembered. If any of you want to, you can come to temple on Saturday morning for my *t'vilah*. My immersion."

"What?" Kellie stopped pouring lemonades. "Really?"

"Your excursion?" Jake asked. "You're Persian? I thought you were a Hebrew."

"Don't be a stooge, Jake," Allie said. "You heard him. Are you really going to be baptized, Sam?"

"We call it immersion—*t'vilah*."

"And you're just telling us now?" Shayne punched him on the arm.

"Well, I meant to tell you about it at lunch, but the other girl was there and I didn't want her to feel uninvited."

Jasmine. She'd been joining us at lunch for the past few days, and I'd come to regret inviting her. She didn't say a whole lot, but what she didn't say said a lot. I wondered why she kept sitting with us if she didn't approve of us.

"Like there weren't a hundred other times you could've mentioned it?" Shayne said.

"I'm mentioning it now."

Kellie laid a hand on Sam's back. "This is wonderful, Sam. I could tell you had something big on your mind this week. We'll be honored to attend, and if anyone else wants to ride with us, we can drive together."

The others promised to go, and in the layers of conversation, I didn't think anyone noticed that I hadn't committed to it. I was trying to imagine the reaction of my mom, who had worried that I might come home from the Front Street Temple a Baptist. I wasn't even sure if I could come home from Sam's temple a Jew. I was pretty sure you had to be born a Jew to be Jewish. Mom would worry anyway.

After the pizza and tossed salad, Kellie pulled out some board games. It wasn't long before we were all making fools of ourselves doing a charades-type game where you might also have to draw the secret word on paper or even sculpt it from a nasty-smelling putty. (We decided the nasty smell wasn't an intentional part of the game, just a gruesome bonus.) I guess friends are people you can make a fool of yourself in front of and know they'll still talk to you the next day. Even Jake's constant stream of wisecracks didn't matter.

I saw the mysterious smile on Ericson's face a lot, and always he would be looking at or talking to Kellie. I didn't want to stare, but I couldn't help but want to study it, something so extraordinary on such an ordinary face. The way they laughed together had a hint of some shared secret, but it didn't shut the rest of us out like an inside joke. They touched a lot, too, without being obnoxious. Little touches like his hand on her elbow, or hers on his shoulder, just in passing. Once he gave her a secret little pat on the belly, and I knew what that was for. Kellie saw me watching, and she gave me a wink. I got the feeling that she hadn't told the others about the baby. For a few seconds, I had my own mysterious smile.

Later, Kellie let us all in on a different secret. "Do you think you'd like to do this again—maybe once a month?" she asked.

"Are you kidding?" Shayne asked. "How about once a week?"

"Or we can just move in now," Jake suggested.

Kellie laughed. "Maybe once a week, eventually. Ericson and I are planning to start a teen ministry out of our home. This whole Armor of God study at Teen Scene started something moving in my heart. Kids your age need a place to go to learn how to stand firm in the battle, to gird up for war."

"And eat lots of pizza," Ericson said.

We all smiled at each other. Jake lifted a finger in wise declaration. "It shall be called The Jesus Machine."

"It most certainly shall not," Allie said.

Kellie laughed, her ponytail swinging. The doorbell rang.

We were disappointed to find that Jeph had arrived to take us home. Kellie hurriedly wrapped up a brownie for each of us, since we'd forgotten all about dessert in the heat of the game. As we pulled on our coats and said our thank yous and goodbyes at the front step, Sam and Jake's ride showed up. We were all on the driveway climbing into cars when Sam called after us, "See you Saturday maybe?"

"You bet," Kellie answered. Shayne and Allie both said, "Definitely," and then tried to jinx each other for saying it at the same time. Jake said, "Yeah, yeah, I told you I'd come." Sam waited for a second or two, but I was already in the car and he didn't actually look at me, so I said nothing. Then everyone was in his or her respective cars and we were off.

Shayne noticed. "You didn't tell Sam if you were going."

"I think he was disappointed," Allie teased. Shayne jabbed her with an elbow.

"I have to make sure with my mom first," I said doubtfully.

I had misjudged my mom. She didn't care anymore if I was a Baptist, a Jew, or a Buddhist monk, as long as I wasn't a crazy. So two days later, I found myself sitting in *B'rit Chadashah* temple. In many ways it felt like another planet.

Or at least another country. It was like what happens when you talk to a person from another English-speaking country. The accent isn't the real problem—it's that half the words are different. To you it's a cookie; to them it's a biscuit. Truck, lorry; bathroom, loo.

Church, congregation. The place felt churchy, the smell of cool stone and wood polish was churchy, but it wasn't a church. It was a congregation. Sam wasn't sitting up in front in his white shirt and brown pants waiting for baptism, it was immersion. And for all the talking that was going on in the service (and there was a lot), I didn't hear the name of Jesus once. Weren't these supposed to be Christian Jews?

I leaned over and whispered to Kellie next to me. "What's this Yeshua they keep talking about?"

She pressed her lips together, but the smile crept out. "Yeshua is Hebrew for Jesus," she whispered back. "They say Yeshua Messiah like we would say Jesus Christ."

I sighed (at least I hadn't asked Jake, who was on my left) and settled in to listen. I figured now I would understand a lot more of what the pastor—or was it rabbi?—was talking about. Of course that's when the Hebrew started. The congregation joined in at alternating parts, but I couldn't follow all the strange syllables printed in the bulletin. Then we were singing a hymn—in English—but I was distracted by the sight of Sam walking up to the podium—lectern—whatever it was called.

Behind him, on a ponderous stone slab, was a large scroll with an ornate roller-thing on both ends. On either side of that, in alcoves in the wall, were two eight-pronged candle holders. It all looked very ancient and solemn. Sam fidgeted, running a finger along the inside of his shirt collar. As the hymn entered its final verse, I peeked ahead in the bulletin for a clue as to what happened next. *Samuel Solomon Newman,* it read, then *t'vilah.*

The room became quiet except for the shuffling of feet on the stone floor and the rustle of paper. From behind us there rang a soft, low sound like a chime. My mouth went dry when I realized that Sam didn't just have to speak, he had to sing. My palms began to sweat on his behalf.

He opened his mouth, and on the very first word his voice squeaked and broke. He cleared his throat while the slightest murmur went through the congregation. I sensed their affectionate anticipation, and I imagined all the other boy-men who had stood up there trying to sing with changing voices, and how the people were remembering them now. Sam began again, and the squeak had gone, replaced by a low, barely shaking voice.

He sang in Hebrew, a very simple melody that repeated like a meditation. The words themselves didn't seem to repeat, but Sam's voice grew stronger as he sang them. It was a complicated string of sounds, sometimes smooth and rolling off the tongue, sometimes choppy and in the throat, yet always musical. It all had an exotic feel. I heard one word repeated many times: *adonai*. In the bulletin below Sam's name was printed *Psalm 27*, so I guessed that was what he was singing.

In a flash of staggering brilliance, it occurred to me that Hebrew was probably the language the Psalms were originally written in, not English. If I closed my eyes, I could almost picture the ancient time when it was first sung. Except for the fact that I didn't know what instruments they used back then, what clothes they wore, and all that. It didn't matter; I felt like I was sitting inside an old, sacred place, right there in a much newer—maybe sacred?—place.

When he finished, the stillness that had settled over the congregation broke, and the people smiled and spoke words of approval. Sam half-smiled and looked down at his shoes. The pastor/rabbi directed him to one side where another man was pulling aside a heavy curtain. Behind it was a short circular wall of stones, and there was water in it, like a fountain that wasn't spraying at the moment. Sam approached it, and that's when the meaning of 'immersion' hit me. This wasn't a sprinkling. He was going in.

Dr. and Mrs. Newman came to the side of the pool, Mrs. Newman looking rather pale. Along with them came a few others I didn't recognize, probably family. One of these, a tall man who looked a lot like Sam's dad, began to read. I followed along in the bulletin.

> But those who depend on the law to make them right with HaShem are under his curse, for the Scriptures say, "Cursed is everyone who does not observe and obey all these commands that are

written in HaShem's Book of the Law." Consequently, it is clear that no one can ever be right with HaShem by trying to keep the law. For the Scriptures say, "It is through faith that a righteous person has life." How different from this way of faith is the way of law, which says, "If you wish to find life by obeying the law, you must obey all of its commands." But Yeshua Ha'Mashiach has rescued us from the curse pronounced by the law. When he was hung on the cross, he took upon himself the curse for our wrongdoing. For it is written in the Scriptures, "Cursed is everyone who is hung on a tree." Through the work of Yeshua Ha'Mashiach, HaShem has blessed the Gentiles with the same blessing he promised to Abraham, and we all receive the promised Holy Spirit through faith.

Galatians 3:10-14

Sam handed his glasses to his father and climbed barefoot up the two steps to the stone pool while the rabbi spoke. "In the waters of the *mikveh* some find ritual cleansing, not of external filth, but of the uncleanness within; others find the death and burial of Messiah and emerge from the waters as Messiah emerged from the grave, sharing in his resurrection. Paul reminds us that we 'were baptized to become one with Yeshua HaMashiach,' and that '...we died and were buried with Messiah by baptism. And just as Messiah was raised from the dead by the glorious power of the Father, now we also may live new lives.'

"As an act of obedience to Yeshua and as a public display of his decision to receive a new life in Him, Samuel comes to the *mikveh* this day. Do you acknowledge, Shemuel Shelomoh, that it is not these waters which wash away sin, but the very blood of Yeshua HaMashiach?"

"Yes."

"Yeshua taught that a man must be born again to see the Kingdom of HaShem, born of water and the Spirit. May these waters symbolize your second birth into the Kingdom, a new man." He smiled at the appropriateness of the words. Then Sam stepped into the water, and took another step down, and another. I counted seven steps down—the pool was sunk down into the floor. Only Sam's head and shoulders were visible above the low wall. The pastor spoke a few quiet words to Sam, who nodded. Holding him behind the neck, the pastor placed the other hand on Sam's forehead and pushed him under the water.

He held him down a little longer than I expected. When Sam came back up, he took an audible breath. The pastor said something quietly again and pushed Sam back down. This time he held him down even longer. I looked around, wondering if it was just me or if it seemed like he was overdoing it a little. Jake noticed me.

"He's either going to be a 'new man' or a dead man," Jake said, a little louder than he should have.

Sam came up, this time practically gasping for air. Then down he went again. What kind of church/temple/synagogue/ congregation was this? A hand patted my knee. Kellie was intent on Sam's ordeal, but she must've felt me fidget and was reassuring me.

Sam finally surfaced again, water streaming down his hair, a grin on his face. As he climbed out of the pool into the towel his mother held open for him, the people around me broke into applause. I couldn't decide if we were clapping for his immersion or his survival.

The service ended soon after that, but not before the Newmans invited everyone to their house for 'food and fellowship.' We waited in the lobby until Sam reappeared in dry clothes. We gathered around him, and Kellie gave him a hug.

"Nice perm," Shayne said, fluffing his damp hair.

"I wish," he said. "I'd shave it off and let it grow back straight."

"Not a chance," said Kellie. "With that curly-wurly hair and those dark, sparkly eyes, you'll have the young ladies melting, just you wait."

"Oh, every boy dreams of being curly-wurly," Jake said with a girlish twirl.

Allie pushed him aside. "Thanks for inviting us, Sam. It was really a neat ceremony. That pool was pretty deep."

"Yeah, and not very warm," said Sam.

"So, Rory and I want to know," Jake said, "was the guy trying to drown you, or is he just absent-minded, kind of forgot you were down there?"

Sam got his faraway look. "Nah, that's just how I wanted it. I let Rabbi Rosenblum know when I needed to come up."

"You didn't even seem nervous," Ericson said.

"In the water? No, that was easy. It was the Psalm that had me shaking in my shoes."

"What is *adonai*?" I asked suddenly.

Sam looked at me. "It means Lord."

"I kept hearing that."

"Yeah. I kept saying it."

I laughed, the dorky nervous kind. I tried to cover it up by talking more. Never a good tactic for me. "Your grandpa must be proud."

"What?" His face fell, or maybe just his smile dropped off.

"Your Hebrew lessons. They must be working. I figured your grandpa must be happy…" My words trickled to a stop. While I was still talking, Sam turned and practically ran out the door.

23

1 sat on the Newman's back porch, alone in my misery. It was only fitting since Sam sat upstairs in his bedroom, alone in his. Thanks to me.

On the drive over, the others puzzled over what had happened. (The kids, anyway. Kellie and Ericson didn't say much.) No one could find anything wrong in it, but obviously something I'd said was to blame—Sam had taken refuge in the family car and stayed there until his parents left for home. I also thought longingly of home and refuge, but Kellie assured me that I had done nothing wrong, and since six of us carpooled in the Greene's van, I didn't feel I could insist on a detour to drop me off at home. When we arrived at the Newman house and learned that Sam had retreated to his bedroom, I wished I had insisted.

I knew Sam was only my friend by default, just because of Shayne, but I sure hadn't needed Shayne's help to screw it up. I poked at the assortment of unfamiliar foods on my plate—

probably authentic, homemade and delicious, but they had as much appeal as a cafeteria Special. At least it warmed my lap on a day that was still a bit too breezy to make the back porch a popular gathering place. Which is why I'd chosen it.

The screen door creaked open behind me. I hoped that by not turning to look I sent a clear message about my desire for company.

"You know," said a woman's voice, "an untouched plate is a terrible crime in a Jewish household."

I looked up. Mrs. Newman gazed down at me with one eyebrow raised.

"Sorry. I lost my appetite."

"That is just what Samuel says." I noticed a slight accent in her voice.

"I guess that's my fault."

"No, it isn't, as I've come to tell you. Samuel is upset because his grandfather was not present today at the *t'vilah*. He wanted to be brave and go ahead as if it did not bother him, but it certainly does. You are not the cause of this."

"But I reminded him of it."

"He did not forget. It is better for him to face his sadness now. Then he will come down and eat with a man's appetite and dance with his family and his friends. And you, too, should come in to eat and dance. It is why Samuel asked you to come." She smiled, just a little, and her eyes looked like Sam's.

I nodded. "I'll be right in." As she turned to go back inside, I asked, "Mrs. Newman? Why—" I stopped. "I mean. What is this called?" I pointed to a dollop of creamy stuff on my plate.

"Pasta salad," she said.

I sighed. Would I never tire of embarrassing myself? The truth was, I was going to ask why Sam's grandpa hadn't come to his immersion, but I managed to stop myself in time. Mrs. Newman struck me as a private person, and if it were any of my business she would have told me.

She leaned against the doorframe, her long skirt draping around her, and once again I saw the poise that reminded me of a dancer. She had seen through my stupid question. "My father is an Orthodox Jew who does not share or understand his daughter's belief in Yeshua. To him it is a bitter betrayal of the true faith. It has long been his hope that Samuel will follow in his path and return the family to its tradition. Samuel's immersion today sealed his decision for Messiah Yeshua—a blessed occasion to us but a grievous event to his grandfather. Perhaps an unforgivable event." Her eyes were not focused on anything I could see. "Sam and his grandfather love each other very much."

There was nothing more to say. She opened the door, and the sound of voices and music poured out, then quieted again when it closed behind her. Almost immediately the voices rose in pitch, calling out in approval, and I knew Sam must've come back downstairs. It started to rain, and the wind blew it right under the porch roof, so I had little choice but to hurry inside. I would stay in the kitchen for a bit, I decided, and avoid the crowded living room.

The kitchen bustled with women pulling casseroles from the oven, removing tin foil from dishes, bringing empty bowls back from the dining room to be replaced with full bowls. I didn't see Mrs. Newman among them. The ceiling was high, but the old farmhouse kitchen not especially wide, so a system of friendly jostling now ruled. I got nudged and bumped and kindly ushered aside all the way into the dining room. There I managed to find a corner occupied only by an older man dozing in a chair, so I tucked myself out of the way and nibbled at some of the unusual goodies on my plate. And the pasta salad.

Sam stood in the center of the crowd, enduring a mix of congratulations and teasing with a pale but genuine smile on his face. There was so much talking that you could barely hear the music playing, but the music was loud enough to encourage people to talk louder to be heard over it, so the place was in a practical uproar. From what I could hear, I gathered that many of the guests were from the temple, and a surprising number of them weren't even Jewish. *B'rit Chadashah* was a gathering of various people all wanting to worship Yeshua in the original Hebrew way that started it all. It made me a little less nervous about going there—too late, since I wasn't there anymore, but now I could remember some of the details of the service more comfortably.

Sam passed me on his way to the food table, and he must have seen me there, but he didn't show any sign of it. I wasn't sure how to feel about that. I tried on a few reactions for size. Mad might fit, since he apparently decided to ignore me when all I'd done was make an innocent mistake. But no, indifference felt even better—a nice *whatever* attitude to show I was above it all. I couldn't manage either of those, but when I slipped back into my previous embarrassment, it was worn thin and didn't fit properly anymore. So I settled for the old Irish standby: melancholy. I fed it with a slow sigh.

After the food there were heartfelt speeches from uncles and neighbors and probably the mailman. All the while Sam had to sit in front of the crowd and endure the attention. It felt like he laughed with, was embarrassed by, or at least looked at every person in the room but me. He even made a joke about the old man snoring in the chair next to me. I wondered if Kellie and Ericson would leave after all the talking, and if they would drop me off first. Instead there was more food, about a hundred different dessert delicacies, then an effort by some cousins to play a duet on tuba and violin, the unlikeliest combo ever to attempt Mozart. They did manage to inspire gales of laughter and an older, more skilled fiddler to grab the offending violin and make real music. Hands clapped, voices sang out, and feet stomped. Someone grabbed someone else's hand, they grabbed another person, and a circle formed on the living room floor.

"Come on, Sam," they called from the circle, which revolved one way and then with a stomp reversed and spun the other direction, all while the fiddle played madly.

Kellie was beside Sam, and she laughed and pushed him towards the dancers.

"Not unless you try, too," Sam said.

"I'm right behind you." Kellie pushed him ahead of her. "But where's Ericson?" As they passed my corner, she spotted me and grabbed my wrist. "Come on, no wallflowers."

My protests were ignored. Kellie had Sam by the hand on her left and me on her right when we were pulled into the moving circle. I stumbled along, trying to follow the simple steps. Every time I got the rhythm, the direction would suddenly change and I'd have to try all over again. Kellie was having the same problem beside me. It was ridiculous; I couldn't help laughing with her.

Suddenly Kellie loosened her grip on my hand and said, "I've got to get Ericson into this. Here." She pulled Sam and I towards each other, pressed our hands together and stepped back out of the circle. She was gone, the dance shuffled us along, and there was nothing to do but clasp hands.

My head spun faster than the circle I was trapped in—horribly, wonderfully trapped. I couldn't look at Sam, and I could feel him not looking at me. We shuffled along with the dance. Someone from the opposite side of the circle called out, "Why so red in the face, Samuel?" Teasing laughter and various theories broke out through the circle, and my face felt pretty red, too.

Sam dropped my hand. I missed a beat and faltered, looking at him before I could stop myself. He met my eyes for just a second; his looked almost black, and his mouth was pressed closed with a certain kind of intensity. He wiped his hand on the leg of his pants and then took my hand again.

The tempo picked up, and we were grateful to focus all our attention on not falling on our faces. Finally the song ended and so did the dance, with a great shout and lots of gasping for breath.

My barrette saved me from that awkward moment when you feel like you should say something to the person you were just holding hands with. Unfairly overloaded for hours, it finally popped under the strain, and all my crazy half-curls fell into my face.

"Um, excuse me," I said from behind my hair, and found my way upstairs to the bathroom. It was delightfully cool up there, away from the crowd of dancing bodies. I reluctantly examined myself in the mirror. My face was flushed but not as much as I feared, and my hair been more disastrous than this on days when I had less of an excuse. I dampened it with my hands to 'reactivate' the curl. The marvels of modern hair product.

When I heard other footsteps on the stairs, I quickly applied apricot glimmer lip gloss and vacated the bathroom. The hall was empty when I stepped out, but I heard voices close by. Sam and Jake stood just inside Sam's room.

"Rory, come here a second," Jake called when he saw me. "Nice hair. Stick a fork in the toaster?"

"Did you stick your head under the lawn mower?" I asked sweetly.

"I never reveal my beauty secrets."

I didn't want to seem like I was peeking into Sam's room, but I was peeking into Sam's room. The walls were a surprising shade of orange, and a guitar leaned against the dresser. Jake noticed me looking.

"Don't be all impressed. It's usually a sty. His mom made him clean it."

"And I found this under my bed," Sam added, holding out a CD case. I took it but didn't recognize the name of the singer. She was a small brown-haired woman behind a rather large acoustic guitar. "You can borrow it," he said.

"Oh. Thanks." I tucked it into my handbag because it was something to do.

"You're dismissed," Jake said.

Leaving seemed like a good plan, but I hesitated. I should say something, even if it was just a lame *I'm sorry*. But with Jake leaning there in the doorway between us, it wasn't quite right. So I wandered back downstairs to wait for another chance. There wasn't one. Kellie met me at the bottom of the stairs.

"Hey, kiddo. Ericson and I have a sunrise Easter service in the morning and a ham-and-eggs breakfast to help serve afterwards, so we've got to get home. You about ready?"

Soon we were shaking Dr. Newman's hand and thanking Mrs. Newman—whom, when I thought about it, I hadn't actually seen except on the back porch. We waved our goodbyes to Sam (except for Kellie the hugger) and headed out the door.

When we arrived at my house, I hopped out of the van. Kellie rolled down her window and leaned out. "So," she asked so only I could hear, "everything all right now?"

"All right?" I asked, but I thought I knew what she meant. I considered her sudden exit during the dancing and gave her a look of deep suspicion that would have done Jasmine proud. "I guess. I think so."

"Good. Happy Easter," she said, winking at me with a little half-smile as they pulled out of the driveway. I never forgot that expression.

My mom was working but Sheelan was in her room on the phone when I went inside. I turned on the computer and put Sam's CD in the slot. After sampling a few of the songs, I pulled the lyrics out of the case and puzzled over them. It was Christian. And yet it was cool music. I'd never realized this combination existed. The singer's voice was much bigger than her little person, and her big old acoustic guitar gave as good as it got. I clicked through a few more songs until I hit one that sounded vaguely familiar. When she reached the last line of the chorus, it clicked. *Can I be made whole again?*

It was the song playing on the radio in the Monstermobile right after I'd had my seatbelt freak-out, the song that had broken the uncomfortable silence. Is that why Sam lent this to me? Or was there some other message buried in one of the songs? I brought the disc upstairs so I could stretch out on my bed with my headphones and really listen, reading all the lyrics. I eventually fell asleep doing that, and so I didn't see the email Sam sent until the next day, when it was too late.

It was Easter morning, and the sun was cooperating—shining, at least, if not very warmly. I sat at the computer waiting for my mom and Sheelan to finish getting ready for church. As planned—and despite Sheelan's recent philosophical objections—we were going to the big church, what I had come to think of as the Super Everything Church. Mom liked to leave things until the last minute, so she was rushing to be ready on time as usual. Sheelan started early and took her sweet time. I just threw on a fluttery dress that felt right at Easter but no other time, strapped on sandals, reactivated my curls and applied a little makeup. Ten minutes.

"You look like you only spent ten minutes on yourself," Sheelan said as she breezed past. "Have you seen my white strappy heels?"

I ignored her and clicked on the mail icon, just for something to do. More hair replacement systems, cut-rate prescription drugs, and something with 'I forgot' in the subject line. It was from Sam.

I meant to tell you guys that you're invited to come to temple again tomorrow for our Resurrection Day celebration. It will basically be more singing, dancing and food, so if today just wasn't enough, here's your chance. I'm sure you'll be doing your own church things, but I thought I'd offer just in case. We can pick you up if you need a ride. Oh, and did I mention it starts at sunrise? —SSN

I checked to see who got the email. Just Shayne, Allie, Jake and me. But Shayne and Allie were Front Streeters and were surely going there, and even I knew that Jake was spending Easter with his mom. Sam had probably included me just to be polite. Or he knew I didn't really belong to a church, in which case… he was mostly inviting me. Or I had a hyperactive imagination.

"Come on Rory, get your jacket. We're going to be late." Mom tossed her makeup bag in her purse, which meant she'd be putting her face on at the red lights. I followed, because what else could I do?

The whole time I sat in the Super Everything Church (when I wasn't being dazzled by the choir or amused by the prowling and pouncing preacher), I kept thinking *Yeah, but what about Yeshua?* The very air crackled with the excitement of Easter, but I wasn't sure what we were getting excited about. The preacher talked about the miracle and the mystery of the empty tomb, and how it symbolized different things to different people. He talked about God loving the world so much that he sent his son to save us, but he didn't mention what we needed to be saved from. Thanks to Pastor Dan and my own heavy conscience, I knew the answer to that already.

Even Sheelan clapped a few times with the rest of the audience, though her eyes scanned the crowd more than they watched the preacher. She was checking out the other teenagers around us, I could tell, and ranking herself in terms of overall stylishness and God-given looks. One or two guys returned her glances. She'd be back.

The preacher timed the service perfectly. He came to the climax of his sermon just as the sun shone through the stained glass windows above the audience, and beams of brilliant colored light fell across the stage, a glowing white-golden beam settling precisely on him. Even as he concluded with a 'Hallelujah!" the choir burst into their final hymn and a full brass fanfare finished up the jubilation.

People were almost giddy as they mingled in the sun-drenched lobby eating gourmet doughnuts and drinking designer coffee. My emotions were all stirred up, too, but I was bewildered. I remembered a Russian egg-decorating project we had done last spring in Mrs. Greene's art class. First we made a pinhole in the top and the bottom of the shell and carefully blew out all the raw egg until we were left with an empty shell. Then we started a complicated decorating and dying process with wax and wooden styluses. The result was a beautiful and intricate, but still very empty, shell. That's how this church felt.

I sat on the front steps at home still thinking about it. Mom had skipped the whole Easter basket farce this year and given us both a box of buttercreams from the fancy chocolate shop. We hadn't gotten her anything, but then we never did. It was always Dad who gave her an Easter lily for a centerpiece and a flower to pin to her dress. We hadn't thought to do that for her.

The Fishers' front door opened, allowing the noise of a house full of family to escape. Kingston came out with it, holding a square leather bag. He saw me and sat down on the same step on his side of the handrail. "Happy Resurrection Day," he said.

"Yeah, you too. You carrying a purse?"

"Naw, this is my Bible. See?" He unzipped it and flipped the pages. "What's wrong?" he asked.

I automatically started to say I was fine, then stopped. It was Kingston. He just knew. "We went to that big church in Westhaven."

"Really? Whadja think?"

I shrugged. "Flashy. Lots of people. But it's like being really hungry and biting into a burger that doesn't have any meat."

"Not good." He shook his head. Clearly I was speaking his language. Then he scratched his head. "But maybe there is something good about that."

"Like what?"

"Well, that you're hungry for meat. And you can taste when there isn't any. My mama's always saying, 'Are you babes in Christ, that I have to feed you with milk and not meat?' She means we have to get beyond the Sunday school stuff and into the hard Monday to Saturday stuff."

I half understood what he was saying. "I'm just not sure what to do next."

"What do you mean?"

"You know how Sweetnam Lane just dead-ends, and you have to go either right or left? I feel like I'm at the end of Sweetnam Lane and I have to make a decision. I'm just not sure what I'm deciding."

He was knotting a broken shoelace, the tip of his tongue poking out in concentration. But he was listening. He asked, "What about a decision for Christ?"

A weird tingle shot down my arms into my fingertips. "I'm not sure what you mean."

"Are you saved?"

It came from nowhere, my reaction to his words, strong and bitter like yesterday's coffee. Who was he to ask that? Who could really know that for sure? Wasn't it arrogant to think you had it all figured out, and then go around and ask other people if they were as clever as you?

I turned on him, ready to accuse. Then I saw something in his fudge-brown eyes that was like antacid on my bile. I deflated, hugging my knees. "I know I believe... I guess you would say that I'm a Christian." I sighed. "How do you know if you are saved?" I asked.

He beamed. "That's easy. When in Rome, do as the Romans do."

"Kings…"

"What I'm saying is, get off Sweetnam Lane and get on the Romans Road. Looky here." He unzipped his Bible again and his stubby fingers flipped to the book of Romans. "Pastor made us highlight them. Starting here, chapter three—"

"Don't say 3:16."

"No, 3:10. No one is righteous, no not one. And 3:23, 'All have sinned and fall short of the glory of God.' Do you think you're a sinner, Rory? Lots of people don't. Most of us think we're basically good people."

"Oh, I have no problem admitting that."

"Okay." He flipped a few pages. "Then move ahead two spaces to… chapter five. Here it's saying that sin came into the world through one man, and death came with it, and it spread to everyone."

"Adam."

"Yep. And then in chapter six, the cost of sin is death."

I remembered Pastor Dan mentioning that. Kind of hard to forget. "Yeah, I've heard that one."

"Don't sound so depressed. Here comes the good news. Back in chapter five it says God showed his love for us when Christ died for us while we were still sinners."

I chewed on that. "You sure know a lot, Kings."

"That's 'cause my mama makes me eat the meat." He chuckled, that rolling, choppy laugh that used to drive me nuts but now I found contagious.

"But guess what?" I went on. "I knew all of that, too. I didn't know where it was in the Bible, but I knew it was in there. But just knowing it doesn't… I mean—" I made wild, ineffective gestures. "So what?"

He was unfazed by my mini fit. "Guess you don't know this one." He pointed to a few highlighted lines and passed his Bible over to me. I read:

> *That if thou shalt confess with thy mouth the Lord Jesus, and shalt believe in thine heart that God hath raised him from the dead, thou shalt be saved.*

I frowned at Kingston. "That's it?"

He shrugged. "It's not a secret initiation rite. If you believe it, say it."

"Should I do it in church or something?"

"You can do it in the grocery store. Doesn't matter, just so you do it. Some people say a sinners' prayer, but there's no special formula or anything. Some people know exactly when and where it happened, other folks have just known and believed and talked about it for as long as they can remember. Doesn't matter how it happens—bolt of lightning or quiet and still—just that you believe it."

"How did it happen for you?"

"Well, I'm pretty sure I just told God that I knew I was a wicked boy, and I knew I deserved to suffer the consequences. But I believed that Jesus died to pay for my sins, and they're forgiven. Then he rose from the dead and proved he had the power to do it. I knew I could trust him to be my Savior, and I wanted to follow him and make him my Lord. Then I said thanks for showing me the truth, and amen."

I took a deep breath. We sat there quietly for a minute.

"Kings?"

"Yeah?"

"I just said a prayer."

"Yeah. Your lips were moving."

I took another deep breath. "I meant it, too. I believe it. It's the Truth."

He nodded, then pulled something out of his jacket pocket. "Want a chocolate marshmallow? I've got two."

"Great." I unwrapped one and ate it while a big sticky smile spread over my face. I looked at Kingston, and he wore the same gooey grin.

24

Behind Kings the door opened. "Kingston, Mama needs your help in the kitchen—oh, honey, you've got to stop eating those horrible things." Mrs. Fisher turned to me. "Hello, Rory. A blessed Resurrection Day to you," she sang.

"Thanks. You, too."

"My, don't you have a lovely glow today?"

"Mama," Kings said as he stood. "Rory just asked Jesus to be her Savior."

Her eyes and mouth went circular. "Today? Just now? Praise the Lord!" She dashed down the steps and up again to give me a hug. "The angels are rejoicing in heaven, Sweetie."

Angels… I smiled. Maybe real ones this time. But who was to say God couldn't use even the angels concocted by my sick brain to accomplish something good? They had comforted and taught me, in their own way. I still missed them a little, but I had just taken the hand of the King of Angels. How could that not be way better?

Now it was my mom's turn to open our door. "Well, hello everyone. What's all the excitement?"

Mrs. Fisher beamed, but she left it to me to share the news. "I just asked Jesus to be my Savior," I confessed, though I couldn't quite look her in the face.

Mom's smile didn't falter, it just stiffened like frosting on a wedding cake. "Well, isn't that wonderful? It is Easter, after all, and isn't that what it's all about?" Now she was being polite. "I hate to drag you away, Rory, but Grandma Judy's expecting us for dinner and we're running a little late."

Mrs. Fisher gave me another squeeze and Kingston just kept smiling his marshmallow smile as I said my goodbyes. When I climbed into the car, she asked, "You haven't converted to anything, have you Rory?"

That again? "No, Mom. It's not like that. I've just finally made a decision. For Jesus."

Her head shook, just barely. "But honey, we're already Christians." Then Sheelan got in the car and we let the subject drop. Like a rock. On my soul. But no, I could still tell Grandma Judy. She would get it.

I had to wait a while for the right opportunity. After the ham and sweet potatoes, she took a can of scraps out to the compost pile in the back of her yard and I followed.

"Oh, don't come out here in your nice sandals," she said. "Ground's still soggy from the rain yesterday."

"I had to tell you, Gran." My heart beat fast, and every breath felt like it was filling me up with newness. "I said a prayer today. I asked Jesus to be my Savior."

She smiled at me as she chopped at the compost with her spade. "That's very sweet, Rory. But I led you in the sinner's prayer when you were six. I asked if you understood and if you were ready, and you told me you were. Surely you remember."

Surely I didn't.

Did that mean what happened today didn't really count? I squished my way back up to Gran's house, wondering why I'd thought saying some words would change anything. It obviously hadn't the first time.

But that night I couldn't sleep. I lay staring at the ceiling, the blankets kicked off, my thoughts bouncing here and there, but a steady sensation warming my middle. It felt like hope, and it wasn't going down without a fight.

Tomorrow I would tell the others.

I exited my bed with a decidedly un-Monday-morning-like bounce in my step. I even gave myself some extra time to get ready, picking a shirt and skirt that actually looked ironed, doing my hair with both eyes open. (I'd gotten in the habit of squinting at myself in the mirror through one eye; it was sort of like the fuzzy lens they used on some of the TV anchorwomen to blur their wrinkles. I wasn't blurring wrinkles, just everything else.)

I played and replayed the scenario in my head: me casually mentioning my good news at the lunch table, enjoying their shock and excitement as it sunk in. Or maybe just me blurting it out the second I saw any of them. It didn't matter that they probably already thought I was saved — except for Sam. That would just add to the surprise. I was so busy imagining, I left without taking my little pill. Once or twice I'd forgotten in the morning but taken it as soon as I got home from school, so no big deal. I did remember my umbrella.

Whitestone Elementary looked perfectly normal on the outside. If I'd known what waited inside, I might have just walked right on past.

I picked up on a weirdness right when I went in. Kids weren't all chatting and scurrying to line up outside their classrooms, the usual rainy day procedure. They were moving slowly, stopping to murmur to one another or to glance towards the main office. The office was all windows around the waiting area, so I could see a small group gathered inside. The principal, Mrs. Knowles, was talking to a man in sweats and a slight remnant of bed head. I didn't recognize him from the back, but he had his arm around someone I did know. Shayne leaned against him, and even from down the hall I could tell she was crying. Was she in some sort of trouble?

Then I spotted Allie sitting in an office chair. The secretary brought her a box of tissues and laid a hand on her shoulder.

I could feel the blood drain from my face. I forced my feet to move towards the office, but the hallway stretched in front of me, and it was like walking up the down escalator. Even as I got closer, the word *no* pounded in my brain to the rhythm of my blood. I was almost floating again, like the coma, looking down on life but refusing to join it. Something waited for me, something with claws. I even—just for a second—imagined the sketchy gray shapes, darting around in an ecstasy of hatred. But it was just in my head.

Down the opposite hallway, in the sea of faces, I picked out Jake Dean. I filed the information with all the feeling of a computer. My hand mechanically lifted to the office door handle.

Another hand grasped it at the same time, and just like that my slow-motion bubble burst. I jerked back and found Sam Newman facing me. "What's going on?" he asked.

The sight of him made something snap inside me, and a kind of fury poured over me that also felt like relief. I nearly hit him. "I don't know," I managed to say.

"Why is Mr. Svoboda here?"

"I said I don't know."

He frowned, either at my sharpness or at what waited on the other side of the office door. Then he turned the handle and walked in, holding the door for me. But my feet refused to take any more steps. Sam finally let the door swing shut.

I was already too close. I could hear some of their words. It was like the coma again: English, but not necessarily in the right order.

...on the way to school...called...Ericson...morning...Kellie... ambulance...blood clot...too late.

I tried not to see Sam's backpack slide to the floor or his hands hang at his sides. Jake was beside me, talking, asking questions I didn't hear. Then he went inside. This time I only heard sniffling and low murmurs, but I very clearly heard the curse word Jake chose for the occasion.

I must've crept backwards around the corner without realizing it, because that's where Sam found me, wedged between the drinking fountain and the wall. His face had no color in it. "Did you hear?" he asked. "Are you sick? Is it a seizure?"

I bypassed all that. "She lost the baby, didn't she?"

"Whose baby? What are you talking about?"

"Kellie. Did she lose the baby?"

He stared, then he swore, much quieter than Jake. "She was pregnant? She told you?"

I finally looked at him, straight in the eye. "You said *was* pregnant."

"You can't tell anyone about a baby. I don't think they know." He leaned against the blue-painted cinderblock wall, carefully, like he was bruised all over. "Rory. Kellie died."

The pill I forgot to take that Monday morning I also forgot to take after school, joined by the next pill I forgot to take Tuesday morning. Maybe by then the medication was out of my system.

I thought the emotional flatline the pills caused had worn off after a while, but I guess I'd just gotten used to it. Now without that drug in me, my true feelings slammed down like a flyswatter. The school had immediately responded to the news about Kellie with professional grief counselors and all that, but that was fighting a grease fire with a squirt gun.

I managed to hide the worst of it from my mom. I know she didn't see it, because she let me stay home from school without Gran, and though it's what I wanted, I should've never been left alone. I spent the morning digging through every junk drawer, cluttered shelf, and dusty closet box looking for my dad's Bible. Honestly, I didn't think it was going to help me. I just felt furious that after weeks of searching I couldn't find it.

While I tore through the desk drawers, I came across my notes from Teen Scene. In that moment, my quest changed direction. I began digging out every scrap, every candy-bar-sleeve photocopy, that had ever come from Kellie or been touched by Kellie. I even printed out her emails. It was a pretty scrawny collection. I wanted her words to speak some kind of meaning to me.

If you ever want to "chat" about anything, I'm here.

No, you're not. Just like that poem we read in English class—I couldn't get the last line out of my head. 'Nothing gold can stay.' Dad was gold, Kellie Greene was gold. But there were always sleeping truck drivers, pulmonary embolisms—gold snatchers.

You ask all the right questions! Never be afraid to question and seek answers.

Fine, here's one: How can a person ever learn to trust God? His ways are *so* not my ways. And I don't like them.

… even when you're sincerely trying to live in a God-pleasing way, the enemy will still harass you—in fact, you should expect it, because you're becoming a more effective soldier and drawing attention to yourself.

Is that what happened to you, Kellie? You were on the verge of a whole new life. A baby, a teen ministry thing. Did you stick your neck out too far? Why didn't God protect you?

Just watch out for the voices of doubt that make you feel inadequate, unworthy… Those probably come from the enemy.

Yeah, I've been wanting to talk to you about that. How do you know if it's coming from the enemy or just from yourself? What if it's coming from God? Pastor Dan said God convicts us of our sin.

The thought of conviction jarred a memory. The angel I called Uri (this was how I described my angels now with Dr. McD—'the angel I called Gabby,' 'the angel I called Rafie'…though for some reason I never spoke to her about Uri) had talked about being convicted of sin. What had I been trying to tell myself through Uri? He had always left me feeling unworthy and inadequate. Was it just a way of getting myself to face up to my sinfulness and admit I needed God?

Bloop.

I closed the email window and uncovered the little IM window.

samIam: *you stayed home too*

237

Long pause.

    REJoyce316: *yes*

Another long pause. What was there to say?

    samIam: *I can't think of anything to say*
    REJoyce316: *me neither*
    samIam: *Shayne called*
    REJoyce316: *she okay?*
    samIam: *pretty messed up. She's gone to FST most of her life. Kellie really helped her through it when her mom died*
    REJoyce316: *oh*
    samIam: *she said the funeral is Saturday*

That word made my skull clench like a fist around my brain. I couldn't type anything.

    samIam: *talk about something else?*
    REJoyce316: *please*
    samIam: *something is bothering me*
    REJoyce316: *something else?*
    samIam: *I guess it's not important now*
    REJoyce316: *if it's bothering you*
    samIam: *it's something you said*

Big surprise. Half of the things I said bothered someone at some point.

    REJoyce316: *I'm sorry*
    samIam: *about what?*
    REJoyce316: *what I said at your baptism, about your grandpa*
    samIam: *oh that. No, I should say sorry. I lost it, felt embarrassed, acted like a jerk. long story.*
    REJoyce316: *your mom told me*

There was another long stretch before the next *bloop.*

> **samIam:** *you talked to my mom?*
> **REJoyce316:** *she talked to me*
> **samIam:** *seriously*
> **REJoyce316:** *yes*

I didn't see what the big deal was.

> **samIam:** *she doesn't talk much to strangers*
> **REJoyce316:** *we weren't really strangers. I met her that other time at your house.*
> **samIam:** *she talked to you then? When?*
> **REJoyce316:** *when I went upstairs. She's nice.*

I felt like I was defending Mrs. Newman from her own son. Was he embarrassed of her for some reason?

> **samIam:** *Yeah, she's great. She just has this thing. Likes to be alone, doesn't go out in public much either. She's been that way for a long time.*

It was probably a big yap moment, but I took a chance:

> **REJoyce316:** *because of Benjamin?*

This time I expected to wait a while, or maybe get no response at all.

> **samIam:** *she told you that too?*
> **REJoyce316:** *she saw me looking at the picture in the hall. We don't have to talk about it, with everything else that's going on*
> **samIam:** *but everything else makes you think about it, doesn't it? Like your dad.*
> **REJoyce316:** *yes*
> **samIam:** *except for you it's recent. Ben has been gone a long time.*

I sensed he wanted to talk about it, but IMs can be tricky that way. I chanced it again.

> **REJoyce316:** *how old was he?*
> **samIam:** *we were three*
> **REJoyce316:** *twins*

I waited a while.

> **samIam:** *we had a way of talking that no one else understood. But it's weird, I don't know if I can remember what he looked like. I might just be remembering myself.*
> **REJoyce316:** *confusing*
> **samIam:** *and I remember the feeling of him all of a sudden not being there. Like how you'd feel if every time you walked past a mirror, there was no reflection of you in it*
> **REJoyce316:** *how long did you feel that way?*
> **samIam:** *still do sometimes*

Somehow, talking about losing my dad and Benjamin became a way of dealing with Kellie. I typed for a while, hunting and pecking. Sam waited.

> **REJoyce316:** *I feel like there's this big hole in the middle of my life, like a meteor hit our house and we're supposed to keep going, just sort of walk around this huge smoking crater and ignore it.*
> **samIam:** *you're doing better than I would*
> **REJoyce316:** *yeah, that's why I'm on pills*

(Even that didn't remind me that I'd missed my pills.)

> **samIam:** *pills that banish angels*
> **REJoyce316:** *and demons*
> **samIam:** *do you think so? That they weren't real?*
> **REJoyce316:** *I guess I believe they could've been real. But they did disappear when I took the drugs, so that settles that*
> **samIam:** *maybe*

REJoyce316: *maybe what?*

samIam: *that's what was bothering me*

REJoyce316: *what?*

samIam: *I was thinking about it. These angels told you things, right?*

REJoyce316: *yes*

samIam: *if it was just your brain coping with stuff, then it was kind of like you telling yourself these things.*

REJoyce316: *sounds right*

samIam: *so they couldn't have told you anything you didn't already know*

I read the words but didn't type back. I read them again.

samIam: *did they tell you things you couldn't have known on your own? Stuff that you couldn't just make up?*

I grasped at memories that were already coated with a slick layer of denial. How many Bible verses had Gabby quoted to me? Verses I'd never heard, ones I certainly wouldn't be able to find in the Bible without direction. Or could it be that I had heard them long ago, and somehow they had survived, buried deep down waiting to be dug up by a cracked-pot mind?

samIam: *you there?*

REJoyce316: *I'm thinking about it.*

samIam: *Shayne just showed up*

REJoyce316: *at your house?*

samIam: *yeah. I have to go*

REJoyce316: *okay*

samIam: *shalom*

I barely had the spare brain cells to process the idea of Shayne being there and all the implications. My thoughts had snagged on Sam's question like cashmere on velcro. I sorted through each of the angel visits, trying to pick out anything that couldn't have been a concoction of my own twisted mind. I scrutinized them with a headshrinker's eye. Everything could be reasoned away if you wanted to badly enough.

All the while I was thinking, my hands shuffled through the small stack of papers I had collected, Teen Scene notes and EZBNGreene email. One of them stood out from the bundle because it was creased and wouldn't lay flat. I pulled it out.

> *For though we walk in the flesh, we do not war according to the flesh. For the weapons of our warfare are not carnal but mighty in God for pulling down strongholds, casting down arguments and every high thing that exalts itself against the knowledge of God, bringing every thought into captivity to the obedience of Christ, and being ready to punish all disobedience when your obedience is fulfilled.*
> 2 Corinthians 10:3-6

It wasn't the words themselves that stopped me cold, though as I read them I could almost feel them pass into me like breath, making sense in a way they hadn't before. It was the paper itself that put the sound of my own heartbeat in my ears. I ran my fingers over the many geometrical folds that hadn't quite been smoothed out. Myself, I didn't even know how to make a basic beginner's paper airplane. This one had been folded in a pattern far more intricate than any paper airplane I'd ever seen.

Uri was right. He did know flying.

25

Maybe because of the forgotten pills, my thoughts were razor blades. No more mental mush—I probed surgically through the memory of each angel hallucination. First Rafie. I'd felt him near me right there in the smashed-up car. I shied away from it—that cut went way too deep. Then Rafie at school, Rafie in the hospital... Rafie when I was hurting.

And Gabby. Gabby told me things. Surely I couldn't have known, without knowing I knew, those Bible verses about testing the spirits, or the fact that Jesus was called the Word in the book of John. Or any of the other things she told me to get my head in the right place. She pointed things out, right from the Book, reading with her fingertip.

Then Uri. Uri messed with my head, for sure, but it was my heart that went like jello when he came around, and not in a fun wiggly-jiggly way. Easily shaken, easily sliced. I poked around in those memories, the most recent. Uri had kept coming after the others took a leave of absence. But even he stopped appearing when I started taking the pills.

Now I was struck by one of the very first things he'd said to me, that I might be getting bad information at Teen Scene. Why hadn't that bothered me more? I suppose back then I hardly understood what Pastor Dan was talking about anyway. Uri had never indicated which exactly had been the bad teaching. Not like Gabby—she would've shown me right where it contradicted the Bible.

Uri had told me that being a Christian wasn't meant to be easy, which I could've told him. But he hadn't been warning me about a tough life on this side of heaven. More like an impossible list of demands that a Christian must live up to. That couldn't be right. Kellie had said grace is a gift, not what you earn by being good enough. So who was the source of the 'unsound teaching'?

I knew next to nothing about the Bible, but I had learned that if I wanted truth, I should go there. Gabby had said so. Even Uri had said so: *All of the answers are in there if you know how to find them. But...* there had been a 'but' *...if you want answers fast, I'm your man.*

I'd assumed his answers were still coming from the Bible.

"Hold on just a minute," I told myself, hands spread like a traffic cop to slow down the thoughts. If I had created Uri in my head, then his thoughts came from me. Didn't he even say...? Yep, he said he'd be around when things got confusing. In other words, when I was confused, I conjured up Uri. He was just a face of my mental illness. I had handsome mental illness.

I felt a little more solid now that I'd worked that out. Just to settle it, I sorted through the other things 'Uri' had told me, certain I could trace it all back to my own warped mind.

You do realize that the armor is symbolic?

Whoa, wait. Not according to Kellie.

It's not a bad rule of thumb to consider everything in the Bible potentially as a symbol—especially those things that seem impossible, or just plain unlikely, in the real world.

Like, say, a resurrection? The preacher's words from the Super Everything Church rang in my ears. 'The empty tomb symbolizes different things to different people...'

None of this made any sense. Unless, said a soothing voice in my head, this is, like you say, all a product of your damaged mind. Then the not making sense makes perfect sense.

No, I answered back. The Truth is truth. The empty tomb doesn't symbolize anything. Even I can see that. The tomb is empty because death couldn't keep Life buried under a rock. The Bible shows me the way to live, but I don't have to check off all the items on a 'Christian To-Do List' to get saved. Jesus catches the fish and *then* he cleans them. He caught me. He's the only one who can sort out my mental mess and make things clear again. He'll give me my helmet.

These words were so calm and clear in my mind, I knew they had to be given to me. But not a brain wash. I knew Truth when I heard it. I claimed every word of it. I grabbed tight.

Then I heard Uri again. *I told you I'd be around when things got confusing.*

Around to help? Or around because he was the one making things confusing? I fingered the creased sheet of paper that had once been an airplane. "Stupid, Rory," I muttered. "You're holding the proof in your hands." Sam was right. How could I be so thick? I had almost convinced myself that I'd imagined it all, and that some stupid little pill had fixed me.

And that's how I finally remembered I hadn't taken my pill that day. I tried to picture myself taking it Monday, but I couldn't. Because I hadn't. My heart sank like a sack of rocks. Two days without pills, and now I was ready to believe in the angels again. How could I be so...

No. Truth was truth.

Maybe I didn't need those stinking pills. But the thought of what might happen without them scared me. Stopping all at once—who knew what effect that could have? I'd better take one. I was in my room, and the pills were down in the kitchen where Mom could be reminded to remind me. A system with obvious flaws.

Evening had come without notifying me. Sheelan had never come home from school; Mom had never come home from work. My stomach growled—I had never eaten dinner. It wasn't late, but it was already dark. My bedroom light was the only light on in the house. It reminded me too much of that evening of the creaky floorboards and my freak out.

I flicked on the hall switch to light my way down to the kitchen. I was already two steps down when my brain registered that there had been something in my peripheral vision, like a person standing at the end of the upstairs hall by my mom's bedroom door. *Stop it, Rory.* But I flew down the stairs and slapped on the kitchen light. And the dining room and family room lights.

No one was upstairs. I was alone.

You're alone.

Not exactly a reassuring mantra. Again I thought of the two missed pills. And a new thought: if the pills 'banished' the angels, now they might return. And if the angels were real and had nothing to do with the pills, there was nothing stopping them from returning, anytime. Suddenly, I desperately hoped Uri would not come to me. The intensity of the feeling shocked me. There was fear in it.

Why? If he had come from God, why did God send him? To test me?

My own words bit me. To test me... No. I was supposed to test him. And I had. That's how I knew he came from God (if he hadn't come from my head).

Sure I had tested him. I sorted through the memories, so clear now. Hadn't I?

Not actually...no.

Don't worry, Rory. I'll be around to help you make sense of things. You could say that when things are gray, I help make them black and white.

He'd already warned me. Black and white, white and black. Good guys, bad guys. Only he wasn't wearing the white hat.

The truth of it passed over me, through me, like a stench. I was physically sick. I barely made it to the sink in time. I fumbled with the faucet, rinsed out my mouth with one hand and groped for my bottle of pills with the other. At this point, I didn't really believe the pills would keep Uri away—I only knew I would try anything. I wrenched at the childproof cap. It wouldn't budge. It didn't matter. There was no delicate rattle from inside the bottle. It was empty. It had been half full three days ago. I dropped it.

Tap tap tap. Something tapped, scratched on the window over the sink. If I lifted my eyes, I would see it. I squeezed them shut and turned away. I could tell myself it was a tree branch.

A familiar rumble—the garage door opening. Heaving a shaky sigh, I dashed down to the back door to see who was home. Mom or Sheelan or both, it was all good. I yanked the door open.

No car in the garage. No headlights coming up the driveway. The automatic light was on, but even while I stared out, bewildered, it blinked off. I slammed the door shut.

Gran's Bible. I would read that Psalm Gabby had shown me. Which one? I would find it, even if I had to read them all. Where was the Bible? By the computer—no. Not there. Upstairs in my room.

I never made it to the stairs. The floorboards right overhead let out their unmistakable creak. Not just once: very distinctly I heard footsteps move from one end of my room to the other.

I dove onto the phone. It shook in my hand, and my finger only hovered over the keypad while my mind blanked. Finally I pressed the topmost button, the first super-speed-dial button. The phone rattled off a flurry of beeps, and I urged the rings to come faster by force of will. One ring. Two. Three. Four rings.

Grandma Judy's voice said, "Hello?"

"Gran, it's Rory. Something bad is hap—"

"—So sorry I missed your call. Could you leave a message? You know, after the beep. I'll get right back to you."

I nearly dropped the phone. I hated that answering machine, sounding like the real, live Grandma.

Beep.

"Grandma, please. Something's happening. I'm home alone— I think—I'm scared because there might be something here with me.. I don't know what's real anymore. Are you there? It's something bad—"

"Rory? Rory, I'm here."

"Gran!"

"What's going on, honey? Who's there with you?"

"I'm not sure. I think I messed up, Grandma. I meant to test the spirits, but I didn't get the words right, or he tricked me—"

"Who?" Her voice changed instantly from granny to gunny sergeant.

"I thought he was an angel, but now I'm afraid. I think he's one of the others, and I'm afraid he's coming back and I'm here alone—"

"Rory, I'm coming over. Can you go to the Fishers?"

"They're not home."

"Where's your mom?"

"I don't know."

"I'll try to reach her. I'm leaving right now, sweetheart. Keep the phone in your hand. If anything happens, call 9-1-1. Do you understand? I'm coming over right now."

"Hurry, Gran."

"I'll call you right back from my car."

I know how I sounded: crazy. I didn't care. I'd rather be safe with someone who thought I was crazy than alone. But Gran was twenty minutes away. I backed myself into the recliner and watched the clock over the TV. The ticking became obnoxiously loud. It occurred to me that the clock had never ticked before. It didn't have a second hand.

Turn on the TV. Drown out the bad sounds. But the remote was nowhere to be seen, and I couldn't move from the chair. The computer's screen saver swirled hypnotically in the corner of my eye, a silent random comet of ever-changing color. Other movements tormented the edges of my vision, and I refused to turn towards them but was afraid to shut my eyes.

I would run outside. It was damp and cold; I'd have no coat on, but I'd be out. Away. In the dark. My mind turned to things cold and dark, of things that could happen to me in the dark. It turned to black and twisted things that I never imagined I could imagine. I fell into a mental open grave, and the walls were slimy-slick, and I just slipped back down when I tried to climb out. In time, it almost seemed easier to just stay down.

Then, a voice—very distant, half-chanting, half-singing in a language I didn't know but recognized. Rolling, musical, sharp and soft. And whether it was another voice translating or I just somehow began to understand, I don't know.

The Lord is my light and my salvation.
Whom shall I fear?

Light. I yearned for it, out here in the dark and filth.

Salvation. Such a pretty word. I wondered what it meant. A child's song skipped through my head. *The helmet of salvation… and the sword of the Spirit, which is the word of God…*

A helmet. That's what I needed. A helmet to keep this muck out of my brain. A helmet of salvation. Hey, I should have one of those already. Hadn't I asked Jesus to be my Savior?

Just the thought of that name was a bolt of light; it seared across the blackness, a hundred thousand times brighter than the feeble little light dancing on the computer screen.

"The Lord is my light and my salvation. Whom shall I fear?" I asked out loud.

Just like that, I was back in the recliner. I'd never left it. My eyes flew to the clock. Only one minute had passed. My eyes slid down slowly and met the eyes of someone leaning against the TV cabinet.

"You shall fear me, for starters," Uri said.

And I did. But it wasn't a fear that froze me—my fingers flew to the keypad of the phone still in my hand. If anything happens, call 9-1-1.

"I wouldn't do that," he said, and this time my fingers did freeze. "Think about it." He stopped, laughed a quiet, acid laugh. "Ah, thinking. Not your strong suit, Rory Erin Joyce." My name coming from his mouth was like needles in my ears.

"But honestly, let's think about it. Either I'm real, and any fools you summon to your aid will be a puny obstacle for me to eliminate…" and he spat the last word, bombarding me with dozens of images of my rescuers' violent disposal. "…or I'm merely a creation of your mind, in which case no one can help you." He smiled. Still drop-dead gorgeous, but there was far more of the dead than the gorgeous about him. "I think we both know which is the case."

No one can help you. The words sounded so true, I could weep at the beauty of their trueness. And there was a nobility to it: me, on my own, tragic and solitary, beyond help.

However, my mouth seemed to disagree. "That's a lie," it said, in the big yap moment to beat all big yap moments. Uri took a step towards me, all casual grace, but behind it was a barely-restrained fury.

"Lie, truth… Meaningless words. Surely you've seen it. There is no truth. So it follows that there can be no lies. All shades of gray." When he said it, my eyes opened to the gray shapes darting and slouching and slithering around him, just for a split second. A sickening split second.

"You said when things were gray, you would make them black and white," I said. He took another step forward.

"So I did. I say many things, Rory. Whatever you want to hear, whatever you need to hear. It is pleasant, no?" He blinked, and his blue eyes were gone, replaced by blackness — empty, gaping blackness.

I couldn't even scream; it was strangled in my throat. "No," I choked.

"Yes. Get used to it. I will always be somewhere close — in your house, in your head — until the day I finally get to take you home with me."

"No! You can't."

"What, don't you want to see your daddy again?"

I covered my ears. "Liar! You say whatever you want, just to hurt. But you can't touch me. I belong to Jesus. I'm one of God's children now."

He bared his teeth, still perfect but now needle-sharp. "Do not presume to tell me what I can and cannot do. This god you claim to serve — you will be surprised how much he allows." He rubbed his hands together. On the last stroke, he slipped something out of his sleeve. It looked to be made of stone, but it was long and slim and pointed. It was a knife.

Tears scalded my cheeks. His power or my own fear pressed me down into that chair. I couldn't move. A horrible weight crushed me.

"The question is," he drawled, fingering the tip of the knife, "fast or slow?" Then he smiled. "Just kidding. I always choose slow."

As stupid as it sounds, in all of this, it never once occurred to me to pray. I was paralyzed, mind and body. Good thing it wasn't only up to me. My memories, so sharp all day, shoved against the frozenness until one broke through.

"The Lord says, *I will rescue those who love me,*" I managed to croak.

"No, he won't."

"*I will protect those who trust in my name.*"

"Shut up," Uri spat, pointing the knife at my face. The stone was pitted like pumice, the holes dark with ancient stain. I trembled inside, but my lips kept moving.

"*When they call on me, I will answer; I will be with them in trouble—*"

"No! You have no *rhema*!" the demon spat, raising the blade over his head. His preferred 'slow way' was forgotten. I knew he would stop my words—no, God's own words from the Psalm, just coming out of my mouth—any way he could. Maybe then I could have moved, I don't know. I didn't feel squashed anymore. But a numb part of me still insisted that Uri wasn't real, and that a delusional demon with an imaginary dagger couldn't hurt me. I watched Uri's hand plunge down.

A dull clang throbbed in the air over my head. Where he hadn't been an instant before, Micah now stood, deflecting the dagger with what looked like a metal TV tray. It only looked like that for a second. Then I saw something entirely different, with the same smudgy, light-and-dark vision of my seizures. There was Micah—black-haired, lightning-eyed Micah whom I'd practically forgotten—with a light around him almost too bright to bear. And in his hands a gleaming sword locked against another blade, a black and oily blade in the hands of a creature I prayed I would someday forget. I would never describe him even if I could.

The two creatures were like statues, their swords crossed directly over my head. It was a moment without time. Then with a surge and a cry, the being of light flung the beast backwards, but the creature's claws lashed out and sunk deep into the angel. They tumbled back, entangled. It was an awful kind of double-exposure: I saw Micah and Uri wrestling in my family room, but also there was purity grappling with filth in a flurry of wings and scaly coils.

Hands suddenly grabbed me and dragged me out of the chair. I was face to face with Gabby. She looked like she had been in a slobberknocker. "Come away from here," she said, dragging me up to the kitchen.

"Where have you been?" I cried.

"Trying to get to you. For a while. He's been fighting us off." I didn't have to ask who. "Give thanks to God that someone was praying for you just now—He answered. We were able to push through. Come outside. We must stay out of the way."

"Micah..."

"This is his battle, to help you cast down every high thing that exalts itself against the knowledge of God. He is finally free to fight it."

I let Gabby push me out the front door; chill evening air spilled into my lungs. Micah was my protector? "Just because somebody was praying for me?" *Grandma.*

"Yes! And because you wear the belt of Truth. Rory, when you were a child, we were near because the Shepherd loves his littlest lambs. But you came of an age when you were old enough to understand and declare your allegiance to the King."

"I did."

"I know." She smiled, and I could see how swollen her lip was. "Uri made a grave mistake. He kept us from reaching you, but he stayed away, too—all to convince you we were not real, so you would choose worldly wisdom over godly wisdom. But he held off too long. And all praise to the Holy One—the Spirit chose that time to open your eyes and turn your heart! Here on these very steps."

"Kingston showed me the Romans Road..."

"And so we became more than the protectors of a child—we became the ministers to a believer."

I never had a chance to respond. Headlights swung around the curve of Sweetnam Lane, and a car tore up the driveway. Before the light could fall on Gabby, she was gone, and because I had been leaning on her, I lost my balance and fell on the steps, smacking my head against the iron handrail. The world went black. But in the fractured moment before it did, I could swear I landed with my head in Rafie's lap.

26

Kellie's funeral was the strangest I'd ever experienced. It was actually was only the second, and I barely recalled the first. I remembered itchy clothes, murmuring people, and a stuffy funeral parlor with dreary organ music.

Kellie's family held her memorial service at the Front Street Temple. Uplifting music played in the background while people gathered around a table full of albums and framed photos. We sat to sing some hymns projected onto a screen—Kellie's favorites, songs filled with hope and praise. Even the speakers laughed as much as they cried, but since laughter can bring out tears, there were more of those than at the other funeral. The sadness was for those left behind to miss her. Kellie was casting her crown at the feet of her Savior. It struck me that he was my Savior, too. I'd see Kellie again.

Shayne sat with her dad and Jeph, Allie and Mary Katherine beside them. Sam sat across the aisle with Dr. Newman; I didn't see his mother. Jake was with a man I assumed was his dad.

My mom had brought me. She watched and listened in silence, reliving my dad's funeral—the one I had missed. She came because of him, not because she was babysitting me. Surprisingly, she'd been a lot less watchful since my Tuesday night incident.

Thanks to Gran Judy. It had all hinged on her whether I'd be institutionalized—or at least whether I'd be under house arrest. But Gran had swept onto the scene, revived me on the front steps, and brought me inside for chicken noodle soup and interrogation on the sofa. The house was peaceful. The soup tasted like the first thing I'd ever eaten. The bump on my head throbbed but in Gran's opinion didn't require medical attention, just a bag of frozen peas.

I told her everything. As much as I could put into words. I included the fact that I'd missed two pills, so she could draw her own conclusions. She didn't say anything, even when she picked up the TV tray off the floor and discovered a gaping puncture through the center of it. But she did give me a certain look.

"I tried calling you on my way over," she told me later. "But I couldn't get a signal. I can always get a signal between there and here." She shook her head. "So instead I just prayed. Prayed for you the whole way here."

"Yeah, I know," I told her. "It worked, too."

For whatever reason, Gran decided not to tell my mom. When Mom and Sheelan waltzed in after a healing evening of spontaneous mother-daughter sale shopping, Grandma played it off as if I'd slipped and bumped my head and she'd come over just to make sure I was all right. She did it without lying, an ingenious approach I decided to someday master. She even backed me up when I suggested to my mom that, since I'd missed two pills and was fine, why not see how a third day went?

I suspect the idea of me being off those things was as appealing to my mom as it was to me. She compromised by getting Dr. McD's schedule for weaning off the medication, with the condition that I'd be back on them the minute I even thought about a seizure or vision. I wasn't worried about it. There was this sense of calm inside me, a feeling that God was taking care of it.

So at Kellie's memorial, my emotions were all present and accounted for, no drugged dullness to make it less real. The crowd that filled the church gymnasium gradually thinned out, with sighs and hugs and tears, and still some smiles. A core group, including Pastor Dan, prepared to drive to the cemetery behind the hearse. Mom and I never said anything. We just climbed into the car and joined the slow procession down Front Street.

A canopy hung over the gravesite, and it flapped in the unpredictable April breeze. Pastor spoke words that reminded me of what he had taught us once in the Scene. I heard his voice in my memory clearer than the real pastor before me: "So instead of Hell, you are ushered into the presence of your heavenly Father, and instead of death, you will enjoy a glorified body that no hurt or decay can touch. The assurance of this can give us a hope and a joy that are as powerful in the battle as any weapon."

Flowers nodded and swayed all around us, so many white lilies that the fragrance almost made me dizzy. Always to me that would be the smell of hope, not of death. The last flowers were those that Ericson placed on top of the casket. He stepped forward, and my legs went shaky when I looked at him, in his gray suit with his gray face. On the casket he placed a bouquet of red roses in a cloud of baby's breath—seven roses, one for each year of their marriage. Tucked in with them, almost too small to see, was a white rosebud. I saw Sam looking at it, too. We were careful not to look at each other.

This life can be so hard.

The church had organized some sort of luncheon after, but Mom had to go home to get ready for work. People left quietly, one by one. I heard Shayne crying again and saw her lean her head on Sam's shoulder. He patted her a little awkwardly and seemed relieved when Mr. Svoboda gently led her away. Then Sam looked at me with a little frown. He pointed to his forehead.

I nodded. He saw my bruise. *It's okay*, I mouthed. He nodded then followed his father to their car.

Mom watched me.

"Which way?" I asked quietly.

She took my hand, and to prove that it was not a normal moment, it didn't feel weird walking along holding my mom's hand. Unless this was part of the new normal.

Dad's grave was in a different corner of the cemetery, not under the spreading branches of a tree as I had sometimes imagined it, but just one stone slab in a long row of stone slabs. It jolted me to see beside *Jonathan James Joyce* the name *Margaret Anne Joyce* carved into the granite. Beside my mom's birth date was an empty space. It made my stomach quiver—who wanted to have their name on a gravestone before they were even dead? But as I thought about it, I softened inside. Maybe it was a way of remembering that they didn't have to be apart forever.

Mom's arm circled around my shoulders, and then I could cry. She cried with me. A thing that had been waiting for months to happen finally did, and without a word spoken, we left the cemetery as slightly different people.

Things began to fall into place after that—not wrapped up neatly like a TV show, but neat enough to make me think the new normal might be acceptable after all. I agreed to continue my McSessions with Dr. McD for a while longer, and she reluctantly agreed to let me stay off the pills once I had weaned off them—on a trial basis, of course. Because life is more or less a trial basis.

She never came right out and said that the end of my seizures and visions was related to Kellie's death, my visit to Dad's grave, and all that, but I'm pretty sure she was writing that in her little notepad. She didn't believe it had anything to do with me hitting my head again, though that's what Sheelan seemed to think. And she never even considered the possibility that there might have been real angels and demons, because that wasn't anywhere in any of those big fandangled books on her office shelf. I thought she was one Book short of a complete library.

I toyed with the idea of showing Dr. McD the thing I had found a few days after witnessing the battle of light and darkness in my own living room. It had hidden quietly under the sofa until a breeze nudged it out: a feather, pure white, that fit perfectly in the curve of my palm. But I doubted a feather, no matter how exquisitely formed, would make any of it real to her.

Honestly, after enough weeks passed, it all seemed a little unreal to me, too. Ordinary events absorbed my attention (a refreshing change). I struggled to catch up in my classes and eventually did, though algebra and I only struck an uncertain peace. Then came the day of the eighth-grade trip—not an educational field trip, but a day of frolicking at the nearest amusement park. The rest of us watched as they clambered into the buses, dressed in shorts and tank tops and sunglasses, ready for water rides and hot dogs and roller coasters. We squirmed in our skirts and shirts and ties with more than the usual distaste that day.

But it got worse. Eating lunch with just Jake, Jasmine, and some other seventh graders actually turned out to be okay— Jasmine handled Jake with a certain sarcastic skill that I had to admire. But the absence of Shayne, Allie and Sam only shone a harsh spotlight on a fact I'd been trying to avoid: They were weeks away from graduating. Then off to Whitestone High they'd go, where sure, they'd be dethroned, no longer the reigning monarchs of the school but demoted to jesters, drudges, scapegoats, and laughingstocks—but they'd face a whole new life adventure together.

Never before had it really bothered me that I'd repeated first grade. Now I gnashed my teeth over the cruel twist of fate that left me abandoned in junior high one more year. Oh, right…I still had Jake. (My teeth were destined to be worn down to stubs.)

It all hung over me like a cloud. I'll admit, I could not be described as pleasant some days. Mom would just sigh and toss her hands in the air when I grumped at home, but I almost detected a smile hiding under that exasperation. She welcomed ordinary teen angst.

Sheelan's angst had reached record levels. She complained mostly over her continued lack of a cell phone and a decent spring wardrobe. I think she was a little put off by the fact that our Teen Scene meetings had stopped abruptly (no one had the heart to resume yet), and she no longer had an opportunity to actively ignore Jeph. If anyone was doing the ignoring, it was Jeph—he'd never called, like he suggested he might. Front Street Temple was still coping with the loss of Kellie, and I knew Jeph's silence probably had something to do with this, but Sheelan didn't see it that way.

Seeing things Sheelan's way was a gift I'd never asked for, like underwear on Christmas, but it kept creeping up on me in unguarded moments (also kind of like underwear). When she freaked out about me using any of her precious products, I realized that she was actually worried about money — she had no job, she had no boyfriend with a job, and Mom had to work two jobs to get us by. When she ignored my very existence, it was because she didn't know what to say to me. This was partly because of everything that had happened to me recently, but it was more than that. I just wasn't predictable like I used to be.

For a long time I thought that if I just came up with the perfect sass-back, the cut-to-the-bone response of all time, she'd shut her mouth and stop nagging, criticizing, mocking. Turns out that NO response worked the best. Or the completely unexpected *nice* reply. That would shut her right up. Only thing was, shutting her up didn't satisfy like I thought it would. I started to feel sorry for her. I know, weird.

Like the day she ambushed me in the bathroom. "I knew you were using my curling crème," she wrongly accused.

I swallowed my instinctive urge to gloat. A lot like swallowing a golf ball. "Look," I said, showing her the bottle. "I found this kind that works almost as well." It worked just as well, but I couldn't risk calling her shopping savvy into question. "Costs half as much. Here, smell it. Pretty nice."

She sniffed it suspiciously. "It's okay, I guess. Probably wouldn't work for my hair."

"Well, try it if you want."

Her eyes did the little *whatever* roll, but she couldn't find any reason for a smart comment. She turned back to her bedroom.

"Sheelan?"

"What?"

"There's something I've been meaning to tell you. I just wasn't sure how."

She stopped in her doorway, leaned against the frame, didn't quite look at me. "Well?"

"You know, going to that 4:30 show…" Sheelan got very still, very stiff. "Well, it was my idea, too. I asked Dad to take us to that one." She said nothing. "I thought you should know."

When she came out of her room a while later, her eye makeup freshly applied but not quite disguising a certain puffiness, she found me back in the bathroom, trying again to tame my cloud of hair. She barged in, grabbed a spray bottle, and without a word started spritzing me. "You have to start damp," she bossed. Then she grabbed my hair crème and squirted some in her hand. "And work this in from the back, where it's fuzziest." She showed me, rather vigorously but with good intentions. "Where are you going, anyway?"

"The graduation ceremony."

"Not wearing that."

Before I knew it, I'd been made over in Sheelan's image. Well, she'd chosen clothes from my closet, just put together in a way I'd never thought of before. And my hair looked almost like hers, only the strawberry and not the blond. She informed me that I desperately needed some new shoes and practically shoved me out the front door before I offended us both by thanking her.

I didn't walk particularly fast. When I arrived at Whitestone Elementary, the graduates had already begun filing into their rows of folding chairs in the gymnasium, their blue caps and gowns blending together in one restless mass. I found a place in the bleachers just as the Ns plodded in, so I got to see Sam, then Allie and finally Shayne walk the aisle to the graduation song. Soon Jake was beside me.

"Does that song have a name?" I asked him.

"Sure. 'Hail to the Chief.'"

"It is not."

"Pom-pom Circle Dance, something like that," he said with a shrug.

I laughed, I couldn't help it. "'Pomp and Circumstance,'" I corrected, remembering. "A pom-pom circle dance would've been more interesting."

Certainly more interesting than the speeches that followed. Jake told me that the valedictorian had edged Allie out by only a hundredth of a grade point. That explained Allie's stony expression during his address. Then the superintendent called the kids one by one to receive their diplomas. Jake hooted and hollered for each of our friends, but I didn't have the heart. With each diploma—Sam's, Allie's, Shayne's—I heard a door slam on the life I had come to know.

Afterwards, we stood around waiting for the photo hounds to finish snapping, then we all gravitated together. Shayne had already misplaced her mortarboard hat-thingy; Allie's was still bobby-pinned securely to her gleaming hair, and Sam's sat slightly askew on his head, matching his slightly askew tie. He fought his way out of the blue robe.

"Man, it's hot in here," he said.

"What're you guys doing now?" Jake asked. "Aren't any of you having a graduation party? No one invited me."

"My mom and dad said the *t'vilah* party counted for graduation, too," said Sam. "Which is fine by me."

"We were planning one at Shayne's house," Allie said. "But we just didn't feel like it anymore, you know?"

We all nodded. Jake heaved a world-weary sigh. "When *I* graduate next year, I'm going to have a huge party. A caterer, a DJ—"

"A bouncy castle?" I put in.

"—and a bonfire. Yes, a huge bonfire to burn all my school ties. Then here I come, Whitestone High, wearing whatever I want."

"That reminds me." Sam loosened his tie and slipped it over his head, putting it on Jake. "This is yours now. I dub thee Jacob Leslie Dean, eighth grader."

Jake pulled on it with bulging eyes like it was a noose.

I desperately wanted to say something without sounding desperate. "So, guys. Do they allow you to hang out with lowly junior-highers once you're in high school? You know you have to learn all the secrets and then pass them down to us when we're pitiful freshman." No luck. It sounded desperate. That year between their entry into the big time and ours was impossibly long.

"Oh, sure," Shayne said. "We'll help you out, except for the sacred Whitestone High initiation rituals. Those you'll have to figure out on your own. Right, Sam?"

"Well…" His eyes drifted off to the side.

"What? Something you're not telling us, Sammy?"

"I wasn't sure how to tell you."

Boy, did that sound familiar.

"What?" Jake demanded. "You mean there's something you haven't told even me? Let me guess—that really is a perm."

Sam cleared his throat. "I didn't know for sure until a couple of weeks ago. I'm not going to Whitestone High."

"What?" asked several voices at once.

"You're kidding."

"Why not?"

"You mean you're going to Holy Angels Catholic? So's Mary Katherine."

He pretended to use his graduation cap like a shield to fend off our questions. "No, not Holy Angels. It's something my parents have been talking about for a while, and they finally decided it was time."

"They're trading you in for a newer model?" Jake asked.

"I'm going to do school at home."

"What?" three voices asked, but mine said, "Oh."

"Homeschooling?" Shayne asked.

"I didn't know your parents were hippies," Allie said with a grin.

"You have got to be kidding," Jake said. I could tell right then that for Sam, Jake was the hardest to tell. No wonder.

"There were a few families at FST that homeschooled," Shayne said. Then she scrunched up her pimple-free forehead. "But I think they stopped when the kids reached high school."

"Can you really do high school work at home?" Allie asked. "Don't your parents need to be high school teachers?"

"Well, duh, his dad's a college professor," Jake said. "Though clearly he's nuts."

I saw the deep color brewing in Sam's cheeks, so I scrambled to think of something to say. "Our neighbors homeschool. They're really nice, and the kids are pretty smart for their age. The boy who's my age... actually, he showed me the Romans Road. That's when I asked Jesus to be my Savior."

"Seriously?" Shayne asked. "When exactly was that?"

"This Easter."

They gaped at me, except for Sam. A slow smile grew on his face.

"You're kidding."

"You mean..."

"Rory, that's...Wow! Really?"

Sam nodded. "I knew there was something different."

"Why didn't you—" Allie stopped and thought about it. "Oh, man. You probably couldn't wait to tell us, then everything happened that Monday..."

I didn't have a chance to respond. A hand settled on my shoulder, and we all looked up at the man in the gray shirt behind me. It was Ericson Greene.

"Do you guys have a minute?" he asked. He was grasping a crinkled paper bag in one hand. "I need to show you something."

27

E ricson stepped outside the gymnasium to an empty alcove of the tan brick building. We followed in silence, not knowing what to say. When he stopped, he looked at each of us, and not one of us could look back for long.

"Congratulations, you guys," he said to the grads, and then to Jake and I, "and hang in there, you two. This fall you'll be at the top of the totem pole." While we thanked him, he folded and unfolded the top of the paper bag.

"I was going through some of Kellie's things, and I found this. I'm sure she would've made a prettier presentation of it, but here." He thrust the bag into Shayne's hands. "There's something for each of you."

Again we managed to mumble our thanks, but let's face it, most adults would be at a loss for what to say in that situation. We were a bunch of fourteen-year-olds (and a thirteen). Ericson seemed to understand it well. He was even able to smile as he said goodbye, and that's when I saw it, that extraordinary thing again. At the Greene's house I'd seen it, and I thought that mysterious something in his smile was because of his love for Kellie. And maybe that was part of it. But Kellie was gone, and that something still lingered in his smile. It ran deeper than I'd thought.

We watched him walk to his car in the parking lot and drive away.

"We should've asked him about the new teen group thing," Jake said.

"No," Allie said. "Too soon. That was his and Kellie's baby."

She meant it in the sense of 'pet project,' but Sam and I couldn't help but flinch at her choice of words.

"So…?" Shayne gestured to the bag in her hand.

"Not here," said Sam.

"Under the tree," I said. Everyone nodded.

The magnolia tree at the near end of the soccer field had a month ago rippled with fat white-and-pink blossoms, just as it must have looked when Kellie painted the mural in the hall. Those blooms were long gone now, but its leafy branches sheltered a pair of park benches. We sat down, boys on one side, girls facing them on the other; Shayne opened the bag. She peered in with a puzzled look, then pulled out a folded piece of paper.

"It says 'Allie.'" Shayne handed it over. "Careful, there's something inside."

Allie held onto it while Shayne pulled out a folded paper for each of us. When I took mine, it was surprisingly heavy, and I heard a scratchy, slithery sound from inside. In silent agreement, we opened them at the same time.

We all held a printed letter. Tucked inside the folds, a silver chain puddled around the white stone attached to it. I rubbed the oval stone between my thumb and finger. It was smooth and dull like a river rock, but the back side had been polished flat, revealing a swirl of pale colors, creams and whites. There was something engraved on the flat side. A small silver tag hung behind the stone.

Allie spoke. "The letter's to all of us."

We stopped our inspection of the stones to read.

Dear Ones,

In my years of teaching, I have enjoyed many wonderful students, but you have found a place in my heart reserved for only a special few. Thank you for brightening my days!

When I saw these stones, I just had to get them. I know, you're thinking, "Oh, a white stone, I get it. How clever...Not!" But do you know the Bible talks about a very special white stone? Read Revelation 2:17.

Pretty neat, huh? Well, I first meant this as a graduation gift, but each of you has been on my heart, and I've been praying for all of you. As I've prayed and gotten into the Word, I've struck upon (or maybe "gotten stuck" on) a certain verse for each of you. Though it is our Heavenly Father who gives you your true new name, I hope these will inspire you on this leg of the journey Home.

With love in Christ Jesus,
Kellie Greene

We all looked at each other. Jake said, "I don't suppose anyone has a Bible with them."

Allie—of course Allie, God bless Allie—dragged up her big handbag. She would be just like Grandma Judy in fifty years' time. "Just the New Testament," she said. She pulled out the small white Bible and flipped to Revelation 2:17.

"'He who has an ear, let him hear what the Spirit says to the churches. To him who overcomes I will give some of the hidden manna to eat. And I will give him a white stone, and on the stone a new name written which no one knows except him who receives it.'" Allie let the pages of her Bible slide closed and examined the polished back side of her white stone. We all did the same. The engraving was subtle but readable.

"I got yours by mistake," Jake said to Sam, showing him.

"I don't think so. Here, see? It says *new man*. And look, there's a verse on the silver tag. 2 Cor. 5:17."

"I'll look it up," said Allie.

"Give me that," Jake said, holding out his hand for the Bible. "I'll look it up myself." He did. "It says, 'Therefore if any man be in Christ, he is a new creature: old things are passed away; behold, all things are become new.'"

"I love that one," Shayne said.

"I'm not sure why she picked it for me," Jake mumbled, flipping the stone over in his fingers.

Shayne had already taken the Bible from him. "My verse is John 15:15. Here. 'No longer do I call you servants, for a servant does not know what his master is doing; but I have called you friends, for all things that I heard from My Father I have made known to you.'" She smiled.

"What about the name?" Allie asked. "Jake is a 'new man,' what are you?"

She turned the stone over. "It says *friend of God*."

"Ooh. That's a good one."

"How about you?"

Allie hesitated for a second. "My stone says *chosen*. The tag says Ephesians 1:4-5. Can you look it up for me?"

We all paid attention. Allie, handing the wheel over to another driver? Shayne steered quickly through the little Bible. "'Long ago, even before he made the world, God loved us and chose us in Christ to be holy and without fault in his eyes. His unchanging plan has always been to adopt us into his own family by bringing us to himself through Jesus Christ. And this gave him great pleasure.'"

Shayne hadn't even finished when Allie's eyes filled up and spilled over. That the gift came from Kellie had something to do with her reaction, but there was more to it than that. I realized that Allie had a story I knew nothing about.

All this time I sat reading and rereading the name engraved on my white stone. Sam watched me now—watchful Sam—but when I said nothing the others looked to him next.

"Mine is *ransomed*," he said.

"Hmm. What about the verse?" Shayne asked.

"There are two."

"Really? Does anyone else have two? Rory?" I shook my head. "Well, I always knew he was Kellie's favorite," she teased. "Here, Rory. Why don't you read Sam's *two* verses." I could see she was just trying to be brave. Allie's tears had shaken her; she didn't think she could read anymore.

Sam explained, "There's just one on the tag, like yours. But she wrote another one at the bottom of my letter."

I offered the Bible to Sam, but he declined. "What's the first one?" I asked, knowing that chances were I wouldn't be able to find it.

He looked at the paper. "1 Peter 1:18-19."

Since the book was just the New Testament, I chanced upon it quicker than I expected. "Here, eighteen and nineteen." I cleared my throat. "'For you know that God paid a ransom to save you from the empty life you inherited from your ancestors. And the ransom he paid was not mere gold or silver. He paid for you with the precious lifeblood of Christ, the sinless, spotless Lamb of God.'"

Sam nodded with a look in his eyes like he was remembering something they'd talked about once.

"That's one of those Jewishy verses, right?" Jake asked. "But it doesn't count. What's the one that's actually on your tag?"

"1 Cor. 6:19-20."

I remembered that Corinthians was after Romans. Still, it took me a while, and the longer it took, the worse my case of fumble fingers got. "Here," I said finally. "Who wants to read?"

"You do it."

My eyes scanned it, flicked up at Sam, darted down again. "Um…here. 'Or don't you know that your body is the temple of the Holy Spirit, who lives in you and was given to you by God? You do not belong to yourself, for God bought you with a high price. So you must honor God with your body.'"

The harder you try not to blush, the harder you blush. I hate that.

"Oooh-kay," Shayne said.

Jake snickered. "I'm really starting to like my verse."

"No, it's a really good verse," Allie said quickly. "Don't you think so, Rory?"

My mouth opened, but for a second nothing came out. Then, "What does it have to do with *ransomed*, though?" I asked. Either I came across as a dope or an intentional decoy, deflecting the attention from Sam and his rather personal verse.

"Duh," Jake said. "'God bought you with a high price'? What do you think ransom means?"

"Jake, isn't it about time you tried being that new man?" Allie asked.

Sam jumped in as my decoy. "What about yours, Rory?"

I looked at my inscription. I didn't know what 'Zeph' was short for. But they were waiting; I didn't have much choice. "It says Zeph. 3:14-17."

"That's Zephtacoccus," Jake informed me.

"It is not," Shayne and Allie said simultaneously.

"Yeah, it's all about that horrible plague."

"It's Zephaniah," Allie said.

"So look it up."

"Jake, you know it's Old Testament. Sorry, Rory. Unless we can find someone inside who's got a Bible, you'll have to look it up when you get home."

"Yeah, that's fine." I did a pretty good job of not sounding disappointed. Old Testament? No cool sayings of Jesus. And who ever heard of Zephaniah?

"Well, at least tell us the name on your stone," Shayne said.

"No, wait." Sam stretched across and put his hand over the inscription. "Don't. That way we all have to go home and look it up, and try to guess. Zephaniah what?"

"Chapter three, 14-17." I could've hugged Sam. Except he was a fourteen-year-old boy, I was a fourteen-year-old girl, and we were both susceptible to hot face. Plus Jake would never let us live it down. And the girls would talk. And Sam might be disgusted. But otherwise I could've hugged him.

"Allie, I think that's your Grandma." Shayne pointed to a white-haired lady standing in the side gymnasium door, waving.

"I guess I have to go. You guys better come and say hi to Grammy, or she'll be hurt."

"Guard your cheeks, Sam," Jake said.

We all greeted Allie's grandmother, only this time I was the one who got my cheeks pinched. "Well, aren't you a pretty little thing," she crooned, even though I was a good five inches taller than her. "Look at all that auburn hair. Would you believe my hair used to be that same color? Don't you think she's a pretty thing?" she asked Sam. If ever there was a good time for a hole to open up and swallow me, this was it.

Sam must've been thinking the same thing. "Um...yes, ma'am," he said, because it was the only polite thing to say. So he had to say it.

"And little Shaynie, and my Allie. All so beautiful. You must all be so eager to start your high school careers in the fall." There was no chance to correct her. A loud honk made us jump—Jake's dad waved to him from a red convertible in the parking lot. Then Dr. Newman spotted us from where he waded through the crowd, towering over most everyone around him. So we five would go our separate ways with Grammy's reminder that we no longer had common ground, no default meeting place like school where we could always count on seeing each other.

"Hang on," I said before anyone could wander off. I had to delay this parting, even if it was just for a minute. "Don't you think we should...?" I held up my necklace to finish the question for me.

"She's right," Shayne said. "Let's put them on. For Kellie."

"For the Jesus Machine," Jake said. "These are our dog tags."

Shayne clasped hers behind her neck and smoothed it down. "Jake's right. *Not* about Jesus Machine—about the fight. We lost our fearless leader, but the battle rages on."

"Kellie wouldn't want us to quit fighting just because..." Allie paused.

"She got promoted," Jake finished for her. Allie punched him on the shoulder, but not hard.

We all looked at each other and the ordinary-looking white stone resting against each person's chest—but on its underside a secret, a name to remind us or inspire us or give us courage. A gift from a friend who had already made the journey Home—for me, a friend I'd only just started to know.

"Is this where we all put our hands in the middle and shout something?" Jake cracked the quiet. "Whitestone!" he grunted, like a football player. A horn honked.

"You'd better go with your dad now, or you'll need a tombstone," Sam said.

"Me, too," Allie said. Her grandmother was already halfway to their car. "We're going out for dinner. Grammy likes to get the earlybird senior special." We exchanged quick hugs—we girls, anyway.

"Bye!"

"Call, okay? IM me."

"Shayne, there's your dad in the car."

"Yeah, I see him. We're going out for pizza. Bye, guys! Talk to you soon."

Dr. Newman came up beside Sam. "Ready, Samuel? Your mother is in the car."

"Yeah, Pop."

"Miss Joyce, would you be interested in a ride home?"

No doubt—but how would that look? "Oh, thanks. But I'm walking distance from here."

"You're welcome to come if you wish," he said with a nod that was sort of like a bow, then he headed back for the car.

"You sure?" Sam asked.

"Yeah, I'm good."

"Well, you know what that means."

I frowned. "What?"

He was already following his dad. "I'm going to get home before you, and I'm going to know what Zephaniah 2:14-17 says before you do."

I gave him the hands-on-hips glare as he drove off grinning at me. Once he was out of sight, I smiled and took my time walking home. It was Zephaniah 3:14-17.

I pressed the stone against my thumb, wondering if the inscription would leave an impression on my flesh. It didn't leave a mark that I could see, but the words were already imprinted on my heart. What could they mean?

Sheelan had the phone attached to her head when I got home. My mom scurried by with her freshly ironed work clothes. She stopped halfway up the stairs to look more closely at me. "Did you grow today? You look like a young lady all of a sudden."

"Mom," I said, the two-syllable way.

I got Gran's Bible. Funny, now it always wanted to open to the 91st Psalm, like the binding was bent right in that spot (it wasn't). I flipped around, was fooled by Zechariah, then found the passage in Zephaniah.

> *Sing, O daughter of Zion!*
> *Shout, O Israel!*
> *Be glad and rejoice with all your heart,*
> *O daughter of Jerusalem!*
> *The LORD has taken away your judgments,*
> *He has cast out your enemy.*
> *The King of Israel, the LORD, is in your midst;*
> *You shall see disaster no more.*
>
> *In that day it shall be said to Jerusalem:*
> *'Do not fear;*
> *Zion, let not your hands be weak.*
> *The LORD your God in your midst,*
> *The Mighty One, will save;*
> *He will rejoice over you with gladness,*
> *He will quiet you with His love,*
> *He will rejoice over you with singing.'*

What an outlandish image. God singing over His people? Weren't people the ones who were supposed to do the singing to God?

Rejoicing over me?

So God really must be love, I thought. But a kind of love I couldn't wrap my brain around. I wondered if I could wrap my heart around it instead. (More likely it would wrap its Heart around me.)

When I turned on the computer, almost immediately there was a *bloop*.

> **samIam:** *okay, you got me—Zephaniah 3, not 2*
> **REJoyce316:** *he he he*
> **samIam:** *but I found it. You got a long one.*
> **REJoyce316:** *well, it's not the same as getting TWO*
> **samIam:** *alright already*
> **REJoyce316:** *so any guesses?*
> **samIam:** *the name on your stone?*
> **REJoyce316:** *yeah. Good luck.*

There were more *bloops*.

> **PBnJake:** *I looked for your verses but there is no Zechariah 3:14-17*
> **samIam:** *it's not Zechariah*
> **AlliG8r:** *Yeah, it's Zephtacoccus.*
> **REJoyce316:** *hi, guys*
> **Shaboda:** *I'm here too!!*
> **samIam:** *we're going to guess Rory's name*

We waited for Jake to read the right passage. Then:

> **PBnJake:** *I got it. Obvious.*
> **REJoyce316:** *well?*
> **PBnJake:** *it's got to be Big Mouth*
> **REJoyce316:** *what??*
> **PBnJake:** *there's a lot about shouting in your verses*
> **REJoyce316:** *is that your final answer?*
> **PBnJake:** *Depends. Am I right?*
> **AlliG8r:** *That's his guess. But I guess "unafraid."*
> **Shaboda:** *I like that! I think Allie's right!!!*
> **AlliG8r:** *No, what was your first guess, Shayne?*
> **PBnJake:** *Jesus Machine*
> **Shaboda:** *JAKE*
> **Shaboda:** *actually I thought it might be "daughter" or "saved"*
> **AlliG8r:** *Well, Rory?*

REJoyce316: *Sam didn't guess yet*
samIam: *I already know it*
Shaboda: *oh really?*
PBnJake: *Enlighten us, o wise one*
samIam: *look at her name, guys*

I shook my head—not because he was wrong, but because it looked like he was going to be right.

samIam: *first I thought "rejoicing" but*
Shaboda: *oh yeah! I think Sam's right. I go with "rejoicing" too!*
PBnJake: *You're pathetic, Shaboda.*
AlliG8r: *Wait, let Sam finish.*
samIam: *I say Rory's is…"rejoiced over"?*

I'd thought that I didn't want any of them to guess, so I could reveal it all on my own. But it wasn't so bad that Sam had hit it right on the head. I'd forgive him.

REJoyce316: *Sam's right.*

28

1'd like to say that the five of us kept in contact all that summer. There were a couple of phone calls, plenty of emails at first and some IM sessions that made me laugh so hard I began to doubt my bladder control. A few times Shayne and Allie even showed up unexpectedly at my front door, and we'd sit on the front steps and talk about stuff—clothes, books, occasionally boys (mostly them on that one).

The conversation would eventually come around to school and all the preparations and orientations they had to go through to get ready for Whitestone High. I couldn't blame them. I'd be obsessing over it myself if it were me. We didn't know quite what to make of the fact that Sam would be homeschooling. I told them how neat the Fishers were, and they agreed it was kind of cool — but what about our fearsome fivesome?

But that's the thing: We hadn't been a fivesome since graduation day. Jake took off to spend the summer with his mom in California, and when he did get home, he only ever seemed to talk about his new next-door neighbor, a fourteen-year-old girl— sort of the opposite of my eight-year-old experience with Kingston. Sam traveled with his dad more often than not. Now Shayne and Allie set their sights on freshman year. It felt a little like Hannah and Kimmie all over again.

But we had the white stones. We girls wore them every day, and I imagined the boys did, too. But wearing them wasn't even the point. They united us in a mysterious way, a unique thing we would always share.

One thing I hadn't shared was the story of my last encounter with the angels. In a way it was just easier to let people draw their own conclusions, especially when the details were so confusing. I hadn't seen an angel, had a seizure or anything since I smacked my head on the handrail, and it felt like that chapter of my life had come to a close. From time to time I pictured myself telling Sam more about it. Of all my friends, he seemed best able to believe. He had actually helped me see the truth. But it was a tricky thing to bring up in casual conversation, and we weren't even having any of those.

Sometimes I pulled out my sketchpad and tried to draw Gabby, or Rafie. I had the hardest time with Micah; I could never get the eyes right. I had no desire to draw Uri. Even though Dr. McD encouraged me to draw, I kept the sketches hidden in a safe place, so no one (Sheelan) would come across them and express lingering doubts about my sanity.

By August the sketchpad had gathered a layer of dust under my bed. Days dragged out hot and slow. School loomed mere weeks away, and I had started the reluctant countdown of remaining free days. In other words, life felt pretty normal.

There was a sort of reunion at the front of the school on the day they posted our class listings. Of the three eighth grade teachers, the only one I definitely didn't want for homeroom was Mrs. Palmer.

"You got Mrs. Palmer," said a voice beside me. I'd been hopefully, desperately, searching Mr. Behrens' list, then Mr.

Hayes'. I looked down at Jasmine Wee. She pointed at the list I'd refused to look at.

"Figures," I said.

"They say she's the hardest."

"Um-hmm."

"I got her, too." And she actually smiled at me. It was probably just because she relished the thought of the painful academic year to come, but she almost seemed glad we were in the same class. Maybe it wouldn't be awful.

Jake came along, took one look at the Hayes list and gave a victory shout, high-fiving the glass door. "Yes! Mr. Hayes rules." Then he scanned the student list as if looking for a particular name. "Oh, yeah," he said. "Thank you, Lordy."

"Hi, Jake," I said.

"Oh. Hi, Rory." He barely spared me a glance.

I wasn't exactly longing for Jake Dean's attention, but seeing him reminded me of the others. I sat around that afternoon feeling like the day was about a hundred hours long. Then all at once I remembered: Teen Scene. Pastor Dan planned to start up again in September. Losing Kellie (I know, she didn't slip into the sofa cushions) had ended the meetings so abruptly in the spring, I'd almost forgotten. Once a week, at least, our white-stone fivesome would be reunited. Suddenly the endless afternoon was full of possibilities.

One night when the humidity and everything else stuck to my skin and the cicadas buzzed and no matter how I flipped it the pillow had no cool side, I lay in bed awake until midnight. When I did sleep, dreams came rapid and vivid, faces of friends and strangers, places I knew and some I didn't. I walked along a path barely wide enough for myself, but as I overtook other travelers, somehow we had room to walk side-by-side. They would look over their shoulder as I approached. My heart skipped when one of them turned and I saw the smiling face of my dad.

Another face turned and beckoned, a face like Rafie's, only not so much childish as ageless, its softness not of pudgy cheeks but of spirit. And another traveler looked back with the face of Gabby and yet not—certainly not the bruised face I had seen last. She was striking in her beauty, but not especially feminine. I had the suspicion that these beings were not male or female in the human sense of the word at all. She (for lack of a better word) pointed to one side.

Another semi-familiar figure stood waiting for me. Micah, of course, looking every inch the warrior. As I came near, he drew his sword from the sheath and light danced on the blade, illuminating a strange, graceful script engraved along its length. Even while I marveled at it, I could suddenly read it: *Rhema.*

"The *rhema* is your Sword," he told me. He extended the hilt towards me. My eyes got wide.

"Learn it," he repeated, still stern but with encouragement in his snapping blue eyes. "The Sword of the Spirit is the *rhema* of God."

I took the hilt, still warm—hot—from his hand. The blade drooped. It took two hands for me to hold it up. I clutched the hilt against my chest, blade down, and looked up to thank Micah—and Rafie and Gabby—but they were gone. There was nothing but me, the sword, and something else. Someone Else; I knew it all at once. Someone who had become flesh and dwelt among us. The Word.

The next moment my eyes opened, blinking against morning light that poured through my window and turned my white bedroom pale gold. The curtains stirred with a cool morning breeze. I had an urge to stretch.

There was a weight on my chest, and my hands were crossed over it. For an instant I expected a sword, though I could barely remember why I did. My fingers explored it, lifted it up. A Bible. Not Grandma Judy's Bible. One with a flexible black leather binding, somewhat scarred. I sat up sharply, flipping through the pages with their familiar smell. My dad's crooked handwriting appeared here and there on the margins.

I stroked it, sighed, then smiled. His lost Bible. Unbelievable.

It will only protect you if you read it.

I probably just heard the voice in my memory. Probably. All the same, it was good advice.

So I started reading.

Continued in Cornerstone

39405594R00156

Made in the USA
Middletown, DE
19 March 2019